PRAISE FOR *THE RADCLIFFE LADIES' READING CLUB*

"In 1955, four young Radcliffe students—Tess, Evie, Merritt, and Caroline—gather at the Cambridge Bookshop to explore the scope of a woman's life using the words of Brontë, Wharton, and Virginia Woolf as their guides. As each young woman discovers what ambition, love, and independence mean to her, friendships shift and evolve until the group's bond is shattered by violence and betrayal. This endlessly charming—at times heartbreaking—novel weaves a gentle spell on the reader. You will never want to leave the Cambridge Bookshop."

—Mariah Fredericks, author of *The Lindbergh Nanny*

"*The Radcliffe Ladies' Reading Club* is a loving, engaging tribute to female friendship and to the intimate power of books. It paints the struggles of four young women in living, blooming color as they come into their own in 1950s Cambridge, Massachusetts, a world that has only begun to crack open the door of opportunities for women. Tess, Caroline, Merritt, and Evie want more than they are being offered—more education, truer love, greater freedom—and they make mistakes as they pursue their dreams. They stumble. They fall. But, like the heroines of the books they love, they stand up and try again. Join the Radcliffe Ladies' Reading Club and dive into this passionate, emotionally rewarding story. You'll be glad you did."

—Mary Anna Evans, Benjamin Franklin Award–winning author of *The Physicists' Daughter*

The RADCLIFFE LADIES' READING CLUB

a novel

JULIA BRYAN THOMAS

sourcebooks
landmark

Published by Sourcebooks Landmark, an imprint of Sourcebooks
P.O. Box 4410, Naperville, Illinois 60567-4410
(630) 961-3900
sourcebooks.com

Library of Congress Cataloging-in-Publication Data

Names: Thomas, Julia, author.
Title: The Radcliffe ladies' reading club : a novel / Julia Bryan Thomas.
Description: Naperville, Illinois : Sourcebooks Landmark, [2023]
Identifiers: LCCN 2022050954 (print) | LCCN 2022050955
   (ebook) | (trade paperback) | (epub)
Subjects: LCSH: Female friendship--Fiction. | Booksellers and
   bookselling--Fiction. | Book clubs (Discussion groups)--Fiction. |
   Radcliffe College--Fiction. | Cambridge (Mass.)--Fiction. | LCGFT:
   Novels.
Classification: LCC PS3620.H6286 R33 2023 (print) | LCC PS3620.H6286
   (ebook) | DDC 813/.6--dc23/eng/20221117
LC record available at https://lccn.loc.gov/2022050954
LC ebook record available at https://lccn.loc.gov/2022050955

Printed and bound in Canada.
MBP 10 9 8 7 6 5 4 3 2

To my daughters, Caitlin and Heather, and all lovers of bookshops and the marvelous books therein

"The world was hers for the reading."

—BETTY SMITH

1

***

SEPTEMBER 1955

> "Dread remorse when you are tempted to err,
> Miss Eyre; remorse is the poison of life."
>
> —CHARLOTTE BRONTË, *JANE EYRE*

It had been raining for hours and still a light pattering soaked the cobbled pavement, fallen leaves swimming in puddles all around. Alice Campbell walked down Simpson Street in one of the oldest parts of Cambridge, Massachusetts, not looking left nor right but straight ahead, waiting for the redbrick building to come into view. It was a beautiful place, the Cambridge Bookshop, her pride and joy. Lifting her umbrella, she took it all in: the cherry-red door set at an angle at the corner; the glossy, black facade and trim; the simple, faded gilt letters spelling out BOOKS. When she opened the shop, there hadn't been room to put the entire name on the plaque, leaving it perhaps a little nondescript. But Alice hadn't minded. The people who were meant to buy her books would find their way inside.

A few titles were exhibited on shelves in the window, newer books that had just come out in the last few years: *The Catcher in the Rye*, *The End of the Affair*, and her favorite, *From Here to Eternity*. The store, however, was located on an unremarkable street without a dress shop or comfortable café nearby, leaving pedestrians to walk past without giving it a second glance. Nor did the titles displayed to passersby reflect the true nature of the bookshop, where both old and new books rested on the somewhat crooked shelves. That, too, did not matter. She had chosen her entire catalog herself. The bookshop and the books in it were her refuge, her life, her mission.

Two windows, also framed in black, were above the shop on the second story, where Alice had made a flat out of an old bookkeeper's office. At night, she read there by lamplight; by day, she organized and ordered and occasionally sold a few books in her little shop downstairs. It was more than she had ever hoped for. Sometimes she wondered at her good fortune.

Stepping around puddles, she made her way to the door, fishing in her pocketbook for the key. It turned in the lock and she pushed the door open, the musty odor of books lingering in the air. After closing the door behind her, she folded her umbrella and slipped it into the stand, setting her bag on the counter. Every time she entered the room, she was overcome by its beauty. The walls were paneled in oak and the window casings were wide and generous, allowing a great deal of light into the room. The secondhand desk in a corner was made of mahogany and was quite grand, she thought, though Jack would have called it wormy. It's true, it had seen better days, but she had polished it until it had a lustered sheen, and as far as she was concerned, the worn places only gave it character.

Alice removed her gloves and unbuttoned her raincoat, then hung it on a hook near the door. Before she locked the shop and went upstairs, she would choose a book to take with her to while away her evening. A box from Doubleday had arrived earlier, and she took a sharp knife from the top desk drawer and cut it open. Unfolding the stiff cardboard, she pulled back the flaps to find copies of a du Maurier novel, *My Cousin Rachel*, which she had been expecting. Nodding in satisfaction, she closed it again and wandered over to a nearly empty shelf where she had stacked several new copies of *Jane Eyre*. She took the one from the top of the pile and tucked it under her arm, wondering who would read it with her.

All around the world, she knew, were kindred spirits who reached for the same book on the same evening for comfort or affirmation, souls who found themselves in the pages of a book. But there were other readers too—readers who didn't yet know who they were and how much a particular novel would mean to them. Alice felt it was her job to find them and give them a book.

She bolted the shop door, took her pocketbook from the desk, and turned off the lights before making her way upstairs. It had only been a few weeks since she had moved into the building, but already she knew the familiar creak of every stair.

The flat above was simply furnished: a bed against the far wall, a wardrobe, a table, and chair. She hadn't a television or even a sofa, but there was an old chaise with cushions one could sink into and a trunk she had found at a secondhand shop that functioned as a perch for a teacup. In the second room, there was a makeshift kitchen, where she plugged in the electric kettle and set out a cup and saucer as she did at the end of most days.

Alice had never lived in Cambridge before. In fact, she had never even been to Massachusetts. After Jack, she had taken a map and traced her way as far from Chicago as she could get, loading her few possessions into suitcases and boarding the train to Boston. It was the most frightening, exciting thing she had ever done. It had taken her three weeks to find an empty shop and then another two as she cleaned it up sufficiently to house the books she had selected and ordered from publishers and used bookstores around the city.

After pulling a dressing gown from the wardrobe, she slipped it on over her dress as the kettle whistled. She brewed a cup of tea and took it to the chaise, where she sat down with her book. It lay unopened on her lap as she contemplated the silence. It was good to have a space to oneself where one could think and dream and plan. And there was much to plan, for it was to be a busy year if things turned out as she hoped.

Taking a sip of her tea, she leaned back into the cushions, lifted her new copy of *Jane Eyre*, and held it to her breast. It was hard to imagine it had been published in 1847, as fresh as it felt to her each time she read it. She understood the loneliness Jane must have felt has a child and even more the struggle to find her way in life. Brontë's heroines, like so many women before and after, were often dependent upon the humor and indulgences of men. Alice's sister lived in a twenty-room mansion in Chicago, but at what expense? To have such a home meant to be as dependent as a child, and that was one thing Alice would never be again.

She opened the book to the first page, content in every way with her situation, and began to read.

The following day was Friday, a good day for a bookseller in Boston. In fact, it was a good day for booksellers everywhere. Readers came in with wages in their pockets and the desire to have a book companion for the weekend. She sold two copies of *Catcher*, a Hemingway, a Nancy Mitford that had only been in the shop for a few hours, and four used books she had picked up at a book stall a week earlier for a quarter apiece.

Around three o'clock, a young woman walked into the shop, and Alice glanced up from her seat behind the oak desk, where she was shuffling papers, writing down accounts. She nodded in greeting, loath to disturb anyone browsing through a bookshelf, though the girl didn't respond. She was likely one of the college girls around town. They were near Radcliffe, after all. The girl wore a plain dress, with sensible shoes and a pair of dark tortoiseshell glasses. Alice tried to turn her attention back to the accounts, but she was interested in which shelves the girl explored. For a moment, she thought of handing her a copy of *Jane Eyre* and then stopped herself. This was not a kindred spirit, she could tell. This was a girl who wanted *A Tree Grows in Brooklyn* or another popular book of its ilk. Not that she disparaged readers of any sort, but she was looking for someone different.

Eventually, the girl turned away from the shelves and brought a book up to the desk. It had been previously owned, a slim volume of poetry, an altogether nice choice.

"That will be one dollar, please," Alice said.

As the girl took a bill from her handbag, Alice placed the book upon a sheet of waxed brown paper, folding it carefully and tying it with a length of string. When she was finished, she took out an ink pad and stamped an image upon the package. "The Cambridge Bookshop" looked elegant in formal, ink-dipped letters. One might not know the name of the shop when one went inside, but if one came out with a purchase, it was stamped upon the paper for everyone to see.

The girl glanced at a flyer on the desk and back at Alice.

"You're having a book club?" she asked. "How does that work?"

Alice nodded. "Once a month, a small group will meet and discuss a different book."

She picked up the flyer, which read:

THE CAMBRIDGE BOOKSHOP

is proud to host a Reading Club

Last Thursday of each month

Serious book lovers only

Inquire if interested

"Will it be a classic?"

"Most of the time, yes," Alice replied. "In September, we'll be reading *Jane Eyre*."

"May I take this?" the girl said, reaching for the paper. "I'll talk to my friends and see what they say."

"Of course," Alice replied, wondering if she had misjudged the girl. "Let me know by next week if you're interested."

The next few days were unremarkable, although satisfying in their own way. Alice loved having a routine, and her days had little variation. Coffee, toast, and the newspaper, in which she read only the fashion page. Selling and ordering books in the morning. Exploring Cambridge during her lunch hour, walking through parks and peering in shop windows until she came upon the luncheonette, where she usually ordered a ham on rye or chicken salad at the counter. Afternoons were spent going over the accounts, followed by no small amount of daydreaming over what to read next. She was anxious about only one thing: to know with whom she would share *Jane*

Eyre, wondering if the girl who took the flyer would return with her friends. Fortunately, she didn't have to wait long.

She knew them the moment she saw them. The weather was as sunny and bright that afternoon as it had been rainy the previous one. Alice was washing the windows, which looked as if they hadn't been cleaned in years, when four girls, smiling and talking, arms linked, came down the street and stopped at the door. A moment later, they stepped inside and Alice smiled in greeting, as if they were very old friends. They were young—not even twenty, if she was correct—and obviously Cliffies. One, a beautiful blond, even wore a sweater with the Radcliffe emblem on the front. She couldn't have been happier to see them.

"Hello!" Alice said in greeting. "Welcome to the Cambridge Bookshop."

2

Tess Collins sat primly on a bench in front of her college dormitory, a light breeze ruffling her skirt about her knees. A copy of *Byron's English Composition, First Edition* was perched on her lap, though she had some difficulty concentrating on the page in front of her. She had been a formidable student back at home in Ohio, but while writing a thesis statement and constructing a topic sentence were familiar territory, she didn't intend to let the grass grow under her feet. She was first in her class in Akron and planned to be first in her class at Radcliffe as well. Ordinarily, she studied for exams in a library, behind a wooden carrel to block out the world. One didn't excel in the academic setting if one was distracted by blue skies and unseasonably warm weather. On the other hand, she thought, she was eighteen now, a college student. A mature young woman could both familiarize herself with the crux of her studies and enjoy the last of the summer air.

The dormitory behind her, Duncan Hall, was a grand-looking building with two tall white pillars on either side of the long porch, where weathered gray benches were lined up in a row. Inside, it was as refined as one might expect from its exterior. A large, comfortable sitting room, full of upholstered sofas and chairs covered in chintz, was flanked by walls lined with shelves and shelves of books. They weren't standard textbooks or dry nonfiction tomes either; someone had filled them with novels and mysteries and volumes of poetry in a heroic attempt to appeal to the varied tastes of the girls who lived there. She'd only been at Radcliffe for two weeks but had yet to see anyone peruse the titles, and though she herself had, she was looking for a book in particular that couldn't be found on the shelf.

The second and third floors housed the inhabitants of the building: two girls to each room, sixteen to each floor. It was overwhelming in its way, and she was glad she hadn't chosen one of the larger dorms, trying to navigate her first year of college in a sea of nameless faces.

Tess pulled her sweater around her shoulders and pushed her tortoiseshell glasses up higher on her nose. She almost smiled. It was a little thrilling to have a book in hand and the opportunity to sit outside to read it. She had just turned her attention back to the page when a blue-and-white Bel Air convertible careened into the drive and came to a sudden halt in front of the dorm, the brakes squealing on the pavement. Her roommate, Caroline Hanson, was in the passenger seat, sitting next to one of the best-looking young men Tess had ever seen. He leapt from the vehicle and came around to open the door for Caroline, who laughed when he leaned in close. Tess sat forward, wondering if he was going to breach all decorum and kiss her in front of God and everyone, when Caroline pushed past him with a laugh and walked up the steps.

"Tess," she said in her breathy voice. "This is Carter Gray."

Tess locked eyes with him for a second, blushing. Like Caroline, he was obviously wealthy. He wore a pair of well-fitting white trousers and a white cable-knit tennis sweater with red and navy bands along the V-necked collar, which emphasized his tan, making him look like he had stepped straight out of an advertisement in a magazine. After a quick nod in her direction, he took Caroline by the hand.

"When do I get to see you again?" he asked, massaging her knuckles with his forefinger. "We could go to the pictures tonight."

Tess closed her book, all hope of studying now impossible. She should have expected such an interruption and studied for her exam in the safe harbor of her dorm room at the minuscule desk, although it was possible there would be distractions there too. Caroline was a vision, an eighteen-year-old Grace Kelly, who would no doubt be engaged by Christmas, and their dorm room seemed to have a revolving door, as everyone wanted a glimpse of the Rhode Island beauty. Her major was art history, but she was so popular even in such a short time that Tess doubted her roommate would finish the year. In the meantime, she realized with a sigh, it would be back to the library and wooden carrels if she wanted to keep to her goal of being first in her class.

"I'm busy tonight," Caroline told Carter Gray with a smile. "Tess and I have things to do, don't we?"

She unexpectedly took Tess's hand and led her inside, closing the door behind them. Curious, Tess followed Caroline up the stairs.

The dorms had large but plain rooms. The college had provided two twin beds and mattresses; two plain wooden desks; and tall, matching wardrobes standing side by side. There were twin closets, none too large, but because they had a corner room, there were double the amount of windows, including two over the beds that swung open from the bottom to allow them to listen to the birdsong and the rustle of the wind in the trees.

In the two weeks since they had met, Tess's life had completely changed. She had arrived at Radcliffe three days before Caroline, which made her both pleased and nervous. Pleased because she had never had so much privacy before and nervous because she had to make decisions on her own. *Which bed should I take?* she'd wondered. She had preferred the one on the right because of its view of the courtyard below, though the one on the left looked out onto a row of dogwoods that would bloom spectacularly in spring. She'd decided on the right, knowing she would give it up if asked to. The room was perfect, if only because it was six hundred and thirty-nine miles from Akron, Ohio, and a house full of irascible brothers and a mother afraid to speak up to her bully of a father. There was noise at the dormitory, too, of course, but the sounds here were happy ones. And though she found girl talk frivolous, it was preferable to a litany on the woes of broken tractors and mortgage payments and arbitrating the boys' fights. The reason she had come to Radcliffe was to change her life and make certain she didn't end up with a future like that.

She'd unpacked her single well-worn suitcase and ironed her five dresses before hanging them in the closet. Her shoes—a pair of sneakers, a pair of white sandals, and serviceable church shoes— were lined up in a row. Though she didn't have a fitted sheet, she'd brought two flat sheets and a pillowcase and made the bed, tucking one of the top sheets around the mattress and securing it with safety pins. She had a thin blanket of gunmetal green, which she'd proceeded to fold over the mattress, tucking it in at the corners.

Afterward, she had gone to the campus bookstore to get her books. Because she was attending on scholarship, she didn't have to give them any money, and she was able to get new copies of the books rather than used. Tess had stroked the covers reverently and took them back to her room, where she arranged them in a neat pile on the desk. Everything was perfect. In fact, after a day and a half, she had almost forgotten a roommate was coming.

Her life had changed with a simple tap at the door, which swung open before she could even respond.

"Your roommate is coming up now," Mrs. Schwartz, the dorm's housemother, had informed her with a smile. "Her name is Caroline Hanson. Do make her feel welcome, Tess."

Tess had been reading in bed but immediately rose as Mrs. Schwartz left the room.

Nervously, she'd begun to straighten her sheet and blanket. She glanced at the empty bed on the other side of the room and wondered if she would like the girl who would live with her for the next year. She had met Evie and Merritt, who had moved into the adjoining room, and liked both of them already. They were down-to-earth, sensible girls, the type one would hope to find at a prestigious college like Radcliffe. She only hoped that her roommate would be as nice as they were.

Caroline had arrived a few minutes later with a chauffeur, who carried her bags into the room. She'd smiled and gone up to Tess, shaking her hand.

"I'm Caroline," she'd said. "You must be Tess."

Tess had been awestruck. There was something mesmerizing about this girl. Not just her beauty, which was enough to take one's breath away, but the way she looked one in the eye and was so self-assured. Even Tess, who was articulate on every subject, felt herself stammering in Caroline's presence. She had never met anyone like her before.

"Is this my bed?" Caroline had asked, but before Tess could tell her she would be happy to switch, she smiled. "It's perfect."

There had been a flurry as Caroline directed her driver to place her suitcases near the closet and he went to fetch boxes from the trunk of his car. Caroline opened the first when he returned and drew out a set of satin sheets and a pink comforter with a rose pattern. Tess immediately felt self-conscious about her own plain bedding. However, the matter had quickly been dispatched when Caroline pulled out a second set and handed them to her.

"I hope you don't mind terribly," she had said. "I like everything to match."

The butter-soft linens were thrust into Tess's arms.

"I couldn't possibly..." she stammered.

"I wasn't sure who my roommate would be, but I had a feeling it would be someone who would like roses," Caroline had replied. "You do like roses, don't you?"

"Well, yes, but..."

Tess didn't have time to finish her thought as Evie and Merritt came into their room. Introductions had been made, and Evie went over to touch the bedding in Tess's hand, rubbing it between her fingers.

"How gorgeous!" she had said, turning to Merritt. "What a good idea. Maybe we should get matching bedspreads too!"

The matter wasn't mentioned again. Tess couldn't even find a graceful way to thank her. But that night, nestled in a bed draped in a soft swath of pink, she had marveled at the change that had overtaken her life. Caroline had filled her wardrobe and closet with an astonishing number of sumptuous dresses. When she had arranged all her clothes and shoes, their room, which had once resembled a nondescript box, now looked more like a Park Avenue dress shop. In addition to the pink comforters, Caroline had filled the room with pillows and candles and a small framed painting of a house. It was white and grand. Tess had looked at it for a long time, transfixed by its beauty. She had never met anyone like Caroline before and was secretly pleased that this glamorous girl, with her beautiful things, belonged to her. Before bed, she had folded the utilitarian green throw that had been on her bed and shoved it down the trash chute.

She was a Cliffie now, and Cliffies did things differently.

From the first day, Tess loved the routine of her new life. She rose early, reread a chapter or two of her assignments, and ate breakfast with Caroline, Evie, and Merritt in the large dining room downstairs. She loved attending class as well. English was her favorite, of course, but she found herself just as interested in the others. Evie was in her American history class, and all four of them were in humanities together. She had never been part of a group of young women before and was surprised at how thrilling it was. In fact, she found herself discussing things she never thought she would talk about with friends.

"I was in a bookshop earlier today, and they were advertising a reading club," Tess told the group over dinner on Friday evening.

They sat around one of the six round maple tables in the residence dining room. The kitchen staff kept a small vase on each one with a carnation or rose inside. Starched cotton napkins were set at each place, and Tess loved spreading one across her lap for every meal, careful not to allow a drop of juice to soil its pristine whiteness. She was unaccustomed to such niceties. She dipped her fork into the mashed potatoes and looked up at her friends to gauge their reaction.

"What exactly is a reading club?" Evie asked, brushing her bangs out of her eyes. "I've never heard of one before."

Evie was a nice-looking girl with a long dark braid and a tanned complexion. Tess didn't know much about her yet apart from the fact that she had grown up on a farm.

"It's a meeting once a month to discuss a book that everyone in the group has read," Tess said, looking around the table at her new friends. "I've never been to one, but the shop was nice. It's not too far to walk either."

"It sounds fun to me," Merritt replied, smiling. "Do you know what kind of books they are going to read?"

"Classics, mostly, I think," Tess answered. "The first one is *Jane Eyre.*"

"I started that once and never finished it." Merritt lifted her cup and took a sip before wrinkling her nose. "I'm not used to coffee. I've never tried it before."

Caroline looked around the table. "Personally, I think a book club sounds like extra homework. You go if you want to, but you're welcome to keep it all to yourselves."

"But they talked to us in orientation about having extracurricular activities to broaden our horizons," Tess urged, emboldened by the comfortable situation. "Book club seems like a fun way to do it."

"And easy," Evie said, nodding. "Just read another book and talk about it."

"Have you seen our humanities assignment for this week?" Caroline lamented. "We have to read a thousand pages!"

"It's not a thousand pages," Tess maintained. "And anyway, you love to read. You've had your nose in a book for the last couple of days."

Of course, it was a lurid romance novel, she noted to herself. Caroline needed a little prodding to set her in the right direction.

"What do we need to do to join?" Merritt asked.

"We just go over and pick up a copy of the book," Tess told her.

"It might be dull," Caroline remarked, stabbing her fork into her pink roast beef. "And I can't stand anything that is dull."

"Compared to what?" Merritt said. "Another night in, studying for another exam?"

"Well, if it means that much to you," Caroline said, relenting. "I suppose I can always have you fill me in if I don't have time to finish it."

"This will be fun!" Evie exclaimed, smiling. "Our first real thing to do together!"

They went to the bookshop the following day and came home with copies of *Jane Eyre*. Even Caroline seemed interested when she had the book in hand.

"This is better than I thought," she said that night as the two of them were lying in bed, reading.

Tess leaned back on her pillow and smiled, toying with the ribbon of the book. It had cost three dollars and fifty cents, and while she had an expense budget from her scholarship, she would have to watch every penny to make it last through the semester until her second check arrived. She thought about buying a dress, something pretty and feminine like Caroline's, to wear about campus, but she couldn't justify the expense. However, she noticed that none of the other girls were buying new dresses even though they were living with a walking fashion magazine as well. Her own clothing was sensible and sturdy, like Evie's and Merritt's, who didn't seem to mind at all. She would have to appreciate the frills from afar. *Besides, look at poor Jane Eyre,* she thought. The girl had almost nothing.

The next afternoon, Tess went to check on Evie and Merritt. She always finished studying first and wanted to help the others if they needed it. Their door was open to the hallway, as usual, and she tapped on the doorframe to announce her presence. That in itself was enjoyable to her. Perhaps this was what having a sister was like.

"How's it going?" Tess asked.

Evie looked up from where she was sitting cross-legged on her bed and held up her Economics 101 book.

"Great," she answered. "This is interesting."

"For economics, you mean," Merritt teased, tucking her hair behind her ear. "I can't imagine anything more boring."

"For any subject," Evie parried, though it was clear she wasn't offended. "You'd be surprised how much fun it can be learning about money. Not that I'll ever have any."

"You'll be a Radcliffe graduate," Tess said. "That'll get you any kind of job you want and you'll be rich."

"What do you want to do after college?" Evie asked, closing her book and setting it in her lap.

"Go to New York, maybe, and work for a magazine," Tess answered, sitting on the edge of Evie's bed. "Or maybe work for a newspaper. Can you imagine how exciting it would be? You could walk up and down Madison Avenue every day and look in all of those shop windows. I can't think of anything better."

"Girls don't do those kind of jobs," Evie countered. "Isn't that just for boys?"

"Speaking of boys, imagine the ones in New York," Merritt murmured. "I can see them now, all wearing tuxedos, with arms full of flowers. Carriage rides in Central Park, just like in the pictures. Wouldn't that be dreamy?"

"What are you working on?" Tess asked, looking at the stack of stationery on Merritt's desk, where she had been writing.

Merritt shrugged. "Nothing special. Just a letter to my father."

"Already?" Tess answered, surprised. Writing a letter home was the last thing she wanted to do. She didn't even want to think of the family she had left behind, the chaos and the anger and the fighting. She hadn't received a letter from them, anyway. They weren't thinking of her either.

"Nothing's even happened yet," Evie said, rolling her eyes. "I'm waiting until we actually do something interesting."

Caroline burst through the door, carrying two dresses in her arms. "All right, girls, which one of these should I wear tonight?" she asked, holding up two frothy concoctions for their inspection.

"Where are you going?" asked Evie, standing so she could examine the dresses from every angle.

"Just to a drive-in for hamburgers," Caroline answered. "Nothing special."

"With Carter?" asked Tess. She couldn't help thinking they made a beautiful pair, both blond and rich and exuding ridiculous amounts of charm.

"Yes," Caroline said. "Although you should see his roommate. He's pretty handsome too. Which of these dresses do you like better, the ocean blue or the green?"

Tess was scandalized at the thought of Caroline ditching Carter for someone else. After all, she had already snagged a beau, someone to escort her to dances and to take her on dates. There was no need to stake a claim on every man on the Harvard campus.

"I like the green," Evie said, reaching out to touch the shiny fabric. "The skirt is so poufy."

"There's another one in my room I'm thinking about too."

Merritt and Evie rose and followed Caroline, leaving Tess no choice but to join them.

"What's wrong with what you're wearing?" Tess asked as they filed into the room.

Caroline looked down at her brown tweed skirt and yellow cardigan and shook her head, fingering the pearl choker around her neck. She wore it every day, and Tess hadn't had a chance to get close to it, although she could tell it was a strand of real pearls. She wondered what it must be like to have something so smooth and cool resting just above her collarbone. She touched her own bare throat, thinking about it.

"This is fine for a boring old class," her roommate replied. "But not when you're going out with boys."

"Carter is so handsome," Merritt said, walking over to inspect Caroline's closet. Evie and Tess followed and sat on Tess's bed, mere satellites in Caroline's world. "How did you meet him?"

Caroline shrugged. "The same way you meet any boy, I guess. He noticed me when I was in the library, getting my library card. He was getting his too."

"I wasn't noticed by someone cute when I picked up mine," Evie said in a wistful tone. "Come to think of it, I didn't notice anybody cute then, myself, either."

Merritt laughed. "There's plenty of time to find someone nice, Evie."

"Nice?" Caroline purred. "Who wants someone nice?"

"The question is, who doesn't?" Tess asked.

"You take everything too seriously," Caroline chided. "You need to let yourself have a little fun. You're only eighteen once, you know."

Tess shivered, suddenly cold. She went over to close her window, pulling it by the handle and locking it before turning back to the group.

"You'll need a sweater," she said to Caroline. "It's getting chilly outside."

"And make sure you're back before curfew," Merritt added. "I wouldn't want to incur Mrs. Schwartz's wrath."

"You worry too much, girls," Caroline answered. "This is the time of our life when we're supposed to be having fun."

Tess never did know what time Caroline returned. She had dozed off rereading a chapter in her humanities book. They had a test the following day, and she wanted to get the top score in the class. Maybe then the others would take her seriously.

She awoke in the middle of the night, her neck stiff from falling asleep in the wrong position.

Sitting up, she put the book on the desk and saw that her roommate was fast asleep in her bed, the green dress tossed on the floor like an old shoe.

Tess rose from her bed and went to retrieve it, shaking it lightly before hanging it up in Caroline's closet. Then she put on a pair of pajamas and went to bed.

3

Everything was ready for the first night of book club. Alice surveyed the room, nodding to herself in approval. Five wooden folding chairs were arranged in a circle in the middle of the room; the backdrop of books on three sides was most appealing. A long, narrow table near the door held a pitcher of water and a freshly opened bottle of chardonnay, along with a handful of tumblers. She had debated whether or not to serve wine and decided any serious lover of books would appreciate it. Perhaps there would be one or two among the group.

Her copy of *Jane Eyre*, which had been new three weeks ago, now boasted notes in the margins and earmarked passages, and dozens of slips of paper protruded from the pages, marking favorite quotes. She had first read the book twenty years ago, when she was not much younger than the girls who were joining her shortly, and found it interesting how the story seemed to change as she aged. When she first read it, all she had wanted for young Jane was to find love and marriage, but as she grew older, she knew there was more to wish for her heroine than simply a roof over her head and a man to lead her into her future. However, she had no desire to influence the girls unduly. *Jane Eyre* was meant to be read at all stages of life, and each reader must glean what she could from her own study of the book. There were certain things she would watch for as they discussed it, things that would tell her whether or not these women were meant to spend this year listening and learning and sharing their own stories. Not to mention, intense book studies informed her a great deal about herself and her own direction in life. She was eager to begin.

Her guests arrived on time, like the proper neophytes they were. Alice opened the door to let them in, turning the sign from Open to Closed when they were all inside.

"May I take your coats?" she asked, smiling.

The weather had turned colder in the weeks since she had last seen them. Gone were the glorious seventy-degree, sunny afternoons. Over the past few days, it had become cooler and damp. One by one, they removed their rain slickers and pulled off their black rubber boots, lining them in a row near the door. Alice hung the coats on the stand and turned back to them and smiled.

"Help yourself to something to drink," she said.

She turned away and went to get her copy of the book to allow the young women to pour themselves a glass. When she was seated in her chair, she was surprised to see them still paused in front of the table, unable to decide. In the end, they each poured a glass of water and came to sit in the circle.

"I'm Alice Campbell," she told them. "A longtime book lover and the owner of the Cambridge Bookshop, which opened just a few weeks ago. Perhaps you can tell me a little about yourselves. And do you mind terribly reminding me of your names?"

The stunningly beautiful girl was the first to speak.

"I'm Caroline Hanson," she said. "I'm from Newport."

She didn't elaborate, and Alice could see that she didn't need to. Caroline's fashionable shirtwaist dress, which looked like spun gold, was fastened with a belt over her impossibly slender waist. She wore a delicate charm bracelet around her left wrist and a perfect strand of pearls about her neck. Her hair was coiffed in smooth blond waves and her bearing was elegant. This was a young woman who might have attended finishing school in Switzerland or France and was adding Radcliffe to her résumé before settling on which of her father's rich friends' sons she would marry. When she did, her engagement photo would be in all the society columns.

"I'm Evie Miller," said the girl to Caroline's right. "My parents have a farm in Upstate New York. I'm an economics major."

Miss Miller looked exactly like what she professed to be. Her dress was homemade, if well done, and her dark-brown locks had been plaited into a braid running down between her shoulders. She was thin but muscular, and it was obvious she could do anything from milk a cow to plant a field. She had a genuine smile, but she was also somewhat shy. She could answer a direct question, but Alice wondered what sort of opinions she had formed about the subject of their book.

"I'm Merritt Weber," the third girl said. "I'm from San Francisco, California, and I'm studying art."

Merritt would have been the pretty one of the group if not for Caroline's overshadowing beauty. She had blond hair that fell just below her shoulders and sharp blue eyes, which held a promising look. She had clearly read the book and was ready to discuss it. She crossed her ankles and straightened her plaid wool skirt, pulling her sweater closer about her shoulders, ready for someone else to take the limelight.

Alice smiled and turned her attention to the girl who most interested her.

"And you're the one who first came into the shop," she stated.

"I'm Tess Collins," the girl replied. "I'm an English major, and I hope to one day soon be editor of the campus newspaper."

Alice found herself nodding at the girl to whom she had sold a book of poetry just a few weeks earlier. This one, she knew, was the girl to watch: the one with secrets. She hadn't referenced her past but instead her aspirations for the future. She was escaping something; that much was clear. Alice knew the feeling.

"You'll be the president of it all one day," Caroline said, nodding. "I've never seen anyone more capable."

Tess blushed. "Don't be silly," she sputtered, though it was evident she was pleased to be noticed in such a manner.

"Has everyone read the book?" Alice asked, holding up her copy.

They all murmured their assent, uncertain how to begin. But beginning things was Alice's forte. And there was only one way to begin a discussion of *Jane Eyre*. She lifted her book from her lap and began to read.

"'Am I hideous, Jane?'" she read, glancing up at the circle of serious faces. Even those few words had brought the young women to rapt attention. "'Very, sir: you always were, you know.'"

Caroline laughed. "What a wonderful line. When I started it, I didn't expect *Jane Eyre* to have a sense of humor."

"*Jane Eyre* is a serious book," Tess protested, a slight frown creasing her brow. "She had a terrible life. I don't think humor is the right word to describe it."

"Ah, but you see, there are no right or wrong answers in book club," Alice said lightly, looking around the small group. "It's all about how a book affects you and how it makes you feel. Tess, what do you think the main point of the story is? What was Charlotte Brontë trying to say to the reader?"

"It's a story of a woman looking for love," Tess replied.

Merritt set her glass on the table between them and gave a hesitant smile. "I think it's a story of a woman searching for a place to belong. Everyone wants to belong somewhere, and Jane started out not really belonging to anyone, didn't she?"

"That's a good point, Merritt," Alice said. "It must have been isolating to live in a house that wasn't your own and then be sent off to boarding school at such a young age. We look to our parents for our first real sense of security, and those growing up without them must have a difficult time."

"Sometimes even if you have parents, it's difficult," Evie said. "I've known people who struggled with that."

Alice nodded. "Do you suppose that's a feeling many people can identify with?"

Tess had gone quiet, but Merritt nodded. "Even coming to college, we're alone for the first time without our families. It's a little scary to be out on our own."

"Is it?" Caroline asked, looking around the circle. "I feel like I've had a thousand eyes on me since the day I was born. I'm ready to make my own decisions and go my own way."

"That's what happened in *Jane Eyre*," Tess said. "When she decided to go out into the world and become a governess."

"It struck me that a girl in Jane's situation had to take what she could get," Evie said, tapping the book on her lap. "She had to take the job as a governess sight unseen. Imagine that. Not knowing who would be living there and having nothing to fall back on."

"What did you think of Mr. Rochester?" Alice asked, eyeing the group.

"He was handsome and romantic," Caroline said. "The perfect cliché of a man."

"But he was troubled from the beginning, that much was obvious," Merritt added. "I wondered a little at Jane's courage at sticking with her position. If she'd only had somewhere else to go. Thornfield Hall was so dark and foreboding."

"But maybe compared to her childhood, it wasn't so bad," Evie reasoned. "At least she had a roof over her head and was finally able to get away from that terrible orphanage."

"Sometimes life is all about comparisons," Alice said, nodding. "What might not seem bearable to one person may be a haven for the next. It all depends on their situation. Caroline, tell us why you associate humor with the book."

"Jane broke through Mr. Rochester's gruff exterior, didn't she?" Caroline answered. "They had both been lonely and enjoyed talking to one another. They even teased each other a little."

"It made them feel like equals," Merritt added. "He wasn't as arrogant as he first came across, and she wasn't just a lowly governess. They were two people with real feelings. At least, that's how it seemed to me."

Alice nodded. She was pleased to see that all the girls were taking book club seriously. It was almost more than she had expected. They had challenged one another's opinions somewhat, which was a good sign as well.

"What role does romance play in the novel?" she asked.

She looked about the room, studying the serious faces of the girls who had not yet experienced love. For them, it was still a notion, a dream that hovered, most likely, in the not-too-distant future.

"Jane found it with Mr. Rochester," Tess replied, now that the subject was back on solid ground. "She was lonely and wanted someone to love."

"Can a woman find happiness without it?" Alice asked.

She was surprised when all eyes turned to her. Evie, in fact, looked at Alice's ring finger, which no longer bore the once-familiar gold band.

Tess cleared her throat. "Have you been married, Miss Campbell?"

"Most people have by my age," Alice said without missing a beat. "Love is an important part of life."

She waited for them to press her further, but etiquette prevented them from asking any more personal questions.

"I think Jane and Rochester were right for each other," Caroline said. "They fit together, it seems to me."

"Ah," Alice said, smiling. "How so?"

"They understood one another," she continued. "They were compatible, or Jane could never have warmed up to him."

"But he was wrong to go after her, you know," Tess interjected. "He was pursuing her as a married man."

"But is it a true marriage if one is shackled to someone who is mentally ill, especially in that day and age?" Merritt asked, frowning. She took a breath and looked at her friends. "It was hardly a normal relationship. Didn't you feel sorry for him at all?"

"'For better or worse, for richer or poorer, in sickness and in health,'" Tess quoted. "And no, I didn't feel sorry for him. There are rules about these things."

"Sometimes I wonder how important rules are," Merritt ventured, looking at her hands, which were folded in her lap. "If everyone has to conform to the exact same ideals and standards even though their situations may be completely different."

"But that's the basis of society in general, isn't it?" Tess asked, looking at her friends. "If we were to do as we please without any regard to social norms, where would we be then? Life would be chaos."

"Maybe there's a little beauty in chaos," Caroline said, looking at Merritt. She shrugged a shoulder. "Isn't that the interesting part of life?"

"What do you think about the fact that Jane had the courage to walk away from Rochester when she felt the situation wasn't right?" Alice asked.

"She should have married St. John," Evie said. "She had the heart and spirit to be a missionary. She could have spent the rest of her life serving the less fortunate."

"At the expense of love," Merritt said, raising a brow.

Tess pursed her lips, then said, "But it was wrong to fall in love with a married man."

Alice set her book on the table. "Who's to say it was wrong? They were two people who found each other in spite of all of the tragedies in life."

Tess stood and walked away from the group and then turned to look at them again. "I don't know what sort of book club this is, pushing people to reject the values we've grown up with. Maybe this isn't a good idea after all."

"We're discussing thoughts and ideas here," Alice said. "This should be a space where we feel free to ask the questions we've always wanted the answer to. Answers to questions like why Rochester fell in love with Jane when he already had a wife."

"You can't help how you feel, can you?" Evie asked. "It's just a matter of not acting on the feelings that are wrong."

"Mrs. Rochester was not a wife in the true sense of the word," Merritt answered. "She had been insane for years. She wasn't even capable of having a relationship. I can't help thinking he must have been so lonely."

"Well, it was wrong to bring a woman to the altar when you have a wife stashed in the attic," Tess insisted, refusing to budge from her position. "A wife who might have been helped with the right kind of care."

"You mentioned St. John," Alice said, changing the subject. "He was a reliable type of man, wasn't he? A clergyman, devoted to serving God. Was he interesting to you?"

"Well, not when I realized he was Jane's cousin," Evie remarked.

"Her cousin!" Caroline sputtered. She turned to Tess. "I knew I wouldn't make it all the way through. I'm afraid I skipped some of the heavier parts. We *are* going to college, you know."

"I skipped through a little too," Evie admitted. "My courses had a lot of reading the last couple of weeks."

"I liked him," Tess replied. "St. John, that is. He was a moral man who wanted to serve by whatever means he could."

"Of course, he specifically wanted to go to India," Merritt said. "He expected Jane to marry him and go along with him, even if it wasn't her dream too. I wasn't sure that was fair of him, myself."

"He felt it was his duty to serve the less fortunate," Tess answered. "And it could have become Jane's duty too."

"What about a woman's duty to herself?" Alice ventured. When no one answered, she smiled. "Anyway, it's something to think about."

She leaned back in her chair and looked out the window. The rain, which had been light earlier, had begun to fall in earnest. Alice couldn't help thinking that in many ways, this newest stage of her life was an expression of her duty to herself. If nothing else, she wanted the girls to at least consider what that might mean for each of them.

"What are we reading next month?" Merritt asked later, when the discussion had begun to dwindle.

Alice rose from her chair and went over to the shelf, where she pulled down several copies of the next book. She went around the circle and handed out the slender volumes, watching as the girls leafed through them.

"Virginia Woolf?" Evie asked. "Who is she?"

"She's a British writer," Tess answered. "And this isn't a novel, is it, Miss Campbell?"

"That's right," Alice acknowledged. "*A Room of One's Own* is a book of essays published in 1929. Does anyone here besides Tess want to be a writer?"

The girls shrugged, looking around the room.

"This book is not just for writers, though," she continued. "This is for all young women as they embark on their life's journey."

"Life's journey," Merritt murmured. "That sounds nice."

"That's why we're at Radcliffe," Evie noted, looking at her friends. "We wanted a chance to start things out the way we wanted. I've never been away from the farm before. I miss it, but I like having the chance to see a different kind of life."

"It's not so different to me," Caroline replied. "Homework and tests and papers to write. It feels just like what I've been doing forever."

"Everyone has had different life experiences," Alice answered. "And while we can agree that there are standards and values—as you said—to ground us, through books we can find out more about the world and see where our imaginations take us."

She rose from her seat and smiled. "Thank you so much for coming tonight. I'll see you on the last Thursday in October."

The girls stood and sorted out their slickers and boots, murmuring their goodbyes. After they had gone, Alice began to clear away the glasses and fold the chairs, wedging them back under the tiny closet below the stairs. When she locked the door and pulled down the shades, she wondered which, if any of them, would be back the following month. Feathers had been ruffled, passions roused. As far as a book club was concerned, however, it was a promising start.

4

_____

OCTOBER 1955

"As long as she thinks of a man, nobody
objects to a woman thinking."

—VIRGINIA WOOLF, *ORLANDO*

Autumn arrived in Cambridge with wet leaves blanketing the
ground. The trees had begun to change color, and to Evie, the world
seemed an impossibly brilliant orange, violet, and red. As all cam-
puses do, the campus looked majestic on a cool fall morning, with
a hint of frost on the box-leaf shrubs and a chill in the air. It was
slow to action in the mornings, with students preferring leisurely
midmorning or afternoon classes under the tutelage of some of the
best professors in the country, rather than racing about at the crack
of dawn.

Evie liked being at Radcliffe. Not that the farm wasn't

wonderful, of course. She would always yearn for the rolling hills and meadows of the place where she grew up. In fact, she wouldn't mind snagging a handsome Harvard beau and talking him into moving back with her. It was something the girls discussed often: what life would be like when they were married, how many children they wanted to have, and what their husbands would do for a living. Evie wanted to marry an engineer, while Merritt thought a lawyer would make a fine husband. When pressed, Caroline merely said she planned to marry someone rich. Tess demurred on the conversation of a future spouse, which Evie attributed to the fact that she had ambitions of her own. That was fine, of course, but it wasn't the life she wanted for herself. She wanted to have a little college experience, find the man of her dreams, and move back to the town where she had grown up. In the meantime, she was happy with her set of friends. Merritt was easygoing, the perfect roommate; Tess was the brainy one who was always willing to help them with their assignments if they needed it; and Caroline was glamorous and fun. Caroline, in particular, intrigued her. Evie enjoyed being in her orbit, except perhaps for one thing: being around so much beauty made her feel self-conscious, as though she were a sunflower in a bouquet of roses. Caroline had that effect on everyone, she supposed.

"Caroline is so gorgeous," Evie said one evening, gazing at her reflection in the mirror over her desk. She was most often complimented on her hazel eyes—brown with flecks of green—and her second-best feature was her wide, generous mouth. She had never thought herself inferior before, but compared to Caroline, she felt exactly like the farm girl she was. She glanced at Merritt, who was sitting in bed with her pencils and sketch pad, watching her. "I can't help feeling like the awkward little sister around her sometimes."

Tess had come into their room to finish writing an essay and was camped on the floor, flipping through her notes. She glanced up at Evie.

"You're fine," Tess replied, pushing up her glasses with a finger. "We can't compare ourselves to her, you know. She's just different."

Merritt put down her book and went over to stand by Evie, reaching out to touch her long braid.

"Have you ever thought of cutting your hair?" she asked.

"No," Evie replied, pulling her plait over her shoulder and hugging it to her chest. She had always been proud of her long mane of hair. In many ways, it had defined her. "What's wrong with my hair?"

"Nothing," Merritt said, studying her with a serious expression. "It's just that you have a great face for short hair."

"Short hair!" Tess echoed, drawn into the conversation. "You can't be serious."

"Look," Merritt said, turning Evie a little to the left. "If you look at her from this angle, she looks like Audrey Hepburn. Can't you see her with a pixie cut like the one in *Roman Holiday*? Then all the boys would be buzzing around."

"I couldn't," Evie said, scandalized. "I mean, seriously, I couldn't. My mother would kill me."

"You have great features," Merritt said. "Such big eyes and a pretty face. The only thing I'd change is your hair. It's hidden in a braid, anyway. If it weren't pulled back all the time, it would frame your face better. You should think about it."

"What would Caroline say?" Evie wondered aloud.

Tess rolled her eyes. "Does it matter?"

Evie nodded. "Well, she does have great taste. Let's ask her."

She went into the adjoining room, followed by the other girls. Caroline looked up from her book when they came in. She reached for a scrap of paper to use as a bookmark and then dropped it on her bed, sitting up to give them her full attention.

"You just rescued me from a particularly dull chapter, girls," she said, drawing her knees up and hugging them to her chest. "What's going on?"

"We want your opinion," Evie said, crossing her arms. "Merritt thinks I should cut off all my hair."

"I didn't say that," Merritt argued, sitting down on Tess's bed. "I said you would look good with a pixie cut."

Evie looked at Caroline, expecting her to laugh. Instead, she had a thoughtful look on her face. She reached under her bed for a stack of fashion magazines and gestured for Evie to sit down beside her.

"When in doubt," she said, flipping through the pages, "consult the experts."

She took several minutes looking through them before spreading them across the bed. Evie moved closer and saw that each page had a photograph of a model selling various products: cigarettes, soda pop, a television set. Caroline studied them for a moment and then rearranged them according to the length of their hair. It was clear that shorter styles were in vogue, as Merritt had suggested, although there were a few with longer hair.

Evie sighed and shook her head. "I don't know. Maybe this is a bad idea. There are too many choices."

"A pixie cut is too severe for you," Caroline pronounced after walking around her, looking at her face from every angle. "You need more fullness around your face. What do you think of this one?" She held out one of the magazines for Evie's inspection, tapping the page.

Merritt and Tess crowded around to look as well.

"A pageboy," Merritt said as they studied the photo of a young woman with hair styled just below shoulder length, curled under all around. "You're right, Caroline. That's much better."

Evie studied the picture, nodding. It was longer than Caroline's, although much shorter than her own nearly waist-length hair. Still, it was stylish in the picture, far more polished than her usual look.

"This hairstyle will show off your waves," Caroline said. "And it won't feel too short once you get used to it."

Evie nodded. If Caroline thought it would look good on her, she would do it. A pixie cut was drastic, she thought; this was merely a change. She could grow it out again if she wanted to.

"What do you think, Tess?" Evie asked. She was the most conservative among them and was the most likely to argue against change, but Evie hoped the opinion would be unanimous.

"It's fine," Tess said, looking over her shoulder at the glossy photo. "And if you don't feel like styling it, you can always wear a ponytail."

"I'll do it," she said, smiling.

"Here," Caroline said, handing her the magazine. "Take this to the salon so you can show them exactly what you want."

The following Saturday, they all went together. While Evie discussed her plan with a hairstylist, her three friends sat in the blow-dryer chairs, flipping through magazines. It was a heady moment. She would never admit it to her sophisticated college friends, but the only haircuts she had ever gotten before were done by her mother as she sat on a milking stool in the kitchen. Evie tensed at the first snip of the scissors, looking to her friends for encouragement.

"I can't do it," she announced, sitting forward. Never mind the lock that had already been cut.

"You want to look stylish, don't you?" Caroline asked, hardly looking up.

Evie wasn't certain she would look stylish, but having Caroline choose a hairstyle for her did make her feel that a little of her friend's glamour had rubbed off on her. She nodded and sat back, looking at the stylist, who waited for her to make up her mind.

"Sorry about that," she said, glancing up to catch the woman's eye in the mirror. "It's just nerves."

She closed her eyes for a minute and then felt her chair swing around so she no longer faced the mirror. Evie took a deep breath and tried to relax. It took several minutes and all her willpower not to wince at every snip of the shears. After the haircut, her hair was rolled onto curlers and she was placed under one of the dryers.

"This is too hot," she complained.

"We all have to sacrifice for beauty's sake," Caroline said.

Merritt was more practical, walking over to adjust the temperature. "There. I turned it down to medium for you."

After twenty minutes under the dryer, Evie went back to the stylist's chair and again was turned away from the mirror as her curlers were removed and her hair was brushed and sprayed with layer upon layer of Aqua Net. When the stylist was finished, she removed the cape around Evie's shoulders with a flourish and held out a hand mirror for her inspection.

"What do you think?" she asked.

Evie stared in the mirror, shocked at her own reflection. It was far better than she had imagined. Sighing, she touched the soft curls.

"I love it," she said.

Merritt came up behind her. "It looks wonderful, Evie."

"But what do I tell my mother?" Evie asked, turning toward Caroline.

"Tell her the truth," Caroline replied, pulling her lipstick from her pocketbook. "You don't have time to care for long hair if you want to get any studying done. Oh, and tell her in a letter, Evie. Never deliver news someone doesn't want to hear on the phone."

Evie nodded. "I'll write Matthew, too, and let him know."

"Who's Matthew?" Tess asked, collecting the magazines from her friends and stacking them neatly on the shelf.

"Her boyfriend," Merritt answered in a teasing voice.

Evie blushed as she gathered her things. "He was my high school boyfriend. We write each other sometimes. He's studying chemistry at Princeton."

"You write each other *sometimes*?" Merritt repeated in a scoffing tone. "You have a box full of letters from him, remember?"

"So what if I do?" Evie answered. "We're just friends. We knew we were going separate ways in August when we went to college. Still, he's nice."

"All boys are nice," Caroline said, tapping the cover of a *Redbook* magazine. "It says so right here."

"This is going to take ages to curl every day," Evie said, trying to change the subject. She looked in the mirror again, pleased with both the hairstyle and the attention.

"No, it won't," Caroline said, brushing off her concerns. "You can sleep in curlers, you know. Besides, we all have to think about being our best selves, especially in a competitive environment like college. It makes professors think you're a good student, and it certainly makes the boys take notice."

"Speaking of boys, there's a Harvest Night mixer this weekend,"

Merritt said, pulling on her cardigan. "Harvard and Radcliffe are both invited. We should go."

"I'm going with Carter," Caroline said, taking her sunglasses out of her pocketbook and perching them on her nose. "You should all come too."

"Where is it?" Evie asked.

"At Wendell Hall," Merritt answered. "Dress is informal. Haven't you seen the posters? They've been pinned up in the halls all week."

"Next to the ones about the domino theory lecture," Tess said.

"What's the domino theory?" Caroline asked, tucking her lipstick in her bag.

"President Eisenhower has a theory that if the world allows Indochina to fall to Communist rule, other nations will fall too," Tess said. "It would turn up the heat on the Cold War."

"You sound like you pay close attention to current events," Merritt commented.

"Of course I do," Tess answered. "Don't you worry about the spread of Communism?"

"Not especially," Caroline replied. "That's happening across the world from us. It doesn't really affect us here in the United States."

Tess shook her head. "Everything that happens in the world has a potential bearing on our lives here at home."

Evie shrugged, stealing another glance in the mirror. "I know you're right, Tess, but let's get back to the dance. Caroline's going with Carter, but what will the rest of us do about dates?"

"A mixer is a place to meet boys," Merritt answered. "There will be lots of single girls there."

"Do you really think we should go?" Tess asked, sighing. "We have book club coming up too. We have to finish Virginia Woolf."

"Of course we're going," Caroline replied, opening the salon door and stepping out into the sunshine. "Never pass up a dance, ladies. Or any chance to dress up and meet boys."

On Saturday, they were in and out of each other's rooms for nearly two hours, trying to get ready. They brushed each other's hair, sharing makeup and clothes and bracelets. Caroline curled Evie's hair herself, styling it as professionally as the stylist at the salon. Merritt loaned Tess a dress in blue gingham with a wide white collar and a bow that hung from the neckline to the waist, which suited her auburn locks. Caroline was the showstopper, however, in a form-fitting, short-sleeved blue sheath with a gathered neckline. It had pleats in the back, giving the skirt a fuller appearance. They had never seen anything like it.

"That is gorgeous," Merritt said, fanning out the skirt with her fingers. "Where have you been hiding it?"

Caroline leaned toward the mirror to apply a thick coat of ruby-red lipstick, then blotted her lips on a tissue.

"This old thing?" she said. "I wore it once to one of my parents' cocktail parties and didn't especially love it. I don't even know why

I brought it with me." She stood back and gazed at her reflection. "I suppose it looks all right."

Evie turned back and examined her own image. "Do you think this blue-violet color suits me?"

"It looks very nice," Merritt said.

"You have the only complexion here that could get away with it," Caroline added. "Come on, everyone. We have a dance to get to."

They walked across the campus to Wendell Hall, Evie a few steps ahead of the others. She pulled up the collar on her jacket to ward off the cold air. It was happening, she thought. It was really happening. Her life had finally begun. As they stepped into the building, they could hear music drifting down the hall. She hesitated at the door, but Caroline took charge and led them inside. They hadn't been in the room for a whole minute before Carter Gray approached Caroline.

"Hey there, gorgeous," he said, holding out a hand. "Let's dance."

She handed her coat to Tess and followed him onto the floor. Evie watched, entranced by the low lights and the music.

"Come on," Tess said, depositing their things on a chair. "There's punch."

They wandered over to the refreshment table and Evie took a cup, taking a sip of the sweet liquid. She'd drank one and just finished another when she noticed a Harvard boy was watching her. Her heart skipped a beat. No one besides Matthew had looked at her like that before.

"Oh my, Evie," Merritt murmured, taking the cup from her hand. "He's coming over."

He was tall, nearly six feet, with a buzz cut and a suit with a blue tie that matched his eyes. He brushed his hand through his hair as he approached and then held out the other, looking her over. "Care to dance?"

"Yes, thank you," Evie said, smiling as she placed her hand in his.

She looked back at Merritt and Tess as he led her onto the dance floor and slipped his arm about her waist. Evie moved closer into his arms and they began to dance, the music pulsing through her veins as the Platters crooned "Only You" from the sound system. Evie sighed, enjoying the intimacy of dancing with a complete stranger. She wanted to ask his name, but she didn't want to break the spell. Looking across the room, she saw that Merritt had been asked to dance as well and was smiling at something her partner said. Tess stood at the refreshment table, eating a piece of cake. She didn't seem to mind that everyone had abandoned her. When her partner spun her around, Evie noticed Caroline and Carter at the center of the dance floor, commanding everyone's attention. Ordinarily, she might have felt a pang of jealousy, but at that moment, Evie didn't mind. She was precisely where she wanted to be.

"This is nice," her partner said in a low voice in her ear.

"Mmm," she answered.

His head dipped close to hers, so close she could feel his breath against her cheek. His hand tightened around her waist, and she felt a shiver go down her spine. She suddenly thought of senior prom with Matthew, but the dance in their small town had nothing of the magic of a night like this. She shook her head for a second, trying to forget him if only for a few minutes.

"Are you all right?" her partner asked.

"I'm fine," she replied.

"Let's get some air," he said, releasing her from his grip and taking her hand to lead her outside. He reached into his coat pocket for a packet of cigarettes and held it out. "Would you like one?"

"No, thanks," Evie said.

She was a mass of contradictions: disappointment at ending the dance and having his arms drop from her waist, fear that he would do something inappropriate, fear that he wouldn't. Worry that the others were watching from the open French doors. But when she looked back at the building, she could see that no one had followed them.

He pocketed the cigarettes again. "I don't really want one, either, I suppose. I guess I just wanted…"

"What?" she asked.

He moved closer, raising a hand to put a finger on her lips. "You have a pretty smile, do you know that?"

Evie shook her head, listening to the leaves rustling in the gentle breeze. Instinctively, she closed her eyes, and in a moment, his lips were on hers and she was lost in a sea of emotion. The kiss seemed to go on forever. When he pulled back, she almost lost her balance. She took hold of his arm to steady herself.

"Are you all right?" he asked.

"I'm fine," she said, touching the lips he had just kissed.

"Come on," he breathed near her ear. "Let's catch the next dance."

She was still caught up in the moment but allowed him to lead her back inside to the dance floor. Later, she wouldn't remember what song had been playing. When the music stopped, she nodded and smiled.

"Thanks for the dance," he said.

Evie watched him walk away, shocked that he wanted a different partner. Then she shook herself. She was a good girl, wasn't she? What was she doing, flirting with a complete stranger and letting him kiss her like that? Another young man asked her for a dance, and she accepted, and then another after that, though she scanned the crowd when they were on the floor, looking for her first partner. She didn't see him again for the rest of the evening.

Around ten o'clock, the girls gathered their coats to walk back to the dorm. They were quiet, each lost in their own thoughts. When they arrived, they stood on the porch in the moonlight, reluctant to go inside and break the spell. Evie sat on one of the benches, looking up at the moon. Merritt sat down next to her and sighed.

"What are you thinking?" asked Merritt.

"About Matthew," Evie said, watching as the clouds drifted across the moonlit sky. "Do you think he's going to mixers and meeting pretty girls?"

"Probably," Tess said, leaning against one of the columns.

"Tess!" Merritt exclaimed. "That's not helpful."

"This was a nice evening," Evie said. "It's exactly what I hoped college would be: a chance to meet people and go to dances and have a wonderful time."

Merritt cocked her head. "As long as you know Matthew's waiting for you."

"Especially if he's not having any fun," Evie admitted. She leaned against one of the columns and ducked her head. "That's not exactly what I mean. I just don't want him meeting new girls."

"You want all of his fun to be the pleasure of figuring out a trigonometry equation," Tess supplied. "Isn't that right?"

"Yes, I suppose so," she admitted. "Does that make me a bad person?"

"Honestly, Evie," Caroline reprimanded. "You're eighteen years old! Why wouldn't you want to meet a hundred boys? And kiss a few of them too."

"Caroline!" she said, scandalized, though she wondered if her friend was right.

"Well, you should," Caroline replied. "Your life is just beginning."

"I do miss him, though," Evie murmured. "Do you suppose it's too late to call?"

"Yes," they all answered at the same time.

"Until you have a ring on your finger, you're not taken," Caroline insisted. "And while I'm thinking of it, stop smiling at boys. It only encourages them."

"Don't smile at them?" Evie protested. "But don't we want to encourage them? Isn't that the whole point?"

"You don't want to look too eager," Caroline advised. She stood and opened the front door. "Well, it's late. I'm going to bed. Good night, everyone."

"I should go too," Tess said, following Caroline inside.

"Come on," Merritt said, coaxing Evie. "Let's go. It's cold out here."

"I'll be there in a minute," Evie answered.

Merritt squeezed her shoulder and went inside, leaving the door slightly open. Evie stared up at the starless sky, thinking of her first college kiss, feeling exhilarated and guilty all at the same time. Maybe Caroline was right. She could keep writing to Matthew and date a few Harvard boys on the side. That's not how she had been raised, of course, but right or wrong, she couldn't possibly be the only college girl to feel like this.

5

"Keep your schedules free for Saturday," Caroline told them on Thursday morning at breakfast as they took a plate and looked at the items along the sideboard. The cooking staff, led by Mrs. Kowalski, filled it each morning with scrambled eggs, sausages, bacon, toast, fried potatoes, fruit salad, pancakes, and oatmeal. The four of them spent a couple of minutes deciding what to have before filling their plates and taking them to the table. Caroline settled on a small bowl of oatmeal sprinkled with a few berries, unlike the others, who took advantage of the full meal.

"You eat like a bird," Evie observed as she tucked into a plate of sausages, bacon, and over easy eggs.

"She has to," Merritt replied, buttering her toast as she smiled at Caroline. "That's the way she fits into her fabulous clothes."

They had settled into a comfortable routine: get dressed and ready for classes, have breakfast together in the dining room, walk to the campus as a group, and then meet for lunch. In the afternoons, they went their separate ways. Their classes were in different buildings. Evie had a part-time job in the bursar's office to help make her tuition payments, while Tess spent extra hours studying in the library. After dinner, they set aside time to go over notes together, wandering from one room to the other, asking each other for help or distracting themselves with magazines and doing their nails or occasionally going downstairs to watch *I Love Lucy* on the communal television in the lounge. It was a schedule they liked, even Tess. Before college, she had been a loner, focused solely on her academic achievements with the hope of applying to colleges like Radcliffe and Wellesley, but she found herself enjoying the companionship of other young girls more than she had expected.

"What's on Saturday?" Merritt asked, pausing between bites.

"We're going to the Harvard game," Caroline answered. "Carter got us tickets."

"A football game?" Tess asked. Even though she had brothers, sports were not her area of expertise and that wasn't likely to change.

"That's right, I heard there was a big game on Saturday," Evie said, sounding pleased. "What time is it, Caroline?"

"It starts at two o'clock," she answered. "We'll leave here around one."

She took a final bite of oatmeal and then excused herself,

floating out of the room as quickly as she had come in. Tess turned to Evie.

"Do you like football?" she asked.

"Sure," Evie said, shrugging. "I have brothers, you know. I've spent a lot of time at their games. Besides, it's a Harvard game, Tess. We'll get a chance to see all the boys we could possibly want."

Merritt gave a wry smile. "You and boys, Evie. Have you forgotten Matthew now altogether?"

"Of course not."

"Well, I suppose there's no harm in hedging your bets," Merritt answered. "Come on. Let's get our things. I have an English test this morning."

On Saturday, quizzes and essays behind them, they began to get ready for the football game. Tess had her misgivings. She ought to be getting ahead in a class or two, but Caroline had gotten tickets especially for them, and she didn't want to let them down. The three of them were not only her roommates; they were her only college friends. It was sensible to get along whenever she could. They had included her in all their activities, which she hadn't expected. When she was dressed, she went into Evie and Merritt's room.

"I'm almost ready," Merritt said. She wore dungarees with the cuffs rolled up and was pulling a red sweater over a white blouse.

Then she took a pair of saddle shoes out of her closet and slipped them on.

"I'm copying you," Evie said, grabbing her dungarees. "I have a red sweater too. What are you wearing, Tess?"

Tess looked down at her brown plaid dress and loafers. She didn't have dungarees. In fact, she didn't have anything more suitable to wear.

"I don't have a red sweater," she said as if that were the only problem.

"Go ahead and wear mine," Evie said, tossing it to her. "It'll go with the dress you're wearing, anyway. I'll wear the gold one. That way we'll both be in Harvard colors."

Tess slipped the cardigan on and looked at herself in the mirror, wondering how much a pair of saddle shoes would cost. Then she shook herself. She wasn't here to be a fashion plate; she was here to get an education. If only there weren't so many extracurricular opportunities, things she had never thought about when she had applied to Radcliffe. Although, to be fair, it was probably no different from any of the other colleges she had considered.

Caroline came into the room and turned in a circle for them, posing.

"What do you think?" she asked.

She wore a gray Harvard letter sweater with a large crimson H on the left side and three thin yellow band stripes on the left sleeve. Around her throat, she had knotted a yellow silk scarf. Her full, pleated skirt was a crimson plaid, and she wore bobby socks and loafers on her feet. Tess had never seen anyone look so wonderful.

"Great sweater," Merritt said to Caroline.

Tess looked back at Caroline. "Is it Carter's?"

"Of course it's Carter's," Caroline replied, adjusting her scarf. "He wants me to wear it for good luck. He's the quarterback, you know."

"Who are they playing?" Evie asked as she tucked her key into her pocket. She shook her head. "I can't believe I don't know this. I've just been busy this week."

"Cornell," Caroline and Merritt said at the same time. They smiled at each other.

"Here are the tickets," Caroline announced, holding them out. "Is everyone ready?"

Evie took hers with a smile. "I can't believe we're going to a real college football game. I could pinch myself."

"Well?" Caroline asked. "What are we waiting for? Let's blow this joint, girls."

Tess buttoned the red sweater and then went back to her room, looking for a scarf. She found one in the back of the wardrobe and wrapped it around her throat, looking in the mirror. After a moment, she unknotted it and put it back in the closet. It looked like she was trying too hard.

"Tess!" Caroline called. "We're ready!"

"Coming!" she replied. She took two steps toward the door and then snatched the scarf from the closet, stuffing it into her purse. She could always put it on if she changed her mind.

They walked toward the football stadium together, Tess watching the festive atmosphere around her with interest. The crowd was enormous, as if everyone in Cambridge were headed to the game. The band played pep songs and everyone waved pennants. The smell of hamburgers wafted through the air, although Tess couldn't tell where it came from. Popcorn dotted the pavement like a trail. They made their way through the turnstiles and Caroline led them to their seats, halfway between the two end goals.

"You're Caroline, aren't you?" a voice called out.

They all turned to look at a group of young men who sat down on the bleachers behind them. The Harvard students were eyeing them with interest.

"I am," Caroline answered, sizing up the one who had spoken to her. "Are you friends of Carter Gray?"

"Everyone's friends with Carter," another answered. "I'm Dexter Hamilton. Who are your friends?"

Caroline introduced everyone, and Tess turned back toward the playing field as soon as she had finished. The others chatted as she feigned interest in the pregame activity below.

"It's Tess, right?" one of them said in her ear.

She turned to see who had spoken to her. He was larger than the others, a muscular young man with dark hair and serious eyes. She was uncomfortable having him so close to her shoulder.

"Yes," she said, nodding. "And you are?"

"I'm Ken Blackburn," he answered. "Are you a football fan?"

She resisted the urge to ignore him and shook her head. "This is my first game."

"Ah," he replied. "Then I'll have to give you some pointers as we go."

The crowd roared when Harvard took the field, everyone jumping to their feet at the sight of the crimson jerseys. Caroline waved over a man with a concessions tray and bought an enormous tub of popcorn, then handed it to Tess.

The weather was cool but not cold, and Tess realized it was not unpleasant to sit and watch the game, even with Ken calling out plays as they went along. The others were interested in the action, even Caroline, which surprised her.

"There's Carter," Merritt told Tess, pointing to a player near the thirty-yard line. "Number forty-two."

"Ah," she murmured.

She watched as he effortlessly threw the ball across the field. It appeared he was as good at football as he was at stealing hearts. It was unfair, she thought, for one boy to get all the best qualities.

"First down!" Evie screamed, jumping to her feet.

Merritt followed suit, clapping her hands in delight. When the roar of the crowd died down, she sat and smiled at Tess. "This is fun, isn't it?"

Tess nodded. She had nothing to compare it to, but it was

certainly interesting, if for no other reason than to observe her friends and the gusto they displayed as fans.

"I love football," Evie said, sitting back down on the other side of Tess. "When my brothers played in high school, I went to all of their games. What about you, Caroline?"

"My father played when he was a student here in the thirties," Caroline answered, never taking her eyes off the field and number forty-two. "I was raised on this stuff. When I told him last night that I had tickets to today's game, he was so jealous!"

"Watch Carter," Ken told them. "He's going to throw the long ball."

He was right. The pass went thirty yards down the field. In spite of herself, Tess felt a thrill run down her spine. The crowd was on their feet, watching as one of Carter's teammates caught the ball, and screamed as he ran all the way to the goal for a touchdown. Tess clapped her hands over her ears as the crowd roared.

However, Harvard couldn't maintain their edge. Cornell took over and the boys in crimson began to struggle. By midgame, the stands were half-empty. Even Carter's friends got up and left after the third quarter.

"Let's get a hamburger," Merritt said. "I'm starving."

"I could use a milkshake," Evie answered.

"Carter's always busy after a game, so I'm free," Caroline told them. "They have to review the game and make a plan for next week."

They filed out of the stadium and walked a few blocks to

Ernie's Luncheonette. Sliding into a booth, Tess pulled the plastic menus from where they were propped against the wall and handed one to each of them, the smell of onions and grease in the air. This was different from the dorm, where they had proper napkins in the dining room and a vase of pansies on the table and a buffet with a silver pitcher of water. Her friends looked so alive and happy, though she was thinking of the lost hours of study that she would have to make up when everyone went to bed. This, she realized, was the price you had to pay to fit in at college. She almost wondered if it was worth it. Then she told herself she wasn't committing to a major life change. It was one day, one football game. Surely they wouldn't be expected to go every game.

"I like Carter's friends," Evie said. She glanced over at Tess. "What was the name of the one who was talking to you? He was pretty handsome."

"Ken," Tess answered, shrugging. "He was all right."

"'All right'?" Caroline laughed. "You have some pretty high standards, Tess. I should think he'd be cute enough for any one of us."

"Don't you like boys?" Evie asked, studying her intently.

"Of course I like boys," Tess replied, blushing. "But we're here to get an education, remember? A diploma from one of the most prestigious colleges in the country!"

Merritt smiled. "You're good for us, Tess. We need you to keep us on the straight and narrow. Otherwise, we'd forget what we came here for."

"I don't know about you," Caroline said, "but I'd be happy to forget what I'm supposed to do sometimes and just have a little fun."

Tess felt a twinge of guilt. She was too fussy sometimes, she knew. It was her stern upbringing. She was well schooled in the art of duty and unaccustomed to fun, although the last thing she wanted to do was spoil everyone's time, particularly Caroline's. Her roommate had been nothing short of wonderful, and she reminded herself to be thankful. She had been asked along on a day out, not to mention being included in all the others' plans. She needed to try to go along with things more.

No one seemed to be put out at her scolding, so she tried to relax. They sat in the diner for a long time, drinking Cokes and eating french fries, chatting with the boys who came up from time to time as well as with girls they knew from their classes.

If she had been the sort to keep a diary, she would have written about the day. It was perfect in every respect, and perfect days don't happen all that often. That evening, for the first time, she had trouble settling down to her studies. After they got back to the dorm, they had enjoyed a cup of steaming cider, taking it outside and drinking it in the cool fall air on the porch. Tess was getting to know some of the other girls, like Anne, who was studying English and wanted to teach middle school back home in Nevada; and Chloe, who hadn't decided on a major but hoped to leave her native Alabama and live in New England when she had graduated from college. They were all so different and yet, in some ways, the same: girls with hopes and dreams who felt they would find them at this college, in this town, just like Tess. She closed her algebra book, knowing it would be impossible to read another word. Instead, she sat back on her bed, arms behind her head, thinking of the gloriousness of fall days.

However, later that week when the campus organized a hayride, she demurred, deciding not to go.

"Come on, Tess," Caroline said. "You have to come with us! This is one of those times when you'll make good college memories."

"I can't," she insisted, refusing to tell her the truth—that she was worried about her studies. She had gotten a ninety-two on one of her exams and that was no way to make it to the top of the class. "Besides, I'm allergic to hay."

"But there will be boys!" Evie said. "Harvard's been invited too."

"You'll have fun," Merritt said, trying to urge her to go.

"There may even be kissing in the dark!" Caroline added. "You never know, Tess. You might meet Mr. Right."

"Sorry," Tess said, holding firm. "You have a wonderful time. Kiss a few boys for me, all right?"

Reluctantly, the others left her and eventually, the building fell silent. Tess took up her books and placed them in order of importance on her desk, with the imminent tests at the top. She had to get serious about her studies. Sitting at the desk, she sighed, wishing she didn't have so much willpower.

And then she saw it out of the corner of her eye: Caroline's diary, tucked under her roommate's pillow. Tess stared at it for a long time before she went over and pulled it from its perch with her index finger. She didn't write in a diary herself because she rarely had anything to say. But Caroline was different. Things were always happening to her. Sighing, Tess pushed it back under the pillow. She was at Radcliffe now, and it was possible that something interesting might happen to her one day too.

6

Alice prepared the shop for the second book club precisely as she had the first. Five chairs sat in a circle around a small table to hold books or glasses. On the side shelf, she had set an open bottle of wine, this time a merlot, and five tumblers alongside a pitcher of water. The shop itself was gleaming. She had been doing a brisk business for the last couple of weeks, but she still found plenty of time to organize the shop and dust and straighten the shelves. Half an hour before the girls were to arrive, she poured herself a glass of wine and sat in the circle, thinking about her own life.

Coming to Cambridge had been the right decision. She had long wanted to come to New England; in fact, she had wanted to go anywhere outside of the Windy City, and Boston was as stunning as she had imagined. The previous day, she had taken the ferry around the harbor. There was a freedom here she had never experienced before, though perhaps that was because of the gift of anonymity. She knew no one here, and no one expected anything of her. But she also loved Boston for its own virtues, especially the salty sea air and the cool breeze on her face. She'd tied her scarf over her ears and stood at the railing, reveling in her first look at the Atlantic Ocean.

Alice had been on boats when she was young, mostly short cruises on Lake Michigan when she and her sister were small. They would go to the beach in Chicago once every summer and gulls flapped occasionally overhead, but everywhere were reminders that they were in the city. She wanted to live in a place that reminded her of summer and warm days and the feeling of gliding on the water like a swan. Boston satisfied that craving.

Her friends and family had been outraged that she made such a move, so far from everyone she knew, but it was precisely what her soul needed. Virginia Woolf had said it best, in her opinion: "As a woman I have no country... As a woman my country is the whole world." For centuries—in fact, for all time—men had been free to go anywhere they wished. But it was 1955 now, Alice thought. Things had changed. Even a woman could dream of such freedom. Some could even attain it.

She wasn't convinced the girls in her book club would understand such a dream. They were too busy having their first taste of independence, such as it was in a dorm with a housemother and a curfew. But it was still independence. No mother to tell them to sit up straight or to finish their meat loaf. No brothers and sisters who knew all one's secrets and badgered them endlessly about their faults and ridiculed their innermost desires. At college, they were experiencing an artificial freedom, not unlike living in a bubble, and it wouldn't be pleasant when one day, sooner or later, the bubble would pop. They would graduate or perhaps grow bored and drop out of college. They would marry. Radcliffe, which at this moment was the ultimate freedom, would recede into their memories like a long-forgotten dream. She could challenge them if she wished, but they wouldn't understand anything until the moment they chose to. The problem was, as Alice was keenly aware, so few women chose to. That had been the problem with her family in Chicago. They looked at everything through the lens of the paternalistic society in which they lived. It was difficult to change minds, even more so to change hearts. She found herself wondering if any of her book club girls would change and grow over the course of the year, thinking it likely they wouldn't. Habits and beliefs are ingrained in one from such a young age. Nevertheless, she was happy to be part of their journey.

Alice looked up when the door opened at precisely seven o'clock.

"Hello, everyone!" she called as Merritt pushed open the door, the others following closely behind her.

There was a flurry of greetings, and once again, they removed their jackets. As a whole, they were a pleasant group, smiling and happy. The room seemed to come to life with the rustle of skirts and the jewel tones of their sweaters. As Alice took their coats, she gestured toward the shelf.

"Help yourself to something to drink," she said, taking the coats to the hook.

Once again, they all chose water. Even Caroline, who seemed so worldly, seemed to have either no interest in wine or, perhaps more realistically, no desire to rock the boat.

"How have you been since I've last seen you?" Alice asked, pouring herself a second glass of wine and settling into her chair. "How are you enjoying life at Radcliffe?"

"I love everything about it," Merritt answered. "We have great professors, Miss Campbell. I feel like I'm learning so much."

"We're having fun too," Evie said. "It's not all work. Caroline took us to a football game last weekend and we had a wonderful time."

"Did you go to college in Boston?" Caroline asked, looking at Alice.

"I went to the University of Chicago," Alice answered, smiling. "That's where I grew up. But I've always wanted to live on the coast."

"I like it here too," Tess remarked. "I hope we can see a little more of the area soon."

Merritt nodded. "I'd love to go to the Museum of Fine Arts sometime if anyone's interested. Everyone says it is one of the best in the country."

"You're an art major," Tess said. "Of course you have to go."

"I'll go with you," Caroline offered. "I've been with my mother several times, and I can show you my favorite paintings."

"I didn't know you liked art," Merritt answered, smiling.

Caroline shrugged. "I like some art. There's a Renoir you have to see called *Dance at Bougival*. It makes you feel alive just looking at it."

The girls looked at her, possibly thinking the same thing that Alice was—that perhaps their golden girl had hidden depths. Of course, that remained to be seen.

"Well, ladies, what did you think of Virginia Woolf?" Alice asked, looking around the circle with a feeling of satisfaction.

She was pleased that all four young women had returned this month and hadn't been put off by the last meeting. After all, she believed that challenging one's ideals was the purpose of studying books, not necessarily to change behavior but to inform one's thought. Let them be housewives if that was their greatest desire, but let them be mathematicians and scientists and professors if they so wished. Women deserved the right to dream as well as men. Alice knew too well, however, the decisiveness with which some women shut down challenging avenues of thought, let alone new experiences. It was a stubbornness she herself had confronted on many occasions.

"I thought because it was a short book, it would be an easy read," Caroline said, pulling her scarf from around her neck and tying it onto the strap of her handbag. "But for a skinny book, it was quite thick, if you know what I mean."

"I thought it was interesting," Merritt ventured, "although I didn't agree with all of it. And if I'm honest, a few parts made me downright angry."

"That's interesting," Alice said. "Like what, specifically?"

"The quote from Alexander Pope, for one, about how 'most women have no character at all.' That was insulting."

"Wasn't it?" Alice agreed. "And it goes without saying that it's simply not true. Why do you think he believed it?"

"Maybe because the lives of women for generations gone by was that of a virtual slave in the household," Tess replied, shuddering. "They worked like drudges, had too many babies, and had no ability to speak for themselves. Women didn't have much of a life then. Some still don't."

"Did anything else make you angry when you read it?" Alice asked the group.

"What about the part where she mentioned that Napoleon thought women were incapable of being educated?" Caroline said, glancing around the circle. "And look at us, won't you? Proving him wrong right this moment at Radcliffe College."

"That's right," Alice said, nodding. "Here you are, fresh, young college students with the world offered up to you on a plate."

"No thanks to men," Tess said. "I don't know why you're all so interested in them."

"Do you think that Virginia Woolf hated men?" Evie asked, glancing at her friends. "She didn't have many good things to say about them in this book. And some of the ones we know seem perfectly nice. Just look at Carter and his friends."

"Let's take a look at one of her quotes, shall we?" Alice said, opening her book. A slender ribbon marked the spot, and she removed it and set it on her lap as she began to read. "Here's a quote from Samuel Johnson that Virginia Woolf used: 'Men know that women are an overmatch for them, and therefore they choose the weakest or the most ignorant. If they did not think so, they never could be afraid of women knowing as much as themselves.'"

"See what I mean?" Evie said, shaking her head. "That's exactly what I'm talking about."

"I think it depends on whether or not the statement is true," Tess murmured.

Alice raised a brow, surprised at Tess's comment. "Do you think it's true? Do men choose women who are weaker or ignorant?"

"Maybe," Tess said.

Caroline nodded. "Some do. Without question."

"Not everyone feels that way, I'm sure of it," Evie protested. She looked at Merritt. "What do you think?"

"I haven't met enough men to know for sure," Merritt admitted. "That's why I'm here at Radcliffe. Most of the other good women's colleges are too secluded. There's no opportunity to get to know the opposite sex."

The girls laughed, nodding.

"Well, Miss Woolf wrote this book in England in 1929," Alice ventured. "And in 1929, do you think men were afraid of women knowing as much as they did and potentially having equal power to them?"

"Yes," Tess said.

"But it's twenty-five years later," Evie persisted. "I mean, look at us. We're here at a prestigious college. We can even attend coed classes. Surely, that's being equal to men, don't you think?"

"Is it?" Caroline asked, shrugging. "Do you expect your opinions to carry the same weight as one of the boys' at Harvard? And what about when they're a lawyer or the head of an international firm? How equal do you think your voice will be then?"

They left the question dangling in the air. Alice slipped the ribbon back into the book and set it on the table.

"Here's a question for you," she said. "Have you ever thought you were smarter than a member of the opposite sex?"

"Well, I'm smarter than my brothers," Evie admitted. "They're a couple of numbskulls, those two."

"I am," Tess answered. "I mean, I'm smarter than my brothers too. None of them cared a whit about going to college. But the same was true in school. Most of the boys I knew were too lazy to work for good grades or to get into a good university."

"I think that's too simple a question, Miss Campbell," Caroline inserted, lifting her glass. "Men might not be smarter, but they have a rigged system. They'll get the jobs and the power and the money. They might not have the intelligence or even the drive, but they're smarter in a different way and use it to their advantage."

"Does that mean that all men are bad?" Alice asked.

"No," Merritt and Evie answered together.

"Not necessarily," Merritt ventured. "Some are perfectly nice. Otherwise, women would never marry them."

"I think it's interesting that you mentioned coed classes, Evie," Alice said. "Harvard has had coed classes since 1943."

"Why 1943?" asked Tess.

"That's when the boys went to war," Merritt replied, looking up at Alice. "Right, Miss Campbell?"

Alice nodded. "That's right. When so many young men went to Europe, they had to allow the Radcliffe women to attend with Harvard men to fill up the classes. But not that long ago, the majority of men in this state didn't even want Radcliffe to be formed. They worried about what it would mean in society for women to be educated alongside men and also about the effect of male and female comingling at a young, impressionable age."

"There needs to be a lot more male and female comingling in my opinion," Caroline said with a laugh.

"You already have someone to go out with, you know, Caroline," Tess reminded her with an arched brow.

Caroline turned toward her, surprised. "My. It sounds like someone has a crush on Carter Gray."

"No I don't," Tess stammered, her cheeks growing pink.

"She was teasing, Tess," Evie said. "Weren't you, Caroline?"

Caroline didn't answer.

"Let's change the subject for a minute," Alice said, opening her book and studying the page in front of her. "Here's an interesting concept. Virginia Woolf mentions a library and then asks whether it is worse to be locked in or locked out. What do you think? Which would be worse to you?"

"Locked out," Tess answered, sitting forward. "Imagine not being able to read whatever you want, whenever you want. You couldn't educate yourself or lose yourself in a good book."

"Locked in," Caroline said, smoothing her skirt. "I can't think of anything worse. I like to read now and then, but I'd a million times rather be driving around the coast, looking at the ocean than trapped in a room full of dusty old books."

"Locked out, I think," Merritt said. "I mean, I'm not the reader Tess is, but it's wonderful to browse around and look up things you're interested in. Being locked out sounds like censorship to me."

"What about you, Evie?" Alice asked.

Evie shrugged, brushing back her bangs. "I don't think I could stand to be locked in anyplace. I'm used to freedom and the great outdoors. It's probably from being raised on a farm."

"What about you, Miss Campbell?" Tess asked, staring up at her. "Which sounds worse to you?"

Alice smiled. "I think I'm definitely in the locked-out camp. After all, as you can see, I live in my own little world of books."

"I love this shop," Evie said. "It's got such a good feeling here."

"Thank you," Alice replied. She turned a couple of pages until she found what she was looking for. "Here's another one. Miss Woolf said that a writer wasn't to forget the importance of writing about food. I have to say, listening to her describe gravy so thin you could see the china pattern through it wasn't very appealing, was it? So what is your favorite food?"

She turned to Tess again, who actually smiled.

"Pork chops with mashed potatoes," she replied after a moment. "Hot butter dripping all over them."

"What about you, Evie?" Alice asked.

"My mother's homemade fried chicken," Evie answered. "You haven't even had fried chicken if you haven't had hers. She wins prizes at the county fair."

"I can't help myself," Merritt said, grinning. "I love a good, greasy hamburger. Lots of cheese. And onions too."

Caroline made a face. "Oh, Merritt, onions, really?"

"Oh, yes, always with onions," Merritt said. "What's your favorite?"

"Well, I don't especially love food," Caroline answered. "But I suppose my very favorite is a cod sandwich that you can get at this place near where I live. The fish is always freshly caught, and it's a little bit of heaven."

"You're making me hungry," Alice said.

They all laughed.

"Not all of Miss Woolf's ideas, as you can see, were controversial," Alice said. "But she was not afraid to explore the heavier aspects of life, things that women were sometimes afraid to discuss. For example, she says quite plainly that for most women, it didn't matter if they made money because their husband would take it from them anyway."

"But doesn't it make sense for one person to be the financial leader in the family?" Tess asked. "And wouldn't those decisions fall to the breadwinner?"

"But what of the wife's contribution to the family?" Alice asked. "Is taking care of a home and a family worth less than what a man makes at a job outside the home?"

"Some husbands give their wives allowances," Caroline said.

Evie nodded. "Sometimes it's a very generous allowance too."

"Let me ask you this," Alice said. "Do you think a woman should be allowed the opportunity to write a book if she wants?"

"Of course," Merritt answered. "Or paint a picture or write a song…"

"Let's say a woman writes a book in her free hours," Alice continued. "She has a wonderful idea, and when she is finished, a publisher wants to publish it. And now let's say that the money she's offered for the book is ten times more than her husband makes."

The girls grew quiet for a moment. Evie finally broke the silence.

"Well, then she should have some say in how it is spent, but she should look to her husband for guidance when the sum is that high. He's used to making decisions and knows how to take care of things better than she does."

"Does everyone agree?" Alice asked.

They were noncommittal, shrugging and waiting to hear what she would say next.

"All right, then, what about a woman who knits blankets in her spare time?" she continued. "Let's say she can ask ten dollars per blanket. She makes ten or twelve of them in a year for a modest hundred or hundred and twenty dollars, perhaps. And imagine that she stashes the money in a jar at the back of the pantry. If her husband comes in one day looking for a packet of crackers and finds it, is he entitled to keep it or not?"

"Of course not," Caroline asked. "She worked for that herself."

Tess shook her head. "No, he can't keep it."

"It's hers," Evie said.

Merritt nodded in agreement.

Alice looked around the group. "It's interesting that when we had a woman making ten times more than her husband, you weren't quite sure if he should have control of the money or not, but when it comes to the pin money in a jar at the back of a cupboard, you are all adamant that the money belongs to her. Why were you more interested in the woman who has little?"

"You can't have nothing," Caroline said. "It's like he's stripping her of all value when he takes everything."

Alice reached for her wineglass and took a sip before setting it back on the table. "We're all that woman," she said. "Whether we knit blankets or write books. It doesn't matter. The money you make belongs to you."

"But it makes a man really angry when he can't control things," Evie answered. She looked around the group. "Everyone knows that."

Alice shrugged. "I suppose the question is whether or not that is fair."

"I'm uncomfortable thinking we do things or don't do things because a man might disapprove," Merritt said. "That doesn't seem like a smart way for a woman to make decisions. Shouldn't marriage be a bit of a compromise? Both people should have their feelings taken into account, right?"

The conversation went on for a while and Alice sat back, watching them, lost in her own thoughts. She thought of her life with Jack, when she hadn't had control over a single cent. How different her life was now, when she was free to make decisions for herself.

"What was your favorite part of the book?" she asked when they had arbitrated decisions of their own.

"The writing," Tess answered. "It was so pretty and lyrical in spots. I'd like to read more of Virginia Woolf's books."

"I like the way she made you think about things you never thought of before," Evie added. "Even if I don't agree with it all."

"Merritt?" Alice pressed. "Did you like anything about the book?"

"I couldn't stop thinking about the story of her inheritance from her aunt and how it allowed her freedom," Merritt answered. "It was something I've never thought of before. She said she didn't have to worry about shelter or clothes or food because of the generosity of her aunt. Because of it, she was free."

"We have a lot of freedom," Alice ventured. "But we take it for granted sometimes, without considering the lack of freedoms our mothers and grandmothers had."

Evie nodded. "I suppose I liked the part where she mentions that men run to and fro trying to make money when a little bit of it and some sunshine were all one really needs."

"Caroline, what about you?" Alice asked.

"This book was a little bit like homework, if you don't mind me saying it," Caroline answered, shaking her head. "I felt like I was plodding through ten feet of snow trying to get through a single page. So I suppose my favorite part was the end."

Alice laughed. "That sounds like a good place for us to stop tonight. Are you ready to get your books for next time?"

"What are we going to read?" Tess asked.

"We're back to another novel," Alice said, rising from her chair. "*The Age of Innocence* by Edith Wharton. Let me get them for you."

Everyone nodded blankly, accepting the books as she handed them out. They probably hadn't heard of it. If not, Alice thought, they were in for something special: star-crossed lovers and the complexities of love. Although, in Alice's view, any experience with love at all was complicated. That was just the way of the world.

7

> "The air of ideas is the only air worth
> breathing."
>
> —EDITH WHARTON, *THE AGE OF INNOCENCE*

The Radcliffe College Library was a grand building, one Tess associated with the beauty of a New England Ivy League college. Whenever she was there, she was in her element. She organized her friends into study groups and set up schedules where they could work together, but even if she hadn't been fortunate enough to make friends at college, which she hadn't expected, she still wouldn't have been lonely. Instead, she would have spent the majority of her time in the library, content to concentrate on her homework and observe other students from a safe distance, just as she had done in the past. Here, she wandered the rooms, inspecting titles of the books, familiarizing herself with the location of her favorite subjects, sitting in various armchairs to determine a favorite. Before coming to Radcliffe, she had planned to spend longer hours there, but her friends took up more time than she had imagined.

Three afternoons each week, they sat at a huge table in one of the large study rooms, books spread out among them, sometimes working together, often in a companionable silence. Since the others had rejected the notion of daily study sessions, she found time to go herself on the days when they did not. It made the college feel as if it belonged to her, as if she knew the heart of the institution was the place where knowledge was stored. Tess had applied to other universities and been accepted, but she couldn't imagine a better place for higher education than Radcliffe.

Her other favorite spot was a bench in Radcliffe Yard. It was almost as if she could feel the wisdom of those who had gone before her. She could certainly use it. Already there were situations—like dances, for instance—that she had not calculated into the scheme of her college experience. She was beginning to think that some of these diversions were educations of their own, in a way, but nothing surpassed the excitement she felt sitting in a room of higher learning, where the air they breathed meant freedom.

"What are you doing tonight?" Merritt asked her at dinner one evening.

The four of them sat around the dining table, picking at

the meat loaf. It was the one meal of which Tess wasn't fond. It reminded her too much of home.

"The usual," she answered. "Studying."

Merritt glanced at Evie and Caroline. "I know it's a school night, but we thought we could all do something fun. Harvard shows movies on Tuesday nights in one of the smaller auditoriums, and tonight it's a good one. I, for one, could use a break."

Tess looked at the other two, who nodded. She had the feeling they had already decided and were trying to gauge her reaction.

"Really?" she asked. "I feel like we're always doing extracurricular activities."

"Extracurricular activities," Caroline scoffed. "You have to live a little, Tess. We're young! We're supposed to be enjoying ourselves."

"Besides, it's a little trip to Italy!" Evie exclaimed. "They're showing *Three Coins in the Fountain.*"

"Has anyone seen it?" Merritt asked.

"Well, I have," Caroline admitted. "But unfortunately, I was on a date and he was an octopus, all hands. I can't remember a single thing about the film. I was too busy playing defense."

"It's a date, then," Merritt said. "We'll walk over after dinner."

Tess started to protest but held her tongue. She didn't want to be overly social, but she had to admit she had enjoyed most of their nights out. She only hoped there wouldn't be any interaction with boys. In her opinion, they had a better time when they were on their own.

After dinner, they went upstairs to get their coats and then walked a few blocks to the Harvard campus. The sun had already set, but streetlamps lit the way. The evening air was cool, but there was no wind, and the walk was pleasant. Dozens of other students were headed in the same direction.

"I'm not usually a spontaneous person," Tess admitted to Merritt as they walked. She was comfortable talking to Merritt, perhaps more than the others.

"Well, maybe you'll be different at college," Merritt answered, her blond locks swinging as she walked. "We can all be a little different than we were at home. Here we can make our own decisions and do what we like."

"No one can say you're not responsible," Caroline added. "You're a great student, Tess—everyone knows that. We just want you to have a little fun along the way."

"I can't wait to see this picture," Evie said. "It's supposed to be dreamy. They're going to go all over Italy."

Caroline smiled. "You know me. I just want to see the clothes. I seem to remember Jean Peters being especially chic in it. And the scenery!"

"Italy must be beautiful," Tess said.

"Not that kind of scenery!" Caroline replied, grinning. "I'm talking about Louis Jourdan and Rossano Brazzi."

They made it to the auditorium and stood in the short line, fishing quarters out of their pocketbooks for the price of admission.

Tess was surprised to see that the room was crowded for a Tuesday, but although the movie was in one of the Harvard buildings, there were mostly young women in the audience. They found four seats together and settled in for the film.

Tess went still as a hush came over the audience. She was sitting between Merritt and Caroline, who were studying the credits, suddenly glad she had come. Perhaps she was taking her antisocial habits to an extreme. There was no reason she couldn't enjoy a night out with her friends. She was caught up on her studying and had made all As on her tests. Not to mention she had finished a piece for the student newspaper that she planned to submit for their consideration the next day, an article on best study habits for incoming freshmen. She was, perhaps, not following her own advice, but studying was not her weak area. In fact, she had spent two hours in the library after her English class and had read a chapter or two ahead in each of her classes. She tried to relax. She deserved to enjoy an occasional small pleasure.

The film was better than she expected. Tess liked the snugness of the auditorium, the popcorn they passed back and forth among themselves, and the proximity of her friends. Normally, she would never watch a romance; she wasn't interested in putting anything above her future academic career, and neither did she believe in frivolous pastimes. But this, she thought, was educational, an examination of the beauty of Rome and Venice. Akron seemed small and unworldly compared to Boston, but now they were treated to a tour of Italy. She couldn't help but wonder if she would ever travel to such a beautiful place.

"All right, let's vote," Caroline said as they were leaving the theater. "Louis Jourdan or Rossano Brazzi."

"Louis Jourdan," Evie said. "Without a doubt."

"I think you may be right," Tess said, smiling.

Evie elbowed Merritt and laughed.

"I vote Louis Jourdan too. He's so handsome," Merritt said. She looked at Caroline. "Want to make it unanimous?"

"Please," Caroline answered, shaking her head. "Louis Jourdan was a boy who didn't know what he wanted until Maggie McNamara told him what to think. She literally pretended to be his dream woman and he fell for it. No thank you. I'm a Rossano Brazzi girl. Now there's a real man."

"He was rugged and good-looking," Merritt admitted. "But he was too old."

"He was classic and mature," Caroline contended. "That never grows old."

"I think his love affair with Jean Peters was the true romance of the story," Evie said. "She loved him even when he was poor."

Caroline smirked. "You mean, she loved him because he was handsome and had good prospects, of course. He was studying to be a lawyer."

"Speaking of handsome, there's Professor Whitman," Evie whispered as they left the building. She cocked her head toward him and waited while the others looked. "How old do you think he is, anyway?"

Tess looked over at their sociology professor. He was tall and thin, not classically handsome in her opinion but definitely good-looking. His blond hair had streaks of brown, and he wore tortoiseshell glasses that accentuated his steel-blue eyes. The only flaw that she saw in him was that he seemed too young to be a Harvard professor. Perhaps she had expected all of them to look like Albert Einstein.

"Thirty-five?" Merritt ventured, shrugging. "Maybe forty?"

Evie frowned. "Do you think he's really forty? That's Rossano Brazzi old."

"Evie, you can't get crushes on professors," Tess insisted. "It's not proper, no matter what they look like. They're just here to do a job. We're here to learn what they have to teach us, not to moon over them like we're teenagers."

Evie made a face. "I hate to break it to you, Tess, but we *are* teenagers."

"Besides," Tess said, ignoring her, "he's with his wife."

They looked back at the professor and then nodded.

"She's pretty," Merritt remarked. "And younger than he is too."

"Do you think she was one of his students once?" Caroline asked.

"Caroline!" Evie and Tess said together.

Evie shook her head. "That would be scandalous."

"You're the one who mentioned how handsome he is," Caroline reminded her. "That's how these things get started."

"That's right," Merritt added.

"Besides, you're forgetting that professors don't make as much money as men in other professions," Caroline said. "You have to take everything into consideration before you let yourself get carried away over a pretty face."

"But you have Carter," Evie pointed out. "And he's just a college boy. He's not out on his own or making a living yet."

"Carter's nice," Caroline admitted. "But in case no one has mentioned it, you can date at college without promising to marry someone. Or didn't you know that?"

"You forgot, Evie," Tess said. "Even if Carter is young now, he has excellent prospects for the future."

Caroline laughed. "That's true. It's better to date someone with excellent prospects than to date someone just because you like how they look."

"Well, Carter has everything, though, doesn't he?" asked Merritt. "Good looks, a future in his father's law firm, and he's a good football player too. He's a trifecta of perfect attributes."

"Why aren't there more boys like that?" Evie asked, sighing. "Think how wonderful college would be if there were."

"Don't give up yet," Caroline said. "We've hardly started mining the resources of this university, ladies."

They went up to the door of Duncan Hall and Merritt took

out her key, then unlocked the door. They had a curfew, but it wasn't strictly enforced in the smaller dorms, where everyone had their own key. Mrs. Schwartz was long in bed by this hour. They went inside, Merritt locking the door behind them. Upstairs, they said good night in the hallway. Caroline and Tess had just gone into their room when Evie leaned in and smiled.

"I still think Louis Jourdan wins!"

"One day, you'll see what I mean," Caroline countered, folding her sweater. "See you tomorrow."

Caroline took her toothbrush and pajamas into the bathroom, and Tess started putting away her things. Her life at Radcliffe was better than she had expected. It was nice to have friends who studied with her and were in and out of each other's rooms like sisters. For once, Tess was no longer on the outside looking in. She was participating in college life the same as everyone else. Satisfied, she grabbed her copy of *The Age of Innocence* to read a chapter or two before she fell asleep.

After her shower, Caroline returned and brushed out her hair in front of the mirror. Then she got into bed and turned out the light.

"Tess," she murmured.

"Yes?" Tess answered, lowering her book.

"Thank you for being a good sport tonight," Caroline said, plumping her pillow. "I loved going out like that, just the four of us. Did you have a good time?"

"I did," Tess replied. "I was surprised how good the film was."

"We should do things like that more often," Caroline said, yawning. "Good night. See you in the morning."

"Will it bother you if I read for a while?" Tess asked.

"Heavens, no," Caroline said. She pulled a pink silk eye mask from her desk and settled it over her eyes. "Read as much as you like. I hope it's our book club book. You'll probably have to tell me the ending anyway. I'm getting bogged down in the middle."

Tess smiled. For some reason, she didn't feel the need to scold her about the importance of finishing things that you start. She knew Caroline was participating as much as she could in their book club venture.

After a minute, she could hear the sound of Caroline's rhythmic breathing. Tess cracked open her window and let in a small gust of cool air. Turning toward the wall, she read three more chapters before she closed the book and shut the window. It had been a good day, perhaps her favorite day at college so far. And when she fell asleep, she would dream of Rome.

"Pack your things, everybody," Caroline said the next morning as they were walking to class. Their first hour was English Composition, and they were all in it together. "We're taking a short trip, leaving first thing tomorrow."

"A trip?" Merritt exclaimed. "What sort of trip?"

"You'll find out in the morning," Caroline answered. "It's just for one night. We've been studying hard for fifteen days straight. We need to get out of here and clear our heads for a while."

"I'm game," Evie said. "What do we need to bring?"

"Nothing special," Caroline answered. "One dress for dinner and something you can wear outside for exploring."

"Exploring?" Tess asked.

"Trust me," Caroline said. "You'll love it."

Tess fretted about it all day. It was one thing to walk a few blocks to go to a movie or over to the stadium when they had free tickets to one of the games, but she was far less comfortable with the announcement of a mysterious trip for the weekend. She couldn't even imagine what it would be.

Later, when they were alone in their room, Tess turned to Caroline, her stomach tied in knots.

"I can't go with you," she said. She had been as spontaneous as she could be for a while.

"What do you mean, you can't go?" Caroline said. "You took your algebra test yesterday. You're all done until after Thanksgiving."

"I don't really have the money for a trip, if you want to know the truth," Tess confessed. "I'm on a pretty tight budget."

"Is that all?" Caroline asked. "Well, don't worry. You don't need money for where we're going, so I'm not taking no for an answer."

Tess didn't argue, but neither did she look convinced. Caroline picked up her book and settled a pillow under her head. After a minute, she glanced up to see Tess still watching her.

"Stop worrying and get back to your reading," Caroline told her. "Or have you forgotten that book club is next week?"

"I haven't forgotten," Tess replied.

She opened the book, just as Caroline had told her to, but for once, she couldn't concentrate on the words in front of her.

8

"Is everyone packed?" Caroline called from the doorway the next morning, peering into their room. "Evie? Merritt? Are you ready?"

She and Tess already had their cases stacked by the door. Caroline didn't have to bring much, and Tess didn't have a lot of clothes—even if her roommate had packed everything she owned, her belongings wouldn't have filled a large suitcase. Caroline sighed. She was going to have to do something about that.

"Ready!" Merritt answered. She came out of the adjoining room, smiling and holding up her smallest case, her handbag looped over her wrist. "Evie needs a few minutes. She packed too many outfits. I had to make her put half of her things back."

"All you need is one dinner dress and some casual clothes," Caroline said. "And make sure you have a coat. We're going to have a little adventure."

"What sort of adventure?" Evie asked, coming out of her room and taking a key out of her pocket.

"It's a surprise," Caroline said. Exams were finished and for once, they could relax, if only for a few days. "You'll have to see when we get there. Is everyone ready? There's a cab downstairs waiting for us."

They locked their rooms and buttoned their coats, then picked up their cases.

"Come on," she said. "Let's go."

Outside, they watched as the driver loaded their suitcases into the trunk before they climbed into the taxi: Tess, Evie, and Caroline in the back; Merritt in the front.

"South Station," Caroline told the driver.

"Where are we going?" Merritt said, turning around to look at her. "Come on, Caroline, give us some idea."

"I'm taking you home with me for the weekend," she answered. "We're going to Rhode Island."

"Rhode Island!" the others exclaimed.

Caroline smiled, enjoying the look of surprise on their faces. None of them had been to Rhode Island before. In fact, they hardly had a notion of what it was like. She was suddenly proud of her beautiful state, and though they would be in Chicago, her parents had given her permission to invite her friends. It was the weekend before Thanksgiving, when everyone would head their separate ways. Caroline's parents were coming to Boston for the holiday and planned to stay at the Four Seasons, where they also had reservations for Thanksgiving dinner. Usually, they gave the help a few days off and spent the holiday weekend in New York at the Plaza, but her mother wanted to get into the college spirit by visiting Caroline's dorm and trying something different.

"That's right," she answered, settling back into her seat. "I thought we could all use a change of scenery."

At South Station, they took their cases from the trunk and made their way into the terminal.

Caroline purchased tickets for all of them, despite their protests.

"You're my guests," she insisted. "All you have to do is relax and have a good time."

Once on the train, they hefted their suitcases onto the overhead racks and sat facing each other, Caroline and Merritt on one side, Evie and Tess on the other. She almost laughed at how serious they looked.

"Haven't you been on a train before?" she asked, looking from one to another.

They all shook their heads, and her eyes widened in amazement.

"Don't worry. You're going to love it."

"Has anyone finished the book yet?" Merritt asked, tucking her pocketbook onto the seat between them.

"I brought it with me," Evie answered. "I got behind when I had to get serious about my exams."

"Two chapters left," Tess replied, pulling it from her bag.

"Top of the class as usual, Tess," Caroline said. "Book club is fine, but there is more to life than burying your head in a book."

"Like men, for instance," Evie teased.

"Honestly, Evie!" Merritt scolded. "Do you ever think about anything else?"

"Why should I when it's such an interesting subject?" she countered. "Come on, we all think about it. What are you looking for in a man?"

"A future husband should be a good provider, of course," Tess said, looking up from *The Age of Innocence*. "Otherwise, why bother?"

"That's a given," Merritt said. "But don't you want more than just someone to pay the bills? I'd like someone I could have fun with."

"Is marriage supposed to be fun?" Tess asked. She studied her friends' faces. "I've never met any couples I thought fit that description."

"Really, Tess," Evie said. "You're way too serious about everything."

"Well, I think if you're going to spend every day for the rest of your life with one person, you'd hope to have a good time," Merritt told them.

Evie sighed. "Every girl wants romance, but it's also nice if he's steady, like a best friend, someone you could tell your secrets to."

"God no," Caroline argued, shaking her head. "Your husband is the very last person you'd tell your secrets to. That's why you have a maid, ladies. Someone to look after you and guard the vault of your personal comings and goings. Men are fun, of course, but they're a means to an end. Period."

"Aren't you all jumping the gun?" Tess asked. "Who wants a husband now, anyway? We've been at college for a total of three months. Aren't you having fun learning new things and having new experiences?"

Caroline gave her wry smile. "That's exactly right, Tess. This is the time to try new things."

As the train rumbled down the tracks, her three friends took out their books and began to read. Caroline hadn't even brought hers. She preferred watching the familiar scene outside and found herself leaning against the window, deep in thought. There was so much she liked about this time of her life, particularly the freedom of being around so many girls her own age, in spite of the fact that they were all so conventional. Everyone was so serious about one thing or another: getting high marks, looking for someone to date, even scouting for a potential husband. Caroline wanted none of it. She was quite certain one could enjoy college without getting serious about anything at all.

She also hoped that this weekend would turn out to be a good idea. She seldom allowed anyone into her personal life, but she was enjoying the unlikely friendships she had begun to form with this unusual group of girls. Despite the differences in their social statuses, she felt more accepted among them than she had even among her boarding school friends, most of whom had been not only rich but jaded as well. She was in danger of being jaded, herself. However, this group of girls, who thought a film night on a college campus was the height of living, made her smile.

Baxter, her father's driver, met them at the station and loaded their things into the car. Caroline noticed how quiet the others were as they drove, with Evie nudging Merritt, raising a brow at their surroundings. Her parents lived in an exclusive area of Newport, of course, but somehow, she had become oblivious to the sheer wealth of their position. When one is born with money, one is used to formal gardens and estates and country clubs. She and her mother had actually been to Rome instead of merely dreaming about it while watching a film on the screen.

However, Caroline was no snob. She liked being at Radcliffe in her snug little room. It was similar to staying at camp, as she had when she was younger. There, she didn't have to take anything too seriously; they were there to have a good time and to amuse themselves as much as possible before they entered the unrelenting phase of adulthood, with its myriad responsibilities and expectations. She was none too eager to begin.

Eventually, they neared her parents' home, the drive lined with perfectly sculpted Japanese maple trees, the scarlet leaves catching everyone's eye. Caroline couldn't help but feel a sense of pride when the house came into view. It was enormous, and it seemed even more so when viewed through the eyes of her friends. The car proceeded into the circular drive, giving them a perfect view of the eight-bedroom chateau whose limestone facade was draped with climbing roses and ivy. She watched as her friends leaned toward the window, speechless. As the car came to a stop, no one moved until Caroline reached for the handle of the door.

"Come on," she said, realizing they would follow her lead. "Let's get our things, and we'll get settled in our rooms."

They followed her, still in awe as she took them through the intricate iron-and-glass doors into the marble foyer. She walked to the grand staircase but turned to see they had stopped to admire the stunning gold-framed mirrors and paintings that graced the hall.

"There you are," Elizabeth Hanson said, coming down the stairs.

"Mother!" Caroline said, startled. "I thought you said you would be in Chicago."

"Your father's business trip was postponed, and I couldn't be happier," her mother replied. "Introduce me to your friends!"

Caroline made the introductions, hoping her father was ensconced in his study and not eager to meet a group of college girls he would never see again. She wouldn't have brought them to Newport if she'd known his trip was canceled.

"Come with me," she told her friends. "I'll show you to your rooms."

Everyone picked up their cases and hurried to follow her. Upstairs, she showed them her room and then chose two of the nearest ones to hers.

"Evie and Merritt, this one has twin beds, so you'll be in here," she said.

Evie set her case on one of the tall four-poster beds and reached out a hand to touch the gold satin bedspread. Then she wrapped her arms around a bedpost and smiled. "This is gorgeous, Caroline. I've never seen anything so pretty before."

Caroline smiled. "I'm glad you like it. And, Tess, you're next door."

They all followed her to the next room, which opened to a small jewel of a space with a white bed covered in red toile. Caroline pointed to the large chinoiserie chest. "You can put your things in here."

"I can't believe you live here," Merritt said, shaking her head.

"I can," replied Tess.

Caroline consulted her watch, choosing to ignore the inference. "We'll rest for a few minutes and then go to the library to play games before dinner. Does that sound all right?" As they murmured in agreement, she turned to her roommate. "Come with me for a minute, Tess."

They left the others and went back to Caroline's room, where she closed the door behind them.

A large maple four-poster bed dominated the room, across from which stood a Louis XVI chest that was finished in a gray wash. Noticing the look on Tess's face, she realized she would never tell anyone that she had picked it out herself in France at an auction with her mother, who was teaching her some of the finer points of collecting antiques abroad. It was Caroline's favorite piece in the entire house, and she planned to take it with her to her future home one day.

"This is such a beautiful room," Tess said. She stood stiffly near the door, as if ready to bolt.

"Sit down at the desk for a second," Caroline told her. "I want to get your opinion on a few things."

Tess obeyed her instructions, watching as Caroline pulled a number of garments from her closet. She spread an array of dresses, blouses, and skirts on the bed and then went back, coming out with a couple of sweaters.

"Your closet looks like a store," Tess remarked.

"Here," Caroline said. "I think a few of these would fit you."

"Oh, Caroline, I can't," Tess said with a stricken look on her face. "I mean, thank you, of course, but really, I can't. Your mother wouldn't want you giving your clothes away, I'm sure."

"My mother doesn't care in the slightest," she replied. "I have so many things, she'd never notice anyway."

"But—"

"No buts." Caroline put another sweater on the bed next to the first two and then rummaged around for a couple of skirts, holding one up to Tess. "Try this one on. I think we're close to the same size."

After a moment, Tess took it and self-consciously unzipped her own skirt, allowing it to fall to the ground. Caroline sat down on the edge of the bed to pick out the next thing for her to try on, concentrating on the clothing in front of her if only to mitigate her friend's embarrassment.

A half hour later, there were four outfits on the bed, and Caroline took down a duffel bag and folded each garment carefully, setting them inside. When she was finished, she handed it to Tess, who took it reluctantly.

"Honestly, Tess, you're doing me a favor," she said, smiling. "I didn't have room for anything new. Now, let's get the others."

The four of them went down to the library, and Caroline opened an armoire and took out a handful of board games.

"Yahtzee or Risk?" she asked.

"Both!" Merritt replied. "Risk first, though."

They played games for hours and everyone began to relax. Caroline seldom brought people home and had no desire to impress anyone. She simply hoped that a couple of days by the sea was the perfect antidote to too much studying and stress. At seven, they cleared away the games and went to change for dinner.

When they went back downstairs, Caroline could once again see how imposing her home might feel to someone who wasn't used to such luxury. The table was set with china and silver. Tapered candles lit the room, which was large, with sideboards along two walls and a pair of comfortable leather chairs in front of the window. No one ever sat there, of course. The house was far too big to take advantage of every little corner. There were four short bouquets of roses and Peruvian lilies in the center of the table, adhering to her mother's view that people want to see one another when they are conversing at dinner, a rule Caroline planned to observe when she had her own home as well. The blooms were subtle shades of orange and purple, matching the plum-patterned china her mother had ordered on her most recent trip to London.

"This is beautiful, Mrs. Hanson," Merritt said as they took their seats. "Thank you so much for having us."

"It's our pleasure," Caroline's mother said. She introduced Caroline's father before they all took their seats.

"What's this plate for?" Evie whispered in Caroline's ear, indicating a small plate above the forks.

"Bread and butter," she murmured in reply. She could see they were all looking to her to model proper etiquette. Taking a roll from the basket, she put it on the plate and handed it to Evie, who followed suit.

"Tell me all about life at Radcliffe, girls," her father said.

Caroline looked up at her father, her muscles tensing. He was a daunting figure in every way, from his large frame to his deep, gravelly voice. He lifted his glass of wine, and she took a deep breath, hoping he wouldn't drink too much. It was one of the reasons she seldom invited guests. He could be confrontational at times. She was used to ignoring him, but most of her hometown friends had found him intimidating when they were younger.

"The campus is lovely," Merritt replied, instinctively sitting up straighter in the presence of authority.

"It is, isn't it?" her mother replied.

"You know, many famous people have gone to Radcliffe," Caroline's father continued, cutting the roast on his plate. "Of course, some of the more famous were Harvard men. You'd recognize more of their names."

"Like whom, Mr. Hanson?" Tess asked.

Of her three roommates, Tess appeared the least intimidated by her father. Perhaps, Caroline thought, it was because she didn't have a high opinion of men in general.

"Helen Keller was a Radcliffe student," added Caroline's mother.

"That's nice, of course," her father replied. "But Harvard has educated presidents, from John Adams to Franklin Roosevelt. It's a fine education. I myself am a Harvard graduate."

Caroline resisted the urge to purse her lips, glancing up to see if her friends were sufficiently impressed. They were, which almost depressed her.

"Mother went to Radcliffe too," she added, smiling.

"Oh, I didn't graduate, of course," her mother said quickly. "I went for about a year and a half and then I met Caroline's father, and that was that."

"I like to say she got her M-R-S degree," he said, laughing. "No doubt that's what Caroline will major in too."

Caroline felt a slight flush at his words and straightened her posture, not even looking up. One never argued with a man like her father. He would always have the final word.

"This is everyone's first trip to Rhode Island," she said instead, hoping to change the subject to something safer than gender norms.

"It's beautiful here," Evie said. "I loved all of the farmland we passed."

"Evie lives on a farm in Upstate New York," Caroline told her parents.

"This is an agricultural state, for the most part," her father boomed. "Chicken, cattle, pigs. Orchards and vegetables as well. Of course, we wouldn't live here at all if it weren't for the beach. All of this oceanfront with great views, and it's more private than any beach you could get in California or Florida."

The door opened and the cook came in with a serving platter filled with lobster rolls and placed it on the table.

"That's fine right there," he said, taking a roll from a silver tray. He looked up at the girls and winked. "She's remarkably good for colored help, aren't you, Pearl?"

There was a moment of silence. Pearl took the tray back into the kitchen, and Caroline got a sinking feeling in her stomach.

"'We all have our pet common people,'" Tess quoted, leaning forward. There was a look in her eye that made Caroline draw in her breath.

Her father put down his fork. "What's that, young lady?"

"Just a quote I noticed last night in the Edith Wharton novel I'm reading," Tess answered, smoothing the napkin in her lap.

Usually, Caroline was a master of aplomb and changing the subject, but she had never been in a situation like this before. All her previous friends had displayed the good sense of allowing her father to spout his nonsense and to let it lie. Clearly, Tess wasn't a *let it lie* sort of person.

"You may be in college, but don't presume you know what it means to make decisions in the real world," he said. "Take Elizabeth and me. We've lived in this beautiful estate with oceanfront property without a single person under the age of consent criticizing us for the way we do business."

"I wasn't criticizing," Tess insisted.

Caroline had no idea what she meant by the remark if not to criticize, but she had one desire: to prevent Tess from going on. Instead, she turned to Merritt. "Pearl is the best cook on the East Coast. Isn't she, Mother?"

"She is indeed," Caroline's mother answered.

They managed to get through the rest of the meal without further incident until dessert was served, a chocolate gâteau with a drizzle of raspberries on top. It was three layers tall and decorated with a delicate design made of hibiscus and lavender. Her mother, the ultimate hostess, had seen to every tiny detail.

"This is so pretty, it's a shame to eat it," Caroline remarked.

"Oh, but you must," her mother replied.

The cake was cut and they ate in silence for a few minutes.

"I think it's the best cake I've ever had," Merritt said to Caroline's mother. "It's so light and delicious."

"I'd love another piece, actually," Evie said, smiling.

"Two desserts?" Caroline's father asked, looking surprised. "There's plenty, of course, but you don't want to get fat, you know. If you do, no one will want to marry you."

Caroline grew completely rigid in her chair, hardly daring to breathe. If she wasn't a coward, she would have said something, but she didn't have the nerve. No one confronted her father. No one. It was shocking how she could forget what he was like when she was away from him for even a short time. He could be a generous man, but when crossed or even questioned, he was ruthless. She wondered what Tess's father was like, or Evie's or Merritt's. Not as rich, certainly, but perhaps not as callous. She was sorry she had subjected her friends to such a display, wondering what they might think of her now. She wanted to apologize, but she wasn't accustomed to doing that either.

"You girls should run along," Caroline heard her mother suddenly say. "You won't want to have a sherry in the library with us when you could have a nice hen party upstairs on your own."

Caroline looked up as her friends rose from their chairs. She stood, placing her napkin on the table. "Thank you so much for dinner, Mother."

She took everyone up to her room and pulled out her

phonograph, spreading the records across the bed. Her friends seized them, flipping through the titles. She hardly noticed, still smarting from the remarks her father had made during dinner. None of the others, thankfully, said anything.

"Here, play this," Merritt said, putting on "Earth Angel."

"My favorite!" Evie cried.

"Everything's your favorite," Tess replied.

Caroline listened to them squabbling for a minute and then stood, taking Merritt by the hand. "Do you want to lead, or shall I?"

Soon, they were all dancing, playing record after record late into the night. The next morning, Caroline brought breakfast up to their rooms on a large silver tray, large glasses of orange juice and buttery croissants. She wasn't taking the chance of letting them sit down with her father again.

"Are you up?" she called, tapping on Merritt and Evie's door.

Evie opened it and yawned. "It's not even seven thirty yet."

"I brought breakfast," Caroline answered, carrying the tray to the dresser. "And then we'll put on our dungarees and go down to the beach."

"The beach!" Merritt said, sitting up. "That sounds great."

They sorted out breakfast and then got ready. When they went downstairs, Caroline carried the tray back into the kitchen, the others following behind. She was relieved to see her parents weren't up yet. Pearl took the tray, smiling at her.

"I made you girls a little something, some thermoses of coffee and some packets of sandwiches," she told them. Then she gestured to a chair. "And don't forget this quilt that you can use for a picnic."

"Thank you, Pearl," Caroline answered, giving her a quick hug. She didn't care what the others thought. Pearl had been her main ally for a long time. "Merritt, can you bring the blanket? Tess, would you help with the basket?"

She led them outside into the cool breeze, the sound of the waves drowning out their voices. When they got down close to the edge of the water, Caroline took off her shoes and rolled up the cuffs of her trousers.

"What are you doing?" Tess cried. "It's freezing out here!"

"Where's your sense of adventure?" Caroline asked, wading out into the water until it was up to her ankles. "It's not that cold. In November, the water is still in the fifties here."

Evie shrugged and kicked off her shoes, and a moment later the others followed suit. They stood in the water, hopping about, laughing.

"What's this?" asked Evie, reaching down to take hold of something small and blue at her feet. She held it up for Caroline's inspection.

"That's sea glass," Caroline said. "Bits of broken bottles get tumbled around in the sea and wash up on shore sometimes. Aren't they pretty?"

They spent half an hour searching for more but only came up with a few shells. When they'd had enough, they got out of the water and collapsed on the blanket. Evie reached over and opened one of the thermoses.

"My dungarees are wet," she said, taking a sip.

They nodded in sympathy, wringing out the bottoms of their own trousers, and then they ate the sandwiches, looking out on the ocean as it lapped on the shore.

"I can't believe you got to grow up here," Tess said. "What a beautiful place it is."

"Thank you," she answered. "I've always loved it."

After a couple hours on the beach, they reluctantly packed their things and returned to the house. Caroline found another sweater for Tess and then made her bed, tucking in the coverlet the way she always liked it. When they went downstairs, her parents walked them out to the car. After the cases were stowed in the trunk, they settled into their seats. Dutifully, Caroline rolled down her window as her father approached so that he could lean in for a final word.

"Don't have too much fun when you get back," he said, drawing a silver cigarette case from his pocket and tapping one out into his hand. "You girls are supposed to be studying."

"Goodbye," Caroline said. She waited a beat before rolling up her window. As they pulled away, she looked back at the house, where her mother waved from the door. She lifted a hand to wave back just as the car turned onto the main road. No one spoke as they watched until the house was out of view.

"Thank you for a wonderful weekend, Caroline," Merritt said. "I'm glad you brought us here."

"Yes, thank you," Evie added. "What a great weekend."

Once they were on the train, everyone was quiet, thinking and dreaming of a glamorous life by the sea, the sour taste in their mouths from the night before forgotten. But Caroline remembered, and it only increased her resolve to get away.

9

Alice was surprised how much she looked forward to book club each month. She liked getting to know the girls and having the opportunity to evaluate their strengths and weaknesses. Evie was opinionated, but in Alice's view, she was the sheep of the group. She would go along with whatever anyone else wanted. Merritt was quiet and respectful. In some ways, she, too, was easily led. She hated to offend others and always tried to smooth over differences among them. Caroline was completely different, having been born into wealth and privilege. In Alice's view, she was an actress playing a role, pretending to be a college student for the sake of the experience rather than putting her heart into it. Perhaps she was. Very likely, her family already had plans for her to marry someone in their circle. Alice sighed. Wealthy girls were rarely given the chance to do what they wanted to do. And then there was Tess, of course, who in every way was still the dark horse. Alice continued to be interested in the secretive yet combative nature of the girl. She was the most guarded of them all, saying little about her past and sharing almost nothing about her own life.

Alice knew something about that herself. She had now been on her own for seven months, the most exhilarating seven months of her life. It still astonished her that she didn't have to answer to anyone: not Jack; not her parents; not even her sister, who had her best interests at heart. Yet she couldn't help but feel that what seemed like Alice's best interest in her sister's eyes wasn't actually in her best interest at all. Women weren't china dolls for men to pamper and care for with the caveat that they never speak their minds. They were living, breathing human beings with thoughts and feelings and emotions that were meant to be expressed however they chose to do it.

Leaving a marriage was hard. Staying would have been harder. She couldn't help but think of the day she'd left him. All the compromises had added up. He would behave normally at times, the epitome of a perfect gentleman, but any problem could cause him to suddenly dissolve into anger. She never knew which she would find at the end of the day. When she told him she was leaving, he had punched a hole in the wall with his fist. Alice shivered. It distressed her to think of such things after putting some space between them and starting over. She shook off the cloud of resentment and resumed her preparation for the evening's book club.

She was happy in the present and didn't care to look back. As she opened the bottle of wine, the bell over the door rang. She looked up to see Merritt stepping inside.

"Hello there," Alice said, smiling.

So far, Merritt was her favorite of the girls, although she planned to keep her mind open. The others could surprise her yet.

"Am I early?" Merritt asked, taking off her coat.

"There's no such thing as too early," Alice answered, watching as she hung it on the hook. "We're open all day."

"I thought I could look around for a few minutes," Merritt said, an apologetic tone to her voice.

"Please do, Merritt," Alice said. "You're welcome anytime."

She went back to her desk and sat down, looking over the latest accounts, having no wish to disturb Merritt as she browsed the shelves. Of all the girls, she seemed the most comfortable in her own skin. She had an effortless grace, even compared to Caroline, whose speech and gestures seemed contrived at times. Caroline was no doubt aware that every eye was on her wherever she went, and she used her mannerisms as a shield against someone getting too close. Merritt, on the other hand, though also attractive, was unself-conscious about her looks and her mannerisms were more natural. Alice wondered if having Caroline around was a shield against scrutiny for her too. Other girls might be jealous of Caroline, but Alice was certain that Merritt was not one of them.

"Do you have any recommendations?" Merritt asked, taking a

book from a shelf to leaf through the pages. After a moment, she put it back where it belonged. "I thought I'd get something to read at home over the holiday weekend."

Alice stood, smiling. "Let me show you where I keep a shelf of my favorites."

Merritt took her time looking through everything, eventually bringing one up to the counter.

Alice waved away her money. "You can borrow that. I've already read it. I hope you enjoy it."

"Thank you," Merritt answered. "I'll take good care of it."

They chatted for a few minutes until the others arrived. Evie and Tess looked like their usual selves, but Caroline appeared subdued.

"It's good to see everyone," Alice remarked. "I can't wait to get started."

They hung up their coats and then Merritt, Evie, and Tess poured a glass of water each. After a moment's hesitation, Caroline poured herself a glass of wine.

"Caroline!" Tess scolded as her friend sat down beside her.

"Did you just get a glass of wine?" Evie asked, ever the busybody.

"It's not a national scandal," Caroline answered smoothly. "I drink wine with dinner at home."

"It's not even legal, you know," Tess protested. "You're not twenty-one yet. You're not even nineteen! You could be arrested."

"Relax," Caroline said. "I took an inch of wine in a small goblet.

I think the police have more important things to do than worry about me becoming intoxicated."

They looked to Alice for support, but she shrugged. "Sorry, ladies. I didn't even think about things like the drinking age. I consider all of you to be young adults."

The subject was dropped, although Alice could see that Tess and Evie disapproved. If Merritt disapproved as well, she kept her feelings to herself, though Alice wasn't surprised. She was the least confrontational of the girls.

"All right, then," she said, ready to steer the subject back to the book. "This month, we have Edith Wharton's novel *The Age of Innocence.* I can't wait to hear your thoughts about it."

"It's a book about the class system," Tess said, starting off the discussion. "And Wharton deals with what it means to be part of the upper class while rejecting those you feel are beneath you, particularly through the fault of their own actions."

"Always the student," Caroline remarked, looking at the ceiling.

"What's wrong with that?" asked Tess, flashing her a look.

"Nothing."

"What else?" Alice asked, trying to fend off an argument, if that was what was brewing. "What sort of book do you think it was?"

"It's a romance," Caroline replied. "It's a love story, even though it's not between Newland Archer and his fiancée, May. It's about the relationship between him and his fiancée's cousin."

"If any cousin of mine tried to come between me and my intended," Evie murmured, shaking her head, "heads would roll."

"*The Age of Innocence* is about upper-crust New York society," Tess said, hazarding a glance at Caroline. "And clearly, they do things differently in the upper classes, in case you weren't aware."

"Does that mean you have a Newland Archer of your own, Caroline?" Evie asked, giving her friend a mischievous smile.

"That would imply that I'm a conventional young woman like May," Caroline replied. "And you never know. Maybe I'm an Ellen Olenska."

"Here's an interesting quote from the book," Alice said, picking up her copy and flipping pages. She donned a pair of spectacles and looked at them over the top before she read. "'There was no use in trying to emancipate a wife who had not the dimmest notion that she was not free.'"

"What does that mean?" Merritt asked. "That May was naive? And was she in reality? Or did she simply follow the customs of the time?"

"What do you think?" Alice asked the group.

"She seemed simple and uncomplicated," Tess answered. "She never seemed to suspect her husband loved someone else."

"Or did she?" Alice asked.

"No," Evie answered. "She didn't. If she had been jealous, we would have known it."

"I don't think she was," Merritt added.

Tess shook her head. "Of course she wasn't. It's never referred to in the book."

"You're wrong," Caroline answered, taking a sip of her wine and setting it on the table in front of her.

Everyone turned to look at her. She smoothed her skirt and folded her hands in her lap.

"You missed the most important thing in the book," Caroline said. "May knew about the relationship and warned off her cousin."

"That never happened," Tess insisted. "I would have remembered something like that."

"Oh, yes it did," Caroline countered. "Remember when Newland points out that May told her cousin that she was pregnant before she actually knew she was? She was making certain that Ellen knew she had no claim to Newland. He was May's, and she had the baby to prove it. It's ironic that she found out later she was pregnant. At the time she told May about it, she merely hoped she was."

"That's an astute answer, Caroline," Alice said, nodding. "There's no other reason for that particular information to be in the book."

"But May was so sweet and loving toward Ellen," Evie argued, shaking her head. "She didn't betray a bit of jealousy toward her. I don't think I could have handled something that well if it happened to me."

"We probably all have no idea how we'd react to any given situation until it's upon us," Alice remarked. "We're all innocents before we have to deal with some of the harsher aspects of life. And what is innocence, anyway?"

"I looked that up when I was reading the book, actually," Merritt answered, leaning forward. "It can be defined as being free from guilt, like May, or free from sin or moral wrongdoing. But I think we usually consider innocence to be comparable to naivety."

Alice privately agreed. The girls here now were naive about many things and would be until they had some life experience. They were all innocents, but perhaps that wasn't a bad thing.

"Were you sympathetic toward Newland?" Alice asked, crossing her arms. "He fell in love with his fiancée's cousin, after all."

"I wondered why he married May in the first place," Evie asked. "They weren't really right for each other. She seemed too young for him, for one thing."

"Lots of people marry who aren't right for each other," Caroline said. "I can think of a lot of people like that myself."

The room went silent as everyone contemplated the marriages of those close to them, Alice included.

"Define what you mean by 'not right for each other,'" Alice said to Caroline.

"He married her because she was the sort of wife society expected him to marry in spite of a clear lack of passion between them."

Alice nodded. "Do you think people are bound by societal expectations now as much as they were in the 1870s?"

"Oh, yes," Merritt answered, looking around the group, studying her friends' faces. "There are always expectations, aren't there? Most parents have ideas about the kind of person you're going to marry. And so do your grandparents and aunts and uncles. And if you bring home the wrong sort of person, aren't they going to be upset with you for choosing someone who doesn't fit the mold?"

"I know mine would," Evie admitted.

"What do you think, Tess?" asked Alice.

She considered the matter. "Merritt's right. As much as most girls would like to marry the person they like best, if he doesn't meet expectations, he'll be forced out of the relationship if the family can manage it."

"But what you said about Newland," Merritt ventured. "I did feel sorry for him. I didn't think he was in the wrong because of his feelings. He truly loved Ellen. He could have been happy with her."

"And yet he could never have bucked social convention," Caroline said. "It's a straightjacket, isn't it? People have to conform or else."

"I thought you didn't finish the book," Tess said, raising a brow.

Caroline gave a wry smile. "I skipped around and read the good parts."

Tess shook her head. "You know, one of these days, you're going to have to read the whole book."

Caroline smiled and lifted her wineglass to her lips. "I managed to get the gist of it."

Alice lifted her book again. "One of the other quotes I liked was something May said to Newland: 'She said she knew we were safe with you, and always would be, because once, when she asked you to, you'd given up the thing you most wanted.'"

"I can't imagine giving up someone if I were in love with him," Merritt admitted. "Wouldn't that be the worst thing that could happen in your whole life?"

"Even if he were engaged or married to someone else?" Tess asked.

No one answered, but Alice could see Merritt blushing. She decided to intervene.

"Like I said, no one knows what they would do in any given situation until you've had to experience it for yourself."

They talked for a while about the history of the book, the setting of early New York City before it was fully formed, the clothing and conventions of that age. The Victorian Era was, in Alice's opinion, one of the most fascinating periods in history.

"There is a lot of beauty in this book," Merritt said. "I, for one, wish I could have lived back then and had the chance to wear those swishy, beautiful dresses."

"They were pretty restrictive, though, weren't they?" Evie argued. "You couldn't live a life of freedom in crinolines and bustles. I can't imagine anything worse."

"Hear! Hear!" Tess replied.

"Another quick subject," Alice said, looking around the group. "Newland was fifty-seven in the final chapter of the book when he goes to Paris to see Ellen after his wife's death. He doesn't go with the intention of seeing her and then refuses to agree when his son tries to set it up. Why do you think Miss Wharton wrote it like that?"

"To break our hearts," Merritt answered.

"But it was years and years later," Evie replied. "Surely his feelings had faded by then."

"Oh, but did they?" Alice asked.

"Of course not," Caroline insisted. "If his feelings had faded, he wouldn't have minded seeing her again."

"I think you can feel love at any age, and a particularly intense love is likely to last through your entire life," Alice said. When no one replied, she closed her book and set it on the table.

"What are we reading for next time?" Tess asked Alice.

"Yes, and when will we meet?" asked Evie. "I'll be going back to the farm on Christmas break."

"We're all going home," Merritt added.

"First, I'll get the books," Alice said.

She rose and set her wineglass on the shelf next to the bottle and went over to her desk. She pulled a handful of books from a paper bag and brought them back, handing one to each of the girls.

"*Anna Karenina*," Caroline said, studying the image of a beautiful woman on the front cover.

"That's right," Alice answered. "It's a Russian novel of romance, love, and betrayal."

"Sounds juicy," Merritt remarked. "But when will we discuss it?"

"Why don't we skip December, since everyone's going home, and discuss it on the last Thursday in January?"

"But that's nearly two months away," Tess complained.

Caroline raised a brow and held the heavy book aloft.

"Take a look at how long it is," she said. "We'll need at least two months to get through it."

10

"Every heart has its own skeletons."

—LEO TOLSTOY, *ANNA KARENINA*

"When are you going home for Christmas?" Caroline asked, wrapping a pearl-white cashmere scarf around her throat.

The four of them were walking around Cambridge, something they rarely had time to do. It had snowed all afternoon, though the temperature had hovered just above freezing the entire day. The town looked like a winter wonderland. It was dusk, but the shopfronts were lit, and small crowds were taking in the Christmas lights in the shop windows, and the wreaths on the streetlamps were festooned with holly. It was magical, and though Caroline wasn't always impressed with things like that, the other girls' enthusiasm was catching.

"I'm leaving the Friday after classes are out," Merritt said, pulling her gloves from her pockets and putting them on.

"Same for me," Evie said, chiming in.

Caroline turned and looked at Tess, who was walking a couple of steps behind her. "What about you, Tess?"

"I thought I'd leave on the fifteenth," Tess answered, her hand-knitted wool cap pulled squarely over her ears. The four of them stopped and looked at each other.

"But that's before the Christmas dance," Evie protested, tugging her muffs closer around her ears. "And you have to go to the dance."

"That's right, Tess," Merritt said, nodding. "Classes will be out, so you won't have any studying to do. You don't have any excuse to miss it."

"I already went to one dance this semester," Tess argued, stepping over a small puddle. "That's one more than I planned to attend anyway."

"We can fix you up with a date, if that's what you're worried about," Merritt said, looking at Evie. "Not that you have to have one, of course. Lots of people go stag, like we did for the last one."

"If you recall, you had a good time," Caroline said, nodding. "You were asked to dance, weren't you?"

"Well, yes," Tess admitted. "With three different boys. Although I can't remember any of their names."

"It's not important to remember their names unless they're special," Caroline remarked. "Save that privilege for anyone you'd like to see again in the future."

They stopped in front of a shop window to admire a mannequin dressed in a floor-length gown made of silk, with a long strand of beads draped around its throat. A Christmas tree stood on one side of the window, papier-mâché birds in every color perched on the branches.

"This is gorgeous," Merritt said, clapping her gloves together for warmth as she stared in the window. "I love it here in Cambridge. I wish we never had to leave."

"We're here for four years," Caroline said philosophically. "It's a little early to start missing the place already."

"You know what I mean," Merritt insisted. "Half a year is nearly gone, which means only three more Christmases left."

"Aren't you looking forward to going home?" Evie asked, cocking her head.

"No," they all answered in unison.

"After the dance, I mean," Evie clarified. "Of course we don't want to miss that. But I'm already thinking about my mom's Christmas turkey and seeing my friends back home."

"Any friend in particular?" Merritt asked, grinning.

Evie colored. "Maybe."

"I have some news," Merritt said, tipping her head toward Caroline. "One of Carter's friends, Dexter, asked me to the dance."

"That's nice," Caroline exclaimed. "You'll have a good time."

"I'm going with one of the boys in my sociology class," Evie said. "His name is Vic. He's from New Jersey."

Merritt turned to Tess. "I can ask Dexter if he knows someone who needs a date."

"No, don't do that," Tess answered.

"Come on," Evie said. "It'll be fun."

Tess pushed her hands into her pockets. "I'll think about it."

They approached a small café, where the shopkeeper was ladling a hot brew, handing them out to the passersby.

"Hot apple cider, ladies?" he asked, wiping his hands on his apron.

"Yes, please," Evie replied.

"Aren't you glad we got out tonight?" Caroline asked, accepting a cup with a cinnamon stick. She stirred the cider thoughtfully. "Sometimes it feels as if the world is shut up at eight o'clock every night. We eat supper, study, and have the occasional date. There has to be more to life than that."

"I know what you mean," Merritt said. "I love college, but it's all work and no play sometimes."

"What do you mean, the occasional date?" Evie asked Caroline. "You're the most popular girl at Radcliffe. You're going out all the time. And you're the only one I know who has a steady beau."

"Come on," Caroline said, ignoring the question. "Let's walk down to the river."

The wind picked up, whipping about their ears as they found a bench. The others sat down to sip their cider, but Caroline stood at the railing, looking out over the water, listening to the sound of the waves lapping against the bank.

"Do you think you'll marry him?" Tess asked, giving Caroline a curious look. "Carter, I mean?"

"Don't be ridiculous," she answered. "He's fun for now, that's all. He's way too young to think about marriage, anyway. A woman has to think ahead. If you want security, marry someone older." She turned from the railing and looked back at her friends, all of whom were watching her.

"'Fun for now'?" Tess repeated, as if the concept were entirely foreign; but then, she didn't seem as if she'd ever actually had any fun before, if it came to that.

"I'm not opposed to girls getting married young if you're not too young," Caroline said. "And I would definitely consider eighteen too young. We have a lot of life to live first."

"But you must love him," Evie argued. "Otherwise, you wouldn't be seeing him exclusively."

Caroline shook her head and laughed. "We can talk about love when we're thirty and not a minute before."

"What if you marry before thirty?" Merritt asked.

"Even then." Caroline turned back to the river for a moment and finished the last of her cider. Then she turned around and smiled. "Why are we wasting a perfectly good evening discussing boys? Let's keep exploring."

The others stood and tossed their cups into a bin. Evie looped her arm through Merritt's, and the two of them led the way back from where they had come. Tess walked beside Caroline but seemed disinclined to conversation, which suited Caroline perfectly. There was something about being out at night under the stars, drinking cider and looking at Christmas lights. Her childhood had been full of structure and rituals, and it was a relief to have the world to herself, as it were, free from thinking about Carter and her parents and life in general. She had no idea what she wanted to do in a year, let alone ten, and all she wanted was the freedom to think about it without being pressured. But that was what college freshmen did best: worry about majors and courses and grades and, even more, the marriage and life that waited beyond their current perimeters. She wasn't ready for it yet. She had barely tasted freedom. She would go to the dance with Carter and then go home for Christmas, all the while looking forward to coming back to the small square room she shared with Tess and a little space of her own. She knew she would marry well and probably not that far in the future, which made these days, so full of promise, as valuable as gold. Because one thing was for certain: when she married, all the unexpected pleasure of life would be behind her. Her future flashed before her eyes. Girls like her didn't have real careers. She would be the mistress of a fine house; she would be president of the junior league; she would host fabulous fundraisers for the local hospitals and the opera and arts councils; and most of all, she would be a status symbol for a man on his way up the ladder. The whole idea made her want to be ill. Perhaps the reason she dated Carter, besides his good looks, was that he was an unserious person and therefore, in regard to her long-term prospects, entirely unsuitable. The short term, however, was a different matter entirely. If she spent time with him, she couldn't possibly be looking for anyone else.

They caught up with Evie and Merritt, and the subject turned to what they should wear to the Christmas dance. Caroline nodded in approval. That was a topic she could definitely warm to. They wandered around the town for another half hour and then reluctantly headed back to the dorm. As she fell asleep, however, Caroline relived the evening one last time. Life would be perfect if every night there were hot apple cider; a brisk, cool breeze; and Christmas lights twinkling under a starlit sky.

"You'll never guess what happened today," Tess said as she came into their room the following afternoon.

She pulled off her coat and straightened it before hanging it up in the closet. Then she sat down on the bed, looking at Caroline with a serious expression.

Caroline was writing her final essay of the semester and put down her pen, glad for the interruption. "What happened?"

"I was asked to the dance."

Tess looked pleased, and Caroline didn't blame her. No one

wanted to be the girl who had to be fixed up with a date for a Christmas dance, not even someone like Tess, who seemed to hate frivolity in all its forms.

"Who are you going with?" she asked.

"It's another of Carter's friends," Tess answered. "His name is Ken Blackburn. He was at the football game we went to. Do you remember? He recognized me in the library and started to talk to me. The next thing I knew, he'd invited me to the dance and I'd said yes."

"That's wonderful," Caroline said, warming to the subject. "He's Carter's roommate, you know. Do you know what you're going to wear?"

Tess nodded. "I thought I'd wear of one of the dresses you gave me when we were in Newport. The blue one."

"Try it on for me," Caroline said.

"Right now?"

"Right now."

Tess stood and went to the closet, taking the dress from the hanger. She went to the mirror and held it up in front of her, running a hand along the smooth lines of the skirt. "The color is so pretty. I think it will look nice."

"We just want to make sure it fits properly," Caroline answered, nodding. "Go get changed."

A few minutes later, Tess was back and Caroline walked around her in a circle, looking the dress over. She stopped and pinched the extra fabric in the bodice, frowning.

"Well, it's a little big there," Tess said, pulling away. "But I don't think anyone will notice."

"I'll notice," Caroline said. "And you'll certainly notice if it doesn't fit right. Let me get some pins."

A minute later, Caroline was pinning the garment around her. After a moment, she stepped back to take a final look.

"I like it," she said, nodding. "We'll just take it in a little on the sides and you'll look perfect."

"What are you wearing?" Tess asked.

"I have no idea," Caroline said, shrugging. "I'll see what I feel like on the night of the dance."

Tess's eyes grew large. "I'd be scared to death to leave something like this to the last minute."

"You're probably scared to death just going," Caroline replied. "Maybe you shouldn't take everything so seriously."

"It's Radcliffe," Tess replied, turning to let Caroline unzip the garment. "I'm on scholarship, remember? I have to take everything seriously."

Caroline raised a brow. "It's not because you're on a scholarship, Tess. That's your personality. You're a stickler for rules. I've only known you a few months, but I can already tell that you'll be conscientious until the day you die."

"You say that like it's a bad thing," Tess said defensively.

"Maybe it is," Caroline said, giving her a look. "But if you don't defy a few rules, how will you ever know?"

She watched as Tess turned and went to change out of the dress, thinking about rules.

Caroline realized she was hardly one to talk. She followed expectations as much as anyone else; she just didn't care as much. Sighing, she tried to put herself in the other girls' shoes. They felt lucky just to get into Radcliffe, wondering how long it would be until their bubbles burst. They already had backup plans for that very contingency, mostly consisting of marriage, while she was simply determined to pass the time and escape her life in a way that would appear acceptable to her parents and her future spouse. Caroline bit her lip in frustration. If that wasn't being a slave to the rules, she didn't know what was.

11

The Christmas dance fell on the following Friday evening. There was merriment in the dormitory on both floors. Caroline had sent the blue dress to a seamstress to have the alterations made, and it arrived just in time. Tess tried it on and then wouldn't take it off, even though Caroline assured her one was only to put on a dress at the last moment before a special evening. She was sitting in her slip at her desk, applying her makeup with a steady hand when Evie and Merritt burst in for her inspection.

"All right," she said, turning to survey their efforts. "Let's see everyone."

Evie and Merritt each struck a pose, and Tess awaited inspection in her usual prim-and-proper manner. The gowns were suitably frothy and colorful: Tess in the blue satin, Evie in a pretty shade of cranberry red, and Merritt in an emerald dress that matched her eyes.

"Gorgeous," she said, nodding. "We'll be the best-looking group of girls at the dance."

"What are you wearing, Caroline?" Tess asked.

"The gold one," she replied, cocking her head toward the closet.

Evie went over and pulled it from the hanger, holding it up to herself in the mirror. Tess and Merritt moved closer to admire it.

"This is gorgeous, Caroline," Merritt said, spreading the garment across the bed.

"It's a dress," she murmured.

She knew she would be the most beautiful girl at the dance, but there was no need to rub it in. The garment cost ten times what the others did put together, and more than any dress they would own in their lifetimes. Yet for her, it was merely another pretty gown for another meaningless event. She would enjoy the swish of the tulle and the distraction of the festivities, but she knew better than to think something would come of it. The way to a stable life was to manage expectations, she believed.

Evie brought her the dress, and the others drifted into the other room to allow her to change. She stepped into the gown, straightening to see herself in the mirror. She hadn't gained an ounce at college and the dress fit perfectly. It was sleeveless, with a deep V-neck hovering just a hairline below modesty. The shell of the gown was a sheath of gold with the faint print of roses, tiny pearls dotting the center of each bud. At the waist, a voluminous tulle in a matching gold cascaded to the floor. The dress was both formfitting and dramatic, with the train of tulle falling behind it. Her figure was mature at eighteen, unlike the other girls, who looked younger than their age, almost as if they were playing dress-up in their older sisters' clothing. She had an unfair advantage. Caroline suddenly realized that it was far too fine for a Harvard-Radcliffe dance, but she didn't have time to change. Neither did she want to disappoint her friends, who had seen and admired the gown already.

After slipping a small comb into her matching bag, Caroline adjusted her earrings and, for a final touch, fastened her pearl choker about her throat. She glanced in the mirror, running a hand lightly over her chin-length waves before going into the next room. She turned her back to the others.

"Will someone do the honors?" she asked, waiting for the dress to be zipped.

All three of them came forward, but Tess got there first. Caroline started at the touch of her friend's cold fingers on her back.

"Are we ready?" she asked after the gown was zipped.

"Yes!" Evie said, squeezing Merritt's arm.

"Wait," Merritt said. She looked at Tess and shook her head. "Can you see without your glasses?"

Tess reached up and touched them defensively.

"A little," she admitted.

"Then you should definitely leave them here," Merritt said.

Reluctantly, Tess removed the glasses and set them on her

desk, rubbing the top of her nose, where there were two pink marks where the spectacles had rested.

"Much better," Caroline said, nodding.

"Now can we go?" Evie asked.

Caroline smiled. "Of course."

They made their way downstairs, where a bevy of young men awaited their dates, corsages in hand. Mrs. Schwartz, dressed up for the occasion in a two-piece brown suit, was organizing everyone as if they were in a play, acting as pleased as a matchmaker about the young women in her charge. The salon had been decorated by the housemother with the aid of a few of the students, and the room looked particularly nice, with a ribbon-trimmed garland of fir draped over the mantelpiece and candles lit around the room. As Caroline and the others reached the bottom stair, their dates came forward to greet them, bowing to Mrs. Schwartz first. Carter looked unusually handsome, Caroline noticed. He wore a black suit with a red tie. The cut of his coat was expensive, one of the reasons she liked to be seen with him. He was of her ilk, an East Coast–bred young man with a fortune in his back pocket. He gave her one of his endearing grins, which was certainly for the benefit of her friends. Their eyes were on Carter rather than their own dates, although they couldn't help it. People notice the Cary Grants and the Ava Gardners of the world and then recede back into their own lives, taking the arms of the less glamorous but still moderately attractive young men and women they had agreed to go to the dance with. After offering Caroline her wrist corsage, a thing of beauty trimmed in white baby roses, Carter kissed her on the cheek in a gesture pure enough to satisfy the housemother and her roommates that he was indeed as good on the inside as he looked on the outside. Caroline, of course, knew better. But she also knew the same was true of herself.

In a minute, they had paired off. Merritt looked lovely on Dexter's arm. Her long blond hair had been pinned up for the event, and she had sparkling rhinestone clips securing her chignon. Dexter was Carter's opposite: dark and olive skinned. Together, he and Merritt made an attractive pair. Evie accepted a corsage from the boy in her sociology class, whom Caroline had to admit was better-looking than she'd expected and therefore worth the opportunity to be seen on his arm. They were well matched: dark hair, dark eyes, and wholesome, all-American looks. Tess held back a little from the group and eventually joined Ken's side, although she did not allow him to slide the corsage on her wrist. She took it from him and placed it in position herself. She had refused to allow Caroline to put up her hair for the evening, but she did accept the loan of a pair of tortoiseshell clips to sweep the hair back from her face. Of the four couples, they were the most mismatched. Ken was handsome, although not so much as Carter, but even in the gifted blue dress, Tess was far plainer than the others. She had refused to allow them to share their makeup with her, barely accepting the loan of a tube of lipstick for the evening.

"Ladies, shall we?" Carter said, taking the lead as the host of the group.

The others nodded in agreement while Caroline was struck anew at their nervous excitement. She tried to remember the last time she had been excited about something as ordinary as a dance. The most she hoped for was that she and Carter would dance as much as possible while talking little and that the punch was good.

The eight of them piled into three vehicles: Caroline and Carter in the first; Ken, Tess, Merritt, and Dexter in the second; and Evie with Vic in the last. They didn't have far to go, but it was cold outside and all the women were wearing heels.

The ballroom was perfect—even Caroline had to admit that. A twelve-piece orchestra was playing at the front of the elegant room, strains of "White Christmas" floating through the air. She tried to imagine what it might feel like to be in love, in actual love, with another human being, one whose arm she would take as he led her onto the floor and whispered romantic things in her ear. Someone who laughed at her ridiculous jokes and could adore her, not just when she wore a stunning gold gown to a beautiful dance but who would touch her face when she hadn't a stitch of makeup on or wake up next to her, nuzzling her neck and not expecting her to get glamorous on his account. If such a man existed, he would love her, flaws and all. Of course, in reality, no such man existed. Her mother hadn't found him; none of her friends had ever found him. He was embodied from time to time on the silver screen in the form of Fred MacMurray or Dana Andrews, but real men, in her experience, were far different: impatient, business oriented, and prone to male-pattern baldness.

Carter, for all his attractiveness, would one day morph into the worst version of himself, and if she was right, it would happen sooner rather than later. However, she still felt a little fondness for him because he didn't realize it himself. It wasn't the perfect situation, but it was a shame to waste this dress on a night as forgettable as this one would surely be.

They checked their coats at the door and stepped to the periphery of the dance floor. Only a few couples were dancing. Most were talking around the edges, still too shy to get out on the floor.

"This is nice," Merritt said, looking around. Caroline wondered if she had ever been to a formal event before. Although it was merely a college dance, it was no doubt the most extravagant evening of her friends' lives.

"It's fine, but it's hard to relax," Tess lamented. "They haven't posted our grades yet. I don't know why you aren't thinking about it too."

Caroline forced herself not to roll her eyes.

"Tess, really," Merritt exclaimed. "Put academics out of your mind just this once. You deserve to enjoy your first date at college without spoiling it with talk of grades."

"Ready?" Dexter asked, reaching out a hand to Merritt.

She smiled and nodded to her partner. "Ready."

They floated out toward the dance floor and several other couples joined in. Caroline crooked her finger at Carter.

"Come on, you," she said. "Let's dance."

He smiled and spun her out onto the floor. Evie and Tess and their dates stood there, as if they had no idea what to do. Caroline decided that for once, she wouldn't step in and take charge. They could dance or not dance; it was their prerogative. When the song came to an end, she was relieved when the orchestra began to play another fast tune. Carter swung her around and for a moment, she let every thought tumble out of her head. She was here to have fun, not to worry about things she couldn't change.

A couple of minutes later, she looked up to see that Evie and her date had finally made it onto the dance floor, and she was giving Evie a smile of encouragement when Vic spun her around and gave her a fresh look. A feeling of disgust came over her. Why did boys have to be such cads? Couldn't he content himself with the fact that he was dancing with a pretty girl at the Christmas dance? Didn't they know how tiresome it was for them to show disrespect to their dates in order to flirt with someone else?

Carter was an attentive dancer, although the possibility occurred to her that she was merely window dressing in his life too. People all around the room looked up as they came near. They danced to three or four more numbers before Carter led her off the floor. They stopped at the refreshment table, where he poured her a glass of punch.

"I'll be back in a minute," he said, handing her the cup.

"Wait!" she called after him.

He didn't seem to hear, so she shrugged and took a sip of the punch. It was good, just as she had hoped. She moved for a better look at the orchestra, who looked smart in their white dinner jackets. They were playing one of her favorite Sinatra tunes, and she could almost hear him crooning along.

Evie and Merritt came up to her a couple of minutes later, their dates giving stiff bows and then following Carter outside. The three of them listened to the music for a while, and then Evie sighed.

"I love 'Don't Let the Stars Get in Your Eyes,'" she said, tapping her foot to the beat.

"Perry Como is so dreamy," Merritt murmured.

Caroline nodded. "Where did the boys go?"

"I think they went out for a smoke," Merritt said, glancing at the door. "At least, that's what Dexter said."

Caroline frowned. "That's no way to treat a date."

It was another ten minutes before Carter returned. She had turned down dances with several people, instinctively knowing that he would be angry if he returned and found her dancing with someone else. When he finally came to get her, she had difficulty keeping the irritation out of her voice.

"Where've you been?" she demanded.

"I was just talking with the guys for a little while," he replied, leaning in too closely. "Come on. Let's dance again."

Caroline looked up sharply. She recognized his manner all too well. She'd seen her father drunk plenty of times after mergers went wrong or whenever he was involved with another woman. Sometimes for no reason at all. He didn't think anyone knew, but he didn't have the delicacy to keep his indiscretions private. Caroline wasn't certain if that was a good thing or not. Perhaps being a good liar was worse.

"You've been drinking," she accused.

Carter gave her an indignant look. "No I haven't. Who needs liquor when there are pretty girls at hand?"

She let the remark pass, trying to decide what to do. He took her by the arm and led her onto the dance floor. To avoid a scene, she allowed him to pull her close. As they started to dance, he lost his balance momentarily and caught himself on her shoulder.

"Sorry," he mumbled.

"Why don't we get something to eat?" she said, looking at the cluster of his friends who were watching them from the sidelines. "It might sober you up."

She had no desire for anything but to get out of that building, but neither did she want a scene. Mentally, she shook herself. Hanson women knew how to put on a good front, and they did it well after long years of practice. Her mother was so skillful at it, Caroline didn't even know what she was thinking anymore.

"I said I want to dance," he snapped a little too loudly.

His arm went around her waist and he pulled her close.

Caroline could smell the alcohol on his breath, but she saw Merritt wave from across the room and attempted to look as if nothing was wrong. The last thing she wanted was for her friends to think she was in a situation beyond her control.

"You know something?" Carter said suddenly. "Girls don't need to go to college."

"What do you mean, girls don't need to go to college?" she retorted. Radcliffe was one of the Seven Sisters, one of the most prestigious women's colleges in the country. "What do men want, to marry a stupid wife?"

He laughed even though she was serious. "What do you need college for? When you're marriage bound, it doesn't really matter, does it?"

The words stung, though she made no reply. Part of the problem was that she knew he was right. She should have been choosing a silver pattern and deciding between Haviland and Royal Copenhagen china, although even that was decided. She would order Winthrop cutlery like her grandmother's and Haviland Du Barry, because after all, who wouldn't prefer gold? She decided never to think of the subject again, but there was a deeper problem when it came to college. She couldn't imagine any occupation she might actually want to do.

She could never work in an office. Men would take advantage of her constantly. And a career was out of the question. Why would one want to work that hard for anything? No, she knew she was most suited for marriage—if not the relationship, certainly the institution. It had an air of respectability that was essential for the well-bred girl. And Caroline Meredith Hanson was nothing if not a well-bred girl.

Of course, there was still a lot of living to do, starting now, with this dance. She smiled at Carter, hoping to win back his goodwill for the rest of the evening. She wasn't his wife; it was nothing to her if he made terrible choices and became a drunk. It's not like she would marry him. But she did want to get through the evening without any further incident or being subject to inquiring glances from her friends.

"I love the music," she said in a low voice, moving her body in perfect rhythm with his.

"I love what comes after the music," he replied.

She gasped as his hand strayed below her waist and pulled slightly away from him to stop it. He'd been overly friendly with her, and she had allowed him small liberties no one else had ever taken, but all that was dependent on the fact that he would never behave with impropriety in public. He gripped her tighter, so tightly, in fact, that she wondered if she would bruise.

"Shall we stop and get some punch?" she asked, hoping to be released from his arms without a struggle.

"I don't want anything," he murmured in her ear. "Except you."

A feeling of dread swept over her. She had known this day was coming but had never believed it would happen when they were among a group of friends. She should have known that his behavior at the dormitory was a means of covering his true motives.

"Carter, we're in public," she warned.

"So what?" he answered. "All the world knows that you belong to me."

His words stirred up long-hidden feelings of anger.

"Women don't belong to men, Carter," she told him. "We're not your property."

"Of course you are," he answered, leaning close to her face. "It's what a girl like you is meant for."

"You're drunk," she said, pulling back. "Why did you have to spoil tonight, of all nights?"

"I'll tell you what's spoiled," he spat at her. "You are. And guess who is going to take care of that?"

Caroline was irritated rather than afraid. They were in a public place, and all she had to do was separate herself from him and not be drawn back in. She would refuse his telephone calls and find someone else, someone more manageable, whose behavior was almost as impeccable in private as it was in public. The only difficulty now was to get away from him without making a scene. She could talk to Tess and say she had a headache. Then they would all have to leave. Carter's fingers bit into the flesh of her upper arm and this time, she knew it would leave marks.

"You're hurting me," she said.

"Don't play so hard to get," he answered. "That game is getting old."

"I don't play games," she replied.

"Are you kidding me?" Carter said. "You're the biggest player of them all."

She pulled away from him, so angry that she didn't care if there was a scene anyway. She was Caroline Hanson, a woman who deserved respect. If Carter Gray wasn't going to behave like a gentleman, it was his reputation on the line, not hers. As she began to walk away, he grabbed her by the arm.

"Don't you dare walk away from me," he said between gritted teeth.

She looked over at the refreshment table, where the chaperones had gathered to chat. One glanced up at the commotion. Caroline made eye contact and the woman started walking toward her when Carter came up beside her.

"Hey, look," he said, running a finger under his collar. "I shouldn't have said that. Let's go back and finish our dance."

"We're finished, all right," she answered.

A feeling of relief came over her as some of the other chaperones turned to look their way.

Merritt had stopped dancing with Dexter and was heading toward them as well, a concerned look on her face. She wished things could have been handled more smoothly, but at least it was over. She would never have to speak to Carter Gray again.

"Are you all right?" Merritt asked when they reached the safety of the refreshment table.

Carter stopped in his tracks and turned to go outside.

"I'm fine," Caroline replied. "Go back to your date."

She was exasperated but upset as well. Her heart was pounding far more than she would have thought over a mere breakup with someone she didn't even like, but that was no reason to spoil the other girls' evening. Caroline smiled at Merritt and nodded as her friend went back onto the dance floor. She watched for few minutes and then went to the door and pushed it open, needing some fresh air. She was going to have a terrible headache in the morning.

"I'm sorry about what happened in there," a voice said in her ear.

Caroline turned and saw Ken standing behind her. She put on her best smile, trying not to show how shaken she was.

"I'm fine," she replied. "You should go back inside. Tess is probably wondering where you are."

"I'm not so sure you're fine," he persisted. "In fact, I thought you might like me to take you home."

Hope surged at the thought. She wanted away from the pawing and arguing. "I am getting a headache," she admitted.

Ken pulled his keys from his pocket. "My car is right around the corner."

Caroline nodded. "I should tell my friends I'm leaving."

"I already told Tess I was taking you home," he answered. "You don't want to go back in there. It might cause a scene. Carter's a little worse for wear, if you know what I mean."

"All right."

She allowed him to walk her to his car and then paused as he reached for the handle. "But you gave Merritt and her date a ride too. What if they want to leave? I should probably stay."

"It will only take a few minutes," he replied, opening the car door.

Caroline slid onto the seat and gathered the tulle around her knees so that it didn't get caught in the door. Ken got in beside her and started the engine, then pulled out onto the street. She closed her eyes, rubbing her temples, thankful that he had gone silent. She didn't want to have to make small talk any longer. They drove for a while, and then she opened her eyes, trying to figure out where they were.

"What are you doing?" she asked as he pulled off the side of a deserted road. Men were so tiresome. They all had the same moves.

"You're such a pretty girl, Caroline," he answered, moving close enough that she could smell his Brut aftershave. In her current state, she couldn't help but recoil.

"I'm tired," she said crisply. "I just want to go home."

He slid across the seat until their hips were touching, putting his arm around her. Then he leaned close and nuzzled her hair. She tried to move away, but he brought up his left hand to her face and pulled her near, settling his lips over hers.

Caroline froze, wondering if he would quit if she feigned indifference. However, he grew more insistent, and she tried to push him away. She had a split second of anger with herself that she had reacted negatively to Evie's date but not to Ken. He'd seemed harmless, a nice-looking young man who could have taken out nearly any girl he wanted. Any, she thought, except her.

"Ken," she cried when she was finally able to lean back and get a breath. "You've got the wrong idea about me. I'm not that sort of girl."

"Not according to Carter," he replied. "He claims you're pretty eager, if you know what I mean."

"Stop," she said, trying to slap him away. "Carter's wrong about me. He's all wrong."

He grabbed her arms and pressed himself up against her again. For the first time, she started to panic. She'd been in difficult positions before and managed to get out of them unscathed, but this was different.

"They'll be wondering where we are," she choked out. "People will be looking for us."

"Well, they won't think of coming out here," he replied. "We're practically in no-man's-land."

His hand drifted to her throat, and with a finger, he began to stroke the pearl choker. She fought back revulsion at his touch and tried to figure out what to do. When he reached over to kiss the spot his fingers caressed, she gasped.

"Get your hands off me," she demanded.

He pulled back momentarily and then wrapped his fingers around the pearls. She caught her breath, regretting the fact that she had worn something tight about her throat. A second later, he jerked the strand so roughly, it broke in his hand, the clasp cutting into the back of her neck. She screamed and he slapped her so hard, she fell back against the seat. He pulled her beneath him, lifting her skirt to her hips and shoving his hand between her legs.

"Looks like the angel is just a woman after all," he murmured, his breath thick on her neck. "You'll love it, baby. Just relax."

"Stop," she cried. "Just stop."

He was deaf to her pleas and outweighed her by seventy pounds, at least. She was crushed beneath his bulky frame, bleeding from the neck, her face numb and sore. She fought for a while, and then he pulled back, punching her in the ribs as hard as he could. It felt like a death blow. She couldn't breathe or move. Suddenly, she was almost outside herself, detached from the body he was violating, hoping she would just die on the spot. After a time, she was aware that he had gone still and was staring at her curiously. Then he startled her by snapping his fingers in her face.

"Is this how you are with all the boys?" he asked. "Because I sure as hell expected more from a girl like you."

A girl like you. The words drifted through her head like leaves on a breezy fall afternoon. What sort of girl was she? She wasn't some trollop; that was for certain, no matter how far she had let Carter go when it came to petting. There was a price to pay for dating the best-looking man at Harvard, after all.

Caroline couldn't speak. Her throat ached from having the pearls torn from her neck, but it was more than outward trauma. She had been raped. She had thought only women who had gone looking for sex would end up having it forced on them. She had never imagined a scenario like this, where someone she had perceived as decent could violate her mind and body and leave her completely defenseless. She didn't make eye contact with him as he rattled off a string of profanities over her lack of response to his foul overtures.

Cautiously, she tried to sit up but found her breathing was ragged. Her chest hurt and the pain was excruciating. Something was wrong inside her—she just didn't know what it was.

He started the car and she slumped against the door. She wanted to close her eyes but didn't dare shut them again. She tried not to breathe as he drove along an empty stretch of road, and then suddenly the car jerked to a stop. He put the car in Park and then reached out toward her.

She let out a small scream, but he leaned across and opened her door. Then he shoved her out in one swift movement. She landed hard on the ground, barely out from under the wheels as he pulled away. The car door swung shut as he drove, but ten seconds later, he stopped again. Bile rose in her throat as she waited for him to get out of the car and assault her once more. Instead, he threw something out the window that landed with a thud on the pavement. Then, with a screech of his tires, he drove away.

Caroline pulled herself up from the ground and tried to stand, stumbling as the taillights of his car disappeared in the distance. She limped forward to see what he had tossed out of his car. As she approached it, she realized it was her clutch. She reached over to retrieve it, tripping again. Every muscle in her body ached, but she pushed herself to put one foot in front of the other.

She didn't know where she was going, but he had to be heading toward town, so she continued along the road, wishing she were dead. It was almost freezing, and her coat was back at the dance. She had never imagined being in a position where she was left so vulnerable. People were predictable in the normal world; some were cruel or unkind and one had to stay away from them, while others were good, although she knew well there were gray areas in the middle. Carter fit into that category, like a lot of other young men, but never had she thought she would come face-to-face with pure evil. She had been a fool trusting Ken to drive her home. It would have been her own fault if he'd killed her right there on the spot.

Caroline stopped to rub her ankle, which had been twisted when she was thrown from the vehicle. Every step was painful, and yet she had no choice but to keep going. She had to get back to Cambridge, or the next person who came upon her would finish what Ken had started.

She heard a sound behind her and crawled to the side of the road, crouching behind a tree. Headlights came into view and she went completely still, cursing the shimmery gown that seemed to glow in the moonlight. The car, full of young men, passed without noticing her. She waited until it was out of sight before she dragged herself back onto the road and continued to push herself to keep on walking.

Finally, she reached an area she recognized and, clutching her bag, she pressed on. The dorm was in the other direction, but she had no intention of letting anyone see her in this condition. When she arrived at her destination, she collapsed on the ground in front of the door. She leaned against it and tried to knock, but she wasn't certain if anyone could hear it. However, she couldn't move another inch if it meant falling asleep in subfreezing temperatures and dying on this stoop. Perhaps that was for the best, anyway, she thought. Her life, as she knew it, was over.

Caroline tried to still her breathing despite the pain in her chest, knowing she couldn't go back to the dorm, not tonight—possibly not ever. There would be too many questions that she wasn't prepared to answer, and the housemother would insist on calling the police. Her parents would be furious if she were to involve them in any sort of scandal, and she didn't want that either. She had dragged herself to the only place she could think of to go. She huddled in the doorway, wondering at her fate. The person she was waiting for would either find her or she wouldn't. She hadn't the strength to even attempt another knock upon the door.

12

Alice was certain she'd heard a knock, and although it stopped after a moment, curiosity made her go downstairs to make certain nothing was wrong. She flipped the lock forcefully, ready to give someone a piece of her mind. There were occasional rabble-rousers in the form of Harvard students who'd had too much to drink and rang the bell of every establishment on their way around the city. Instead, Alice's jaw dropped when she saw Caroline crumpled on the doorstep, her dress torn and her face and neck bloody. Recovering herself, she bent down to kneel near the injured girl.

"Oh my God, Caroline. Come in," she said, reaching out a hand to help lift her. As they made their way inside, Alice glanced outside to see if anyone else was around. When she was certain no one else was there, she closed the door and locked it behind her.

"What happened, dear?" she asked. "Can you tell me?"

The girl eased herself into a chair, shaking her head.

"Can you make it upstairs?" Alice asked. "I'll get you a cold compress and you can lie down."

There wasn't much privacy downstairs. The large picture windows illuminated everything at night when she had the lights turned on, and any passersby, however unlikely it was for someone to happen by at this hour, would be able to see everything. Caroline didn't speak or even cry, though her face was streaked with tears. It wasn't clear what had happened, but Alice had a fair idea. The girl tried to stand, and it took three attempts before she was able to push herself to her feet and shuffle to the stairs.

Alice put an arm around her to steady her, and with difficulty, they made it up the stairs. She took a robe from the back of a chair and unzipped Caroline's dress as carefully as she could. When she saw the bruises, she bit her lip to keep from gasping.

"We should take you to the hospital," Alice said. The girl's injuries were worse than she had imagined.

"No," Caroline protested.

"But you could have internal bleeding," Alice argued. "I can do very little for you here."

"No hospital," Caroline murmured. "And no police."

Although she hadn't voiced it, that was Alice's next suggestion. Something terrible had occurred, and whoever had done it was wandering the greater Boston area, capable of doing the same thing again.

Alice turned on a second lamp and inspected the girl. Caroline's face was bruised and her chin scraped. The blood had dried, leaving smears down to her neck. Her left knee was bleeding, too, and her right ankle was scraped and swollen. Alice knew they had to get it elevated as soon as possible. A strange mark slashed across Caroline's throat, where it was clear something had caused bruising. Caroline looked up to see Alice's face and touched the spot where Alice was looking.

"My pearls," she murmured.

Tears stung at her eyes as Alice realized the choker had been ripped from the girl's throat. She went behind Caroline and carefully lifted her hair. There was a gash on her skin where the gold filigree clasp had cut into her neck before giving way. Alice was even more certain they needed to call the police, but Caroline had trusted her, and she did not want to cause her any more distress than she had already been through.

"I have to call your dormitory," Alice said. At Caroline's panicked look, she shook her head. "I won't tell them anything now. Give me the number."

Caroline murmured the number as Alice dialed the rotary with shaky fingers.

"May I speak to the housemother?" she asked in a low voice.

"This is Mrs. Schwartz."

"Mrs. Schwartz, my name is Alice Campbell, and my friend Caroline Hanson is here with me tonight. She's sprained her ankle after the dance and is not able to walk on it. I don't feel right about putting her in a cab to have her try to manage on her own."

"This is most unusual," Mrs. Schwartz answered.

"I've spoken to her mother," Alice continued, looking at Caroline. "She said it would be perfectly all right for Caroline to stay with me for a couple of days until she's able to put some weight on it."

"Most of the others will be gone by then," Mrs. Schwartz answered. "It's Christmas break, you know. I myself plan to go to my sister's in Portland day after tomorrow."

"She does have a key to let herself in later," Alice prompted. "I'm afraid she can't walk on it at all. We don't want to cause her to have a more serious injury than she already has."

"Well," the housemother said, hesitating. "I hate to have her in here all by herself, but if you'll tell her to please be certain to lock the building when she leaves, I suppose that would be all right."

"That's most kind of you," Alice said. "And would you mind telling her roommate, Miss Collins, what has happened so she doesn't worry?"

"I certainly will," the woman answered. "Thank you very much for calling."

Alice set the receiver on the hook and looked at Caroline. They had to get her out of the torn, bloodstained gown. It was an expensive dress, obviously, but it was beyond repair.

"Can you lift your arms?" Alice asked. "We need to get you out of this dress."

Caroline shook her head.

"I'm afraid I'll have to cut it off you, then. It can't be salvaged, anyway."

She took a pair of shears from her sewing basket and started at the hem, her heart sagging as she cut through the satin and tulle. Caroline was completely still as Alice worked her way up the garment to the waistline. As she made small snips to the bodice, several pearls fell onto her lap before clattering on the wooden floor. She froze, wondering what sort of person would do something like this. Nothing less than a monster could have savaged another human being.

Alice brought a quilt over to cover the girl and then brushed her hair back from her eyes carefully. The girl didn't even seem to notice.

"I'll run you a bath," she said. "If you think you can manage it."

"I think I can," Caroline replied.

Alice went in and turned on the tap, getting the water as hot as possible. When it was ready, she helped Caroline get in. Then she got a cloth and began to help her wash off the blood around her face and neck. Her lip was swollen and her left eye was already turning a dark shade of purple.

Alice left her to soak for a while in the warm water. As it grew tepid, she boiled a kettle of water on the stove and poured it into the tub. Afterward, she found a towel and a gown and helped Caroline out of the bath, wrapping her in the towel. Then she slipped the nightgown, her best, over the girl's head and helped her to the bed.

Alice put the kettle on and made a strong cup of tea with extra sugar and then took it to the table beside the bed. Caroline tried to lift it but didn't have the strength, so Alice held it to her lips. After a couple of sips, the girl fell back onto the pillow, then turned away from Alice and began to cry.

Alice put the cup into the saucer and sat down on the bed beside her, rubbing her back until the wracking sobs stopped and her body went still. After a few minutes, certain Caroline was asleep, she pulled the blankets over her shoulders and took the cup to the sink, staring out the window onto the street below. The lone streetlamp shone in a circle on the pavement. Somewhere in the distance, a dog barked and a car passed below. She turned back to look at Caroline, who hadn't moved, wondering if she should go against her wishes and notify the police. The desire was strong, not only to help the girl but to have the authorities searching to find out who had done this to her. Instead, she sighed and made a fresh cup of tea, then took it to her chaise and pulling a quilt across her knees.

She hadn't felt unsafe in a long while, but having Caroline there, so badly injured and emotionally overwrought, she was reminded of how vulnerable women could be. She didn't malign the male sex as a whole, but one had to be careful getting too close.

They were innocents, these girls, all of them. Perhaps especially Caroline, who had been able to command all the attention her parents had probably never given her with the crook of her finger. It was the reason she wanted to educate young women, to teach them to discern and to think. Their provincial dreams of getting married to fine young men and having bushels full of children might well prove true, but Alice knew very well that there were many times when young brides trusted the men they married for no good reason. People could be cruel—both men and women but particularly men, who could overpower and exert undue pressure on the opposite sex.

Sighing, she lifted Caroline's gown from the floor and folded it carefully, placing it into a box with the pearls that had fallen around her. She put it behind a folding screen to hide it from view.

The next morning, Caroline looked worse, if that was possible. Her bruises were darker, her lip completely swollen. The bruises on her rib cage were terrifying.

"What shall we do?" Alice asked. "It's not too late to go to the hospital."

"I can't," Caroline mumbled. "It would be in all the papers."

"I don't want to scare you, but I'm worried for your health," Alice replied. "You were badly beaten last night."

"It doesn't matter," the girl answered. "I still can't go."

Questions lingered in Alice's mind, questions she couldn't bring herself to ask. Caroline had sought her help but only to a point. She wasn't prepared to go to the police.

On the third day, it was decided that Caroline would pack a suitcase and take the train home. Alice called for a taxi and they drove to the dorm. There, Caroline changed clothes while Alice carried the case down the stairs. Eventually, Caroline came downstairs and put one arm through the sleeve of her coat. Alice helped her with the other, managing the buttons as well. She noticed that the clothing the girl wore were loose garments, at least as loose as Caroline probably owned, though she said nothing about it. They both knew she was in terrible pain.

"What are you going to tell your parents?" Alice asked.

Caroline slid on a pair of sunglasses, but there was nothing she could do to hide the bruise on her lip.

"I'll tell them I was in an accident," she answered. "After all, that much is true. It was an accident that I happened to get into a car with someone who had the desire to hurt me that night. And it's best to tell the truth, or at least a version of it, in my opinion."

Alice didn't comment. She waited as Caroline locked the door of the building, and then they went out to the taxi. The driver lifted the suitcase into the trunk, and Alice helped Caroline into the back seat. They drove in silence to the station, although once, Caroline reached out and touched Alice's hand. Before she could react, the hand was withdrawn and the girl turned away, studying the sky outside the window.

When they pulled up to the station, they alighted from the car, and Alice bought Caroline's ticket and found a porter to help with the suitcase.

"Who will meet you at the station?" she asked.

"Baxter," Caroline replied. "My father's driver."

Alice gave her a final look. "If you need anything…"

Caroline nodded. "I know. That's why I came to you, Miss Campbell. I knew you would help me."

A lump rose in Alice's throat as Caroline turned to board the train. She stood on the platform until it rumbled into the distance and then went over to a bench to sit and collect her thoughts. A ball of rage rose up in her. One should be able to trust the person who offers help, but that was not always the case. She knew Caroline would blame herself for the rest of her life, and for no reason. Evil existed and was an ever-present threat. Their only hope was to avoid it as long as possible.

13

JANUARY 1956

> "Rummaging in our souls, we often dig up
> something that ought to have lain there
> unnoticed."
>
> —LEO TOLSTOY, *ANNA KARENINA*

For Merritt, the bus trip from Sacramento to Boston was grueling, three and a half days of sheer torture. When she had first come to Radcliffe in August, it was a novelty seeing a broad swath of the country she had never seen before. Everything was new and exciting to an unseasoned traveler like herself. This time, she had endured the three-thousand-mile trip twice in two weeks, and there was nothing left to enjoy. It was all too much: Exhaust fumes permeating every article of clothing she wore. Being enclosed in a tight space with too many irritable passengers. Being forced to sit in one seat for an extended, uncomfortable ride as they were jolted through mountains and deserts and plains and hills. She hadn't minded going home, but during the final hour of the return trip, she decided she would look for a summer job in Cambridge and stay put for at least a year.

Her father had been glad to see her in his own way, though she suspected it wouldn't have mattered if she hadn't gone home at all. He wasn't a paternal sort of man. Her mother had passed away three years earlier and she didn't have siblings, so he was the only person to go home for. And there was Penelope, his girlfriend, she supposed, who made things complicated. Merritt didn't have strong feelings about the woman, but over Christmas, she got the impression that they would get married, probably sooner rather than later. It was awkward being home again, even after just a few months. Her father had adjusted to his solitary life in her absence. After she had been home for a couple of days, she realized he had removed many of her mother's things, no doubt to avoid offending Penelope, which meant it was no longer the familiar place she had left. A week later, she found a small painting her mother had done when she was young tossed on top of boxes in the back of a closet. Merritt took it out and examined it. Lara had painted many ocean scenes, but this one was different, perhaps her best work. It was small, only seven by eight inches, depicting their favorite beach in Monterey, where they had gone often together when Merritt was young. The colors were arresting, swirls of pink and white and lilac, the water mesmerizing shades of blue. It had been propped on a kitchen shelf through most of her childhood, no doubt reminding her mother of the possibilities of life while she took care of the practicalities. Merritt wrapped it carefully and tucked it into her suitcase to take it back with her to Radcliffe.

Her father had quit his job teaching science at the University of California to write a book on the genomic basis of beetles, and he talked of doing research around the world, including Africa, where he had written his doctoral thesis. His notes and reference books were strewn all over the house, and Merritt wondered if he would ever complete the project. Without someone to keep him organized, he was hopeless. She sighed, thinking about it, knowing she could never change him. Instead, she would write newsy letters once a month and worry about the rest later. In the meantime, she was eager to get back to Radcliffe and her friends.

Evie had written her two letters detailing her time spent with Matthew, and she had received a Christmas card with a hastily scribbled "Love, Caroline" written inside. Merritt hadn't heard from Tess, but she hadn't expected to. Tess wasn't demonstrative, which was fine. She wasn't a demonstrative person either.

During her weeks at home, Merritt thought a great deal about book club and Alice Campbell, whom she had already come to admire. It was a daring and exciting prospect to have a business of one's own, especially a bookshop. It seemed an ideal place to work. Merritt daydreamed about it from time to time, having no idea what she would eventually do with her life. She love painting and drawing and was in fact good at it, but her passion for art couldn't possibly support her, and it was time to think seriously about what she could do that might. The alternative was succumbing to the pressure to get married and start a family. Personally, she was somewhere on the spectrum between Evie and Tess: not boy crazy like the former but not impervious to love like the latter. However, she was certain of one thing: she was not ready to settle down with one man and raise his children, certainly not before she was twenty years old.

Her relationship with her mother had been strong, but she couldn't imagine following in her footsteps either. Lara Weber had given up her own dream of being an artist to take care of a child and become a slave to a house. While Merritt liked children and looked forward to having a home of her own, she didn't want to give up her freedom just yet. College was more satisfying than she had imagined, though book club complicated everything. The books they had read so far were interesting and yet, at the same time, confusing. Until this point, she had generally read romances, where men were protective and romantic, if in a somewhat cynical way. This appeared to be in direct opposition to the men she met in real life. Granted, her experience was small, consisting of a couple of bland high school boyfriends and a handful of boys she had met at Harvard who were more experienced. Either way, she wasn't ready for it. In fact, apart from Caroline, whom one imagined could handle anything, she didn't know who could.

Her painting was all that interested her. Her father considered it a passable hobby for a young woman but not a vocation. She had to admit, even with a degree in art history from Radcliffe, she had no guarantee of finding the sort of job she wanted. Yet she wasn't ready to give up on her dreams.

The bus hit a pothole as they pulled into Boston, jolting her in her seat. It would be a relief to get back onto solid ground. The weather had been bad since Pittsburgh, the East Coast having been hit with its first major storm of the season. She glanced at her watch, surprised. Although the bus had trudged through sleet and snow for hundreds of miles, it appeared to be on time. They would pull in shortly after seven o'clock. When the bus finally ground to a stop, the gears protesting loudly, she sighed in relief, eager to disembark and get back to her dorm room. It had become more of a home to her than her own, although she wasn't certain when that had happened.

Merritt stood and waited her turn to get off the bus, watching through the window as the driver opened the luggage compartment below and began pulling out suitcases, lining them up on the icy pavement. It was freezing in Boston, almost another season from what it had been in California. Snow fell in fat, wet drops on her head as she collected her cases, and she tried to remember which suitcase held her umbrella. She was going to have to get a warmer coat, too, one with a hood. It had been cold before Christmas, but now it was miserably wet as well, the frigid air penetrating her bones. Merritt struggled with her heavy cases, dragging her things to the curb, where there were no taxis lined up and little traffic on the street. She wanted a hot shower and to crawl into bed, perhaps even for days. Evie wasn't expected back until Sunday, and she would relish the silence of a completely quiet dorm room, without dealing with her father and Penelope. That is, if she ever made it back to Duncan Hall.

"Need a ride?" a voice called over a gust of wind.

She looked up to see Caroline approaching. Surprise and relief soared through her. She'd never been so glad to see a friendly face in her life.

"What are you doing here?" she asked, rubbing her arms to keep warm.

Caroline took one of the cases. "I missed you. And I didn't want you to have to get a taxi in this weather. Although, from the looks of it, you would have had a long wait."

"I can't believe you came," Merritt said, a lump rising in her throat. "How long have you been here?"

"An hour or so," Caroline admitted. "I wasn't sure what time you were supposed to arrive. But I brought my book, so at least I managed to get some reading done."

Merritt followed her to a sleek white Thunderbird, giving Caroline a look when she opened the trunk.

"This is a beauty," she said. "We'll be riding in style."

Caroline shrugged. "I rented it in case we needed to get around in this weather. And look, it's come in handy already."

They loaded the cases and climbed into the car, where Caroline put the heater on to let it run for a couple of minutes before easing the car into Drive.

"I didn't get to say goodbye to you before Christmas," Merritt said as they pulled out onto the street.

"I sprained my ankle," Caroline answered, her eyes fixed on the road. "Of course, it's better now."

There was something in her voice that made Merritt wonder if she was telling the truth, and then she decided she must be. She had always been truthful with her before. There was no reason to lie about something as innocent as a sprained ankle, but still, the feeling lingered that she wasn't getting the entire story.

"How was your Christmas?" Merritt asked, trying not to think about her own difficult experience. "Newport must be beautiful at the holidays. And I'm sure your mother decorates your house like a dream."

On the surface, Caroline appeared to have the perfect life, but after meeting her parents, Merritt knew that wasn't true. There were compromises and difficulties for everyone, she supposed, although one could possibly put up with a few to live a life like that, in a perfect house by the ocean. The beauty of it all had been stunning.

"It was fine," Caroline replied, slowing down as she turned left at the corner. "Pearl made too much food, as usual. It could have fed half our dorm, I think. What about you? How was your Christmas?"

"It was fine," Merritt answered, thinking how most of the time she'd been at home was time spent on her own.

She didn't want to get into the messy realities of her life, not when Caroline had been so kind. No one needed to hear how awkward it was with her father either. She had the sense that he had been waiting eighteen years for her to grow up and move out, which put more pressure on her to figure out how to do just that.

"Have you heard from Tess?" Merritt asked. "I've had a couple of letters from Evie but nothing from Ohio."

"No," Caroline answered, driving slowly through the slushy streets. "Although, I really didn't expect to. Everyone is busy at the holidays, of course."

"You're right," Merritt replied, stifling a yawn. "Sorry about that. It was just so exhausting to travel for three and a half days straight."

"I don't know how you managed it," Caroline answered. "You should fly when you have to travel that far."

"I've never been on a plane before," Merritt admitted. "Have you?"

"Mother and I go to Europe most years for the fashion shows and things," Caroline answered. "But air travel is nothing to get excited about. It just gets you there in a day instead of half a week."

They pulled up to the dormitory building a few minutes later and Merritt sighed in relief. She was tired from the trip, but also from worrying about her father and what she was going to do with her life, which suddenly seemed like an imminent decision.

The dorm was silent as they brought their things inside. Even

Mrs. Schwartz had turned in early. They hauled the luggage upstairs and Merritt unlocked her room. Caroline followed her inside, turning on the lamps.

"There," Caroline said. "That's better."

"Thank you for coming to get me," Merritt said. "I don't know what I would have done without you."

"Shall I hang some of these up for you?" Caroline asked as Merritt unloaded the contents of the cases onto her bed.

"I think everything will have to be washed," Merritt answered, lifting one of the dresses to her nose. "Everything smells like the inside of a bus."

"What's this?" Caroline asked, lifting the hastily wrapped parcel.

Merritt opened it and held out her mother's painting, looking at it before handing it to Caroline.

"My mother made it," she answered proudly. "I miss her, so I decided to bring it back with me. It's like having her with me in a way."

"It's beautiful." Caroline sat down across from her in the small desk chair and tucked her hair behind her ears. "Tell me about her."

Merritt sat on the edge of the bed, shoving the pile of laundry to one side. Some things could wait until tomorrow.

"She was beautiful, Caroline," she replied. "Really pretty. She was a delicate, fragile sort of person. She was pretty independent of my father, and I always wondered why they married. They didn't fight exactly, but they did seem to live separate lives. She died of ovarian cancer when I was fifteen, and sometimes I feel that I never really got to know her. You always think there will be time to have heart-to-heart conversations and learn your mother's deepest secrets when you grow up. But you can't when they pass away so young."

"She was an artist too," Caroline murmured.

"For a while," Merritt replied. "And then eventually, she stopped. I never got to ask her why."

"You must miss her terribly."

Caroline had a thoughtful look on her face, and Merritt nodded. Perhaps they had more in common than she had realized.

"I do," Merritt answered, pulling her hair back and securing it with a band. "If she were here now, there are so many things I could ask her. She was only forty-one when she died, and she was ten years younger than my father. She had so much more life to live. Life's not fair, sometimes, is it?"

Caroline made a low sound in her throat instead of an answer. Merritt worried once again that she had said too much. She didn't want to sound pathetic, but she was keenly aware of the fact that she'd never had a confidante. Not a true one, anyway, with mature thoughts and ideas. Caroline was sophisticated beyond any of them, though she hadn't been one to share confidences, at least not so far.

"Tell me about your mother," Merritt said. "I know I've met her, but I don't really know anything about her."

"Oh," Caroline answered, surprised. "Well, she's busy with all of her committee meetings. She's on a lot of local boards and runs half of the events that go on in Newport. And of course, she's wrapped up in the house too. It takes so much thought and planning to run a place like that."

Merritt nodded. "It's a beautiful home."

"What's yours like?" Caroline asked, handing back the painting. "Do you have a picture?"

"No," Merritt answered. She'd never even considered bringing one. Perhaps because it hadn't felt like a home in a long time. Three years, to be precise. "It's a bit of a mess, if I'm honest."

"A mess?" Caroline studied her face, intrigued.

"It's my father," Merritt said, placing the painting on her desk, where she could look at it when she worked. "He's completely disorganized, papers everywhere. Seriously, I have no idea how he's managing to keep the lights on while I'm away." She sighed. "I suppose when I went off to college, it was a test for both of us to see if we could manage on our own."

Caroline nodded, staring at the painting in an absent-minded fashion. Once again, Merritt sensed that something was wrong.

"Did you have a good break?" she asked.

"It's always good to change your routine," Caroline said. She suddenly stood. "Come on. Let's get some food in you. If I know you, you've been living on bags of peanuts and root beer from vending machines. You're probably starved."

Merritt smiled. It was good to be mothered, even in this small way. They went downstairs, passing through the empty rooms.

"It's nice that the others aren't back yet, isn't it?" Caroline asked.

"I'm glad," Merritt answered. "I need some time to rest after that long bus ride. It was the most miserable experience ever."

Caroline nodded. "I need some time to rest from life."

Merritt didn't answer as they went into the kitchen. Even though it was too late for supper, there were always things to eat if anyone had a late-night craving. Merritt pulled roast beef and cheese from the refrigerator while Caroline found a loaf of bread. They made sandwiches and then took them into the salon.

"I don't think I've ever been alone here before," Caroline said, taking a seat near the empty fireplace. There had been a fire earlier in the day, but Mrs. Schwartz was careful to put it out early in the afternoon to make sure no embers were left burning, particularly since so few students were back from the holidays.

"When did you get back?" Merritt asked.

"The day before yesterday."

Merritt mulled on the remark but didn't inquire about it. Most students came back the day before classes, particularly if they lived as close as Caroline did. She had wanted to get away from home. Merritt didn't blame her. Something was definitely wrong, not that she could ask what it was. If Caroline wanted to confide in her, she would when the time was right.

"I love this room," she said, sitting on the large gold sofa across from Caroline. "No one ever seems to sit here."

"We should claim it for our own," Caroline said, spreading a napkin on her lap. "I might even look at some of these books."

Merritt spied the piano at the far end of the room. "Do you play?"

"Terribly, to be honest. Do you?"

"Probably worse than you," Merritt admitted. "I had lessons when I was small and I cried every time I was supposed to practice, so my mother let me quit."

"My mother should have let me quit," Caroline retorted. "But a Hanson never quits anything, ever. Under penalty of death."

Merritt stacked their plates and set them on a table, careful not to look at her friend. Instead, she went over to peruse the titles of the books on the shelves, selecting a couple of books on gardening. She could remember her mother planting petunias and carrots and onions in the spring, and she wished she could ask her mother now what she had loved about growing things. But questions could no longer be asked, of her mother or of Caroline. Merritt knew instinctively that she had to be protective of her friend. No matter what was wrong, it wasn't her place to interfere. Instead, the two of them spent the rest of the evening in a companionable silence, reading.

14

_____

When the nightmare of Christmas break was over, Tess was relieved to be back at Radcliffe in January. After adjusting to life among her good-natured peers at Duncan Hall during the fall, it had been a shock to be thrust back into her home environment, which was even worse than she had remembered. Her father picked on her mother mercilessly and sometimes on her, too, ridiculing her for always having her head in a book. He was one of those men who didn't believe women needed to be educated. In his mind, they existed merely to take care of men. As soon as she got back on campus, Tess decided she wouldn't go home for summer vacation, thinking she would take summer school classes instead. In fact, it had been so stressful, she thought she might never go back at all.

From everything she read, a career for a single woman might not be sufficient to support her and she might have to entertain marriage at some point. Still, it was difficult, if not impossible, to imagine being head over heels in love with anyone after seeing her mother's experience. She didn't feel temperamentally suited to it. The other girls' constant desire to dwell on the opposite sex grated on her, especially Caroline's flagrant displays with Carter. Tess told herself she wasn't jealous; she just didn't like to flout propriety. Life should be lived in a circumspect, discreet manner. All this flashing of pearls and lipstick and lording it over drooling young men was too much for her to handle. She was all too aware of what happened behind closed doors.

Tess planned to have a different life altogether, one that she decided upon herself. She wanted different values than she had grown up with and felt that hard work and discipline along with strong moral underpinnings was the best way to get ahead in life, whether or not a husband ever factored into the equation.

That was one reason she disapproved of the other girls' constant need for entertainment and distraction. *Aren't they here to get an education?* she wondered. Or was their time at Radcliffe merely something they dabbled in to brag about later at dinner parties when they were married and running households of their own?

Tess admired Miss Campbell, who lived an independent life, though perhaps she was a touch too liberal. As far as Tess was concerned, a woman could maintain conservative values and still have an independent spirit. At least, she would, if she were lucky enough to find herself in the same position. From time to time, she wondered about the future, but usually she shook off the feeling. The most important thing she could do now was apply herself to her studies. The better her grades, the better her opportunities for the future. It was as simple as that.

The telephone rang in the hallway outside their door. It was for Caroline, of course; Tess knew without even answering it. She had only gotten one phone call in the entire semester she'd been at Radcliffe, and that was when the dean's office wanted to reschedule an appointment she had made with them the week before.

"The phone's ringing," she said to Caroline.

Her roommate didn't even look up from her desk, where she was studying. "Let it ring."

Tess sighed. She could no more ignore an insistent phone than she could a mosquito buzzing about her ears.

"Hello?"

"Is Caroline there?"

Tess recognized Carter's voice, having heard it on so many occasions. She had to admit his voice was one of the most pleasant things about him. She covered the receiver and leaned into the room, looking at Caroline.

"It's Carter."

"Tell him I'm busy," Caroline said without pausing.

Tess frowned. It was the third time in two days that she had refused to take his call. Whatever they had argued about at the Christmas dance must have been more serious than she thought.

"But it might be important," Tess argued.

"I said I'm busy."

Tess uncovered the receiver. "She's busy, Carter."

"Give her a message for me," he answered. He was irritated. She could hear it in his tone. "I'm going to be out in front of your building in twenty minutes. Tell her to meet me out there, or I won't call again."

He hung up before she could answer. Tess put the receiver on the hook and looked up at Caroline.

"He'll be outside in twenty minutes," she said, tapping the telephone with her index finger. "He said if you're not there, he won't call again."

"That's a relief," Caroline answered, still not looking up. "I was afraid he was going be hard to get rid of."

"What exactly happened at the dance?" Tess couldn't help but ask.

One thing she knew, nearly every girl wanted a boyfriend, and Caroline wasn't just any girl.

She thrived on the attention of the opposite sex. Had she gotten bored with Carter? Or was she interested in someone else? That wasn't out of the question. She hadn't said much since they had returned for the new semester. Perhaps she had found someone over Christmas break whom she liked better.

"He's just a bore, if you really want to know." Caroline closed her book and put the pen on her desk. "Listen, I'm tired of having vapid conversations, Tess. Like this one, in fact."

"Should I go down and tell him you're not coming?"

Caroline turned her back. "I don't care what you do."

Tess stood for a minute, trying to make a decision. Curiosity, however, got the better of her.

If she couldn't get the truth out of Caroline, perhaps she could get it from Carter. She slipped on her shoes and glanced at her hair in the mirror, running a comb through it to secure a stray lock. Afterward, she took her coat from the back of her desk chair and went downstairs.

He hadn't arrived yet when she stepped onto the porch and shut the door behind her. It was a cold day, and she buttoned her coat, reaching in her pocket for a scarf, which she tied over her head. After twenty minutes, he still hadn't shown up. She stamped her feet, trying to keep her circulation going, wondering how much longer she should wait. A minute later, the front door of the dorm swung open and Merritt leaned outside.

"What are you doing?" she asked. "In case you haven't noticed, it's freezing out here. In fact, I think it's below freezing."

Tess thrust her hands into her pockets, wishing she had brought her gloves. "Carter was coming by to speak to Caroline, and she didn't want to talk to him. I thought I'd let him know she's busy."

"Oh, no you don't," Merritt replied sternly, taking hold of Tess's arm. "Come inside right now. We can't interfere in their business, Tess. If Caroline doesn't want to see him, she doesn't want to see him. We have to let it go."

"But they're so perfect for each other," Tess said, refusing to budge. "What's the matter with her, anyway?"

She believed they were perfect for each other but not for the reason it appeared. They were both beautiful people, but they also had the arrogance and high-mindedness of the very wealthy. In that way, they were infinitely suited for each other. She could imagine them married in ten years, with four portrait-worthy, attractive children and a martini in each hand. She didn't think Caroline could possibly love anyone, let alone someone who would attract as much attention as she could. Everything she did was about appearances.

"I don't know," Merritt said, crossing her arms. "Maybe he hurt her feelings or something. Boys aren't that sensitive, you know."

"Caroline doesn't have feelings," Tess retorted.

Merritt looked shocked and Tess immediately regretted the remark. She suddenly remembered Caroline's kindness to her, giving her clothes when they were in Newport and decorating their dorm room. For a second, she felt a sense of shame that she was so judgmental. What sort of person was she to turn on someone who had been so generous to her?

The only answer was that she was jealous of Caroline. What must it be like to have the world in the palm of your hand? Only the Carolines of the world knew for certain.

"I'm sorry," she muttered. "I shouldn't have said that."

"No, you shouldn't have," Merritt replied.

Merritt was usually the peacekeeper, not the scold, although

Tess knew she deserved it. She normally kept her feelings to herself, but somehow she had gotten carried away.

"Anyway, don't stand here waiting for him," Merritt said, opening the door wider. "He might not even come."

Tess turned away from the window and nodded. She followed Merritt into the salon as Evie bounded down the stairs. The three of them sat down, and Merritt picked up a book she had left on a table. Tess suddenly recalled seeing her and Caroline there several times in recent evenings and tried to remember how long it had been since she had noticed Caroline going out. It was possible she hadn't left the dorm apart from classes and their study sessions at the library since they had returned after Christmas. In fact, Caroline had even missed a few classes. Something was definitely wrong. She wondered if she could get to the bottom of it.

"How was Matthew when you saw him at Christmas?" Merritt asked, looking at Evie. "We've been so busy, I haven't thought to ask."

Evie smiled. "We had a nice time, as a matter of fact."

"Nice, as in 'nice'?" Merritt asked.

Evie nodded. "Really nice. In fact, we spent nearly every day together. My parents just love him. They've known him since we were thirteen, you know."

"He spent time with your family?" Tess asked, curious.

She couldn't imagine introducing anyone to her relatives. Her brothers would punch each other and get into fights, and her parents would probably start a shouting match. No, she would never bring anyone home if she could help it. Not in a million years.

"He gets along with my family really well," Evie answered. She stretched her arms and then settled in on the sofa. "Of course, we spent a lot of time alone too."

"Define 'time alone,'" Merritt prompted.

"You know, we went to the movies," Evie explained, her cheeks turning pink. "We went for hamburgers at Eddie's. Stuff like that."

"So, just casual dating," Merritt said.

"Well, not exactly," Evie admitted. "We had some serious talks too. Like what we thought about the future and things like that."

Merritt sat back in her chair and rested the book in her lap. "Serious talks? That sounds intriguing."

"He actually mentioned marriage," Evie answered, smiling, clasping and unclasping her hands. "He was trying to decide if we should get married in four years when he has his degree or if we should go ahead and get married this summer and live in married-student housing until he's finished."

"*He's* trying to decide," Tess echoed in a scolding tone. "Isn't your future something you need to decide on too?"

"I meant 'we,'" Evie said, grabbing a pillow and hugging it to her chest. "We made a pros and cons list of which was the better decision."

"That's good," Merritt replied. "It's important to weigh your options. If you get married this summer, I assume you'll give up college when you move to Princeton, right?"

Evie pulled her legs up and crossed them. "That's right. I'd keep house and probably get a secretarial job while he finishes his degree."

"I hate to state the obvious," Tess said, giving her a look, "but weren't you trying to meet a lot of people so you had more candidates to choose from? Aren't you still planning to date boys here before you decide on a husband?"

Evie looked offended. "We're at college, you know, Tess. We're allowed to have a little fun before we settle down."

"If there's time," Tess replied.

"What do you mean, if there's time?"

"We're here to get an education, you know."

Evie shook her head. "I take my classes seriously, but I'm not like you. I'm not interested in being a career woman. And I'm not like Caroline, either, running around with boys constantly."

Merritt's mouth flew open. "I can't believe you said that, Evie. You know she isn't that sort of girl."

Evie shrugged. "She's not here to plan for a future career, either, you know. She's here to pick a husband, most likely."

"That's a terrible thing to say," Merritt answered. "Yes, she's dated Carter, but she's getting good grades too. Like I told Tess, I think we should mind our own business."

Tess looked out the window, realizing Carter had still not arrived. Men were so unreliable. She remembered the night of the dance, realizing suddenly that her date, Ken, had disappeared and so had Caroline. It had been a mystery at the time, and she hadn't connected it before, but Caroline was capricious. She had probably gotten bored and demanded he take her home.

Tess sat back on the sofa, thinking. When they had gotten back to the dorm after the dance, Caroline wasn't there. Mrs. Schwartz had told them she had sprained her ankle and was staying with a friend. There was only one obvious answer, Tess thought. Caroline was easy. She wondered why she hadn't thought of it before. And to think, they had all been friends with her. Being the wild girl at college was just about as low as someone could go.

"Maybe Caroline has other irons in the fire, if you know what I mean," she said to Evie and Merritt. "There could be other boys besides Carter Gray in her life."

"I don't believe it," Merritt said firmly. "And shame on you for trying to spread gossip. You know better than that."

"Do we?" Tess asked, unconvinced.

Merritt stared at the two of them and then stood. "I'm going upstairs and getting back to work."

"You aren't going to tell her what I said, are you?" Evie called after her.

Merritt paused at the bottom of the stairs, her hand on the rail. "I have no intention of hurting her feelings by telling her anything like that. I certainly hope you don't either."

When she was gone, it was as if a blast of arctic air rushed in the room, chilling everyone left in her wake.

15

For the first time, Alice wasn't looking forward to book club. It wouldn't be a simple discussion of books as usual. She was worried about Caroline, wondering if the girl would turn up or if she had even returned to Radcliffe for the second semester. Alice hadn't heard from her since before Christmas. As sophisticated as she was, Caroline was still at an impressionable age. To have her trust in humanity completely stripped from her in one horrible night was too much to bear. Somehow, Cambridge had felt safer to Alice than Chicago, perhaps because of the comfortable life she had created for herself here. In reality, there was cruelty and suffering everywhere. One must always be on one's guard to avoid being hurt.

She'd gathered that Caroline's home life wasn't all that it should have been either. Nothing in particular was said between them that night, but it was clear she couldn't confide in her parents. That in itself was a shame, one Alice knew well. A lack of understanding in her own family had forced her to become more self-sufficient, but that wasn't always the case. Tragedies could make or break a woman, and it was impossible for anyone to know how she might respond until she went through it herself.

Alice had been lucky, she supposed. Jack had never struck her. Yet there had always been the knowledge that he was her superior in the relationship. It was a construct that she could not endure. He was controlling, never allowing her any freedom. His suspicious nature had resulted in endless interrogations and accusations. If she'd been late for an appointment, he was upset. If the trip to the market cost five dollars more than he'd supposed, he would tell her to return an item. The constant conflicts had worn her down, and she felt little for him by the time she asked for a divorce. She wasn't his property, although neither her parents nor her sister understood her view. In any case, she'd drawn a boundary and she would live with the consequences.

It was a difficult thing to draw boundaries with others. Less so with Jack than it had been with her family, who had taken his side, expecting all marriages to last forever. But what was done was done. And to Alice, it was all for the best. Sighing, she decided to put it out of her mind. There were better things to think about.

Just that week, she had acquired a new friend. A woman had come into the bookshop one snowy morning, apologizing as she tracked in slush on the bottom of her boots.

"Please don't worry about it," Alice assured her.

The woman hastily pulled off her boots, standing there in her stocking feet.

"I'll be happy to clear this up if you have a mop," she said, setting her handbag on Alice's desk.

"Nonsense," Alice replied. "It will take two seconds. Go ahead and look around."

It took hardly a minute to mop away the melting snow, and then Alice went back to her desk to continue working on her catalog. From time to time, she glanced up at the woman, who was approximately her own age, smiling when she met her eye.

"I love your shop," the woman said after a few minutes. "My name is Eleanor. You'll have to remember it because I'm going to be a regular."

They chatted for twenty minutes before Eleanor finally decided on a book, bringing a copy of *The Razor's Edge* to the counter. Alice took extra care wrapping it and stamping "The Cambridge Bookshop" on the brown paper.

"Paper and string!" Eleanor exclaimed. "What a lovely package this is."

"You have good taste in books," Alice replied. "I read it again last year, myself."

"We should discuss it, then," Eleanor said. "I'll call in when I've finished, and we can talk about it over dinner some evening."

Alice smiled, thinking about it. But for now, she readied herself for another evening spent discussing books with her Radcliffe girls. She prepared the room, pulling the chairs into the familiar circle, and waited for them to arrive.

A few minutes before seven o'clock, all four girls came through the door. Alice greeted them as usual, aware she was holding her breath until Caroline came into view. The girl didn't make eye contact right away. It was only after everyone had hung up their coats that she finally glanced in Alice's direction. She gave a slight nod and then went over to take a glass from the shelf. Everyone else had poured a glass of water but Caroline lifted the bottle of wine and poured herself a drink. Alice noticed Evie nudging Tess, but Caroline didn't appear to notice. She took a sip of the wine, lingering away from the group, and then came and sat down beside them.

"I'm so glad to have you all here," Alice said, though she was speaking to one person in particular. "I hope you had a nice Christmas break."

"Thank you, Miss Campbell," Evie answered. "I had a wonderful time on my family's farm. My older brother, Phillip, was recently engaged and we had quite a celebration."

"Congratulations to the happy couple," Alice said, smiling broadly. "Did you have a lot of snow?"

"Tons of snow," Evie answered. "We went sledding on Chandler's Hill. It was a really great holiday."

"Lucky you," Merritt said. "At least you weren't stuck on a bus for most of the time. I feel like I never want to go home again."

"What about you, Miss Campbell?" Caroline asked.

Alice knew she was heading off any possible discussion of the last few weeks and shifting the focus off herself. Tess, likewise, appeared disinterested as usual in personal topics.

"We got quite a lot of snow here too," Alice said. "So in that regard, it was a lot like being at home."

She smoothed her skirt and smiled. "Tonight's book is *Anna Karenina*," Alice said. "I hope everyone has had the chance to read it."

The girls all nodded. Tess probably had a thousand opinions about the book, but Alice wanted to draw out the others more if she could. Caroline was the only one who usually didn't finish, skimming through each book for the juicy parts, she presumed. But she couldn't complain. At least she had been reading.

"I love reading Russian novels in the winter," Alice confided. "There's something bleak and beautiful about them."

"This book was very atmospheric," Merritt said, nodding.

"Let's start with a quote, shall we?" Alice turned the pages until she found the one she wanted. "Here we are. 'All the variety, all the charm, all the beauty of life is made up of light and shadow.' What do you think of that?"

Somehow, without the ability to speak directly to Caroline, she wanted to convey to her that she was going to be all right. Perhaps it didn't seem like it now, and possibly it wouldn't seem like it for some time, but Alice knew that pain, no matter how intense, eventually faded and wounds healed. If only she could find a way to get that across to them all.

"I endured the bus ride from Sacramento in a snowstorm," Merritt replied. "I think given our subject matter that certainly counts."

"Anna didn't endure her situation, though, did she?" Tess asked. "She was trapped in an unhappy marriage with a love affair that grew cold, as well as being separated from her son. How could anyone endure that?"

"Let's break it into parts," Alice answered. "I think some of Anna's difficulty was that she didn't handle her problems as they occurred."

"I know what you mean," Evie said. "There were issues in their marriage long before Count Vronsky came along and swept her off her feet."

"I'm not so sure she was unhappy enough with her life to do something about it until Vronsky came along," Caroline replied. "Yes, her husband was self-absorbed and tied to his rituals. But she lived the life of a pampered woman and had the love of her son to keep her happy."

"It was wrong of her husband, Karenin, to use the boy as a weapon against her," Tess said. "In fact, I'd say it was nothing less than evil."

"That must have been a common practice for the day," Alice

observed. "Women were considered the property of their husbands. They had a role and were expected to fulfill it. Thinking of herself violated Karenin's expectations, so he lashed out in the most hurtful way he could."

"The real issue in this book is that she was unfaithful," Tess said. "I think we need to talk about that."

"Don't you think she had the right to be happy?" Merritt asked, brushing her hair out of her eyes. "Whatever her reasons were, she deserved the chance to find love."

"Don't you think that if one is determined to be content within a marriage, it's possible?" Tess argued. "Her husband offered her everything she needed. He gave her a child. She could have devoted herself to duty, and love would have followed. He was willing to even look the other way if she would give up her lover and not bring scandal upon their family. Is that so unreasonable? What did Vronsky offer that was worth losing everything?"

"Let's look at Tess's point," Alice said. "Why was Anna drawn to another man if she had everything she needed?"

"She had an independent spirit," Caroline said. "She didn't want to be tied down to monogamy and routine for the rest of her life when she wasn't in love with her husband."

"Some people find monogamy and routine satisfying, even comforting," Evie argued. "I hope to be in that position one day."

"Maybe it depends on your personality," Merritt answered, looking at Evie. "But I had the feeling that Anna was beginning to feel like she was trapped in a cage once she met a man she was attracted to."

"She wasn't looking for a way to disrupt her marriage," Alice ventured. "But after she met Alexei Vronsky, her feelings got out of control."

"But look at the repercussions," Tess insisted. "She ends up angering her husband, losing her child and even her life."

"She didn't deserve a bad end, you know," Caroline murmured. "Anna wasn't a bad person. She just didn't make the same choices you or I might have. In some ways, she reminded me of Ellen in *The Age of Innocence.* Her husband didn't treat her as an equal. In fact, he set her aside like a cast-off shoe. A lot of women are treated badly when it comes to love."

"Remember Anna's friend who says something to the effect of 'She's so dear and beautiful, she can't help it if everyone falls in love with her'?" Merritt asked. "She had more temptations than an ordinary girl would have had. A handsome count was never going to fall in love with someone less beautiful and exciting than Anna. Which makes me think it wasn't her fault as much as some might think."

"She was beautiful, so she didn't have to be held to society's standards?" Tess asked. "Is that what you're trying to say?"

Merritt looked down at her hands. "That's not what I mean. But her beauty meant she would have more problems throughout her life: men constantly hounding her, opportunities to see what different lives would have been like. Karenin was boring and much older than Anna. He called all the shots in the marriage. That's all there was to it. And when women get married for money or social positions or to start having a family or whatever, sometimes they end up having regrets. Anna certainly did."

"Is there any reason to justify straying in a marriage?" Alice asked.

The girls looked from one to another, none of them willing to answer in front of the others.

She wasn't surprised.

Alice set her book on the table. "All right, let's look at it another way. In 1874, when *Anna Karenina* was set, what options did she have to get out of a marriage that had grown stale or was unsatisfactory in some way?"

"She tried to divorce her husband," Tess replied.

"Yes, there were avenues for divorce," Alice answered. "But the laws weren't made to protect the interests of women."

Merritt nodded. "She could have gotten away from him, but then she never would have seen her son again."

"Did she deserve to?" Tess asked. "Could she have been a good mother in those circumstances?"

"I think she loved her son very much," Evie said, frowning. "We could all see that."

"But that wasn't enough, was it?" Tess argued.

"Should it be?" Caroline asked, breaking her silence. "Is a

woman only good for one thing: to raise children? What about her feelings? What about what she wants in life?"

"That was 1874, and you can see how complicated it was to fall in love with someone outside of marriage," Alice said. "But what about now? What are the options for a woman who decides she's in a bad marriage or let's say even a dull one, and she wants something else? Remember, Anna was only twenty-seven. Could she really have settled for an unsatisfying life with the potential of decades of unhappiness ahead of her?"

Tess turned to Alice, crossing her arms. "Are you advocating for divorce, Miss Campbell? Because I think it's immoral. That's the reason it's important not to rush into marriage, but once you do, you should honor your commitments."

"I'm not advocating for divorce," Alice replied calmly. "I'm asking what you think is acceptable. Sometimes a woman marries but then, for a multitude of reasons, finds her partner isn't as kind or good or wonderful as she had hoped he would be. One thing about Karenin, he was set in his ways. Whatever you think of his character, he was never going to change."

"Women can get divorced now," Merritt answered. Alice could see she was trying to intercede. "But they can still lose their children if they are leaving because they have fallen in love with another man."

"I wonder if Anna really ever loved her husband," Evie remarked. "Like you said, there are many reasons women marry.

And if she was mercenary or trying to secure a social position, then she should have lived with her decision, like Tess said. She knew it wasn't going to be a bed of roses when she married him, but she still got a lot of what she wanted."

Caroline eyed her carefully. "So you think women should settle?"

Evie shook her head. "I think they should stay true to what they signed up for."

"Heaven help you if your husband doesn't turn out to be an angel," Caroline muttered.

"I think I'm a very good judge of character," Evie said indignantly.

"Maybe Anna stopped loving her husband after a while due to his coldness," Merritt said, trying to change the subject.

"Maybe she never loved him at all," Tess said. "Maybe she was a gold digger who deserved what she got."

"What's your problem, Tess?" Caroline asked.

Although she had said it in a quiet voice, it silenced her friends.

"There's no reason to fight about it," Evie said, tucking her hair behind her ear. "After all, no one here is going to get married and then divorced, are we?"

Alice could feel Tess looking at her, wondering what had happened in her life, if she had been married and divorced, but again, she didn't have the nerve to make an accusation.

"Sometimes there are just no good options, I'm afraid," Alice said. "And a girl feels she needs the conventions of marriage and family to move forward in her life."

"What makes good people fall in love with bad people?" Merritt asked. "Are some men masking their true selves until they've got a ring on a girl's finger?"

"What about women who get pregnant?" Tess asked. "They're just as bad as the man whose fault it is."

The whole room went quiet, and Alice had a sudden feeling of dread sweep over her. Another worry crept into the back of her brain.

"Why do these discussions always end in a fight?" Merritt asked, looking at Tess. "Can't you ever see more than one point of view?"

"There's right and wrong, that's all," Tess answered. "It's as simple as that."

"Well, I think sometimes there is more than one side to a story," Merritt said, holding her ground. "It's important to listen to all of the information, instead of making a snap decision about every single situation. People go through tough things, things that hurt, and if we don't show a little compassion, then what sort of people are we?"

Tess leaned forward. "The sort that believes in common values."

Alice did her best not to sigh. "I think we'll have to agree to disagree on this point. I definitely believe it's important to have all of the information before a conclusion can be drawn, whether we're talking about literature or even more importantly, someone's life. Any other thoughts about *Anna Karenina?*"

As the girls began talking, Alice thought about their conversation thus far. She was surprised that Merritt had gone as far as she had with Tess. And she wasn't alone. It was clear that although Caroline had been unwilling to step into the argument, she felt the same. Evie, she wasn't so sure about. It seemed to Alice that the group had effectively divided itself in two: those who had open minds and were willing to consider new ideas and those who conformed entirely to society's expectations rather than to think for themselves. If pressed, she would put Evie in the latter category.

She stood and went to the shelf to take down the next book for February's discussion. There were only a few books left, and their time together was dwindling. She was certain they would never change Tess's mind about anything, but perhaps with Evie, there was still a chance.

Alice reminded herself that she had not intended to try to change an impressionable group of girls, but then she wondered if that was true. Wouldn't it be easier if girls were aware of the dangers lurking in the world for women who didn't think for themselves? Or would they be carried along on the breezes of life, taking whatever comes and never wishing for something more? It was time for her to examine her own motives, she realized. She had no intention of creating anarchy or destroying norms or, as Tess had said, advocating for divorce. She was certainly for marriage when it benefited both partners equally and there was mutual love and respect, as well as devotion. But she had seen far too many unequal relationships in her time, not to mention the one she had recently left. She wanted to save others the trouble of finding themselves in such painful situations, but then something her mother had always said came to mind: *You can't learn from the mistakes of others.*

Her mistakes were her own, that was certain, although if she could save someone the heartache she had been through, she would. But her mother was right: people had to make their own mistakes. It had been that way since the beginning of time.

"What are we reading for February?" asked Caroline.

"I hope it's not another dreary Russian novel," Evie said. "How about something exciting this time?"

"I think you'll like this one," Alice replied. "We'll be reading *The Great Gatsby*. It's a favorite of college students all over the world."

After she passed out the books, everyone rose and took their coats from the hooks. She stood at the door, rubbing her arms as the cold air rushed in.

"Have a good month," she told them.

They murmured their goodbyes. Caroline was the last to leave and though she didn't say anything, she reached out a hand and touched Alice lightly on the arm. The gesture was reassuring. Alice put her hand over Caroline's briefly and then, just as quickly, allowed it to drop. When they had gone, she closed and locked the door behind them, pulling the blinds to prevent anyone seeing in.

She sighed and then went over to clear away the glasses from the table. Caroline's glass sat among the others, nearly full. Alice smiled and shook her head. She carried the glasses upstairs and washed them in hot water, then let them dry on a fresh towel.

Their conversation had been spirited, nearly combative at times, but one thing she knew: these young women were certainly able to think for themselves. What they did with their knowledge, however, was another matter entirely.

16

FEBRUARY 1956

> "The loneliest moment in someone's life is
> when they are watching their whole world fall
> apart, and all they can do is stare blankly."
>
> –F. SCOTT FITZGERALD, *THE GREAT GATSBY*

On the twelfth of February, the weather turned severe. Another storm, rivaling the one that had hit at Christmas, overtook the East Coast from Washington, DC, stretching as far north as Nova Scotia. Eighteen inches of snow had fallen in Cambridge, with another foot expected. Harvard and Ratcliffe classes were canceled for the week, and with students snowed in, the dorms lost their clockwork precision. Most of the girls took advantage of the opportunity to sleep in late. When they had finally roused themselves, board games were set up on the dining tables and in the salon. A table was brought in for cutting aprons from Butterick patterns, allowing students to practice their stitches on cherry and gingham fabrics to save for future kitchens of their own. Some gave each other manicures while others played chess by the fire, Nat King Cole crooning from the communal record player. In the kitchen, Mrs. Schwartz was teaching a group how to make a devil's food cake from scratch, with a lesson on pineapple upside-down cake to be held the following day. Everyone enjoyed the chance to relax and have a break from work. A few of the more diligent students used the extra time to study, but they were in the minority.

Tess noticed on the third day that Caroline hadn't been downstairs except for meals and sometimes not even then. She appeared to be losing weight as well, looking thinner than she had before Christmas. She never ate much, but it seemed that lately she was pickier than ever. Carter had stopped calling, which Tess supposed was the reason.

"Why don't we go downstairs for a while?" she asked Caroline, who was reading in bed. It seemed that was all she wanted to do these days. Tess tried to adopt a friendly, cheerful tone to placate her.

"You go ahead," Caroline answered. "I'm busy."

"You've hardly moved in two days."

Caroline looked up for a minute. She noticed for the first time that Caroline wasn't even wearing makeup, not that she needed it. Tess frowned, wondering how long that had been going on. No one she had ever known was more particular about her appearance.

"My stomach's a little off," Caroline said, pulling her knees up under her. She was wearing a pair of blue silk pajamas with white trim. Tess wondered how much such a pair would cost. "I just want to enjoy my book."

"Can I bring you something?" Tess asked. "A glass of milk, maybe?"

If Caroline was really sick, Tess had to make sure she was doing all she could to make her comfortable. She tried to think of home remedies her mother used but couldn't recall any. In their household, they were left alone until they were better, except for dire circumstances.

"I'll let you know."

Caroline gave her a faint smile and then turned her attention back to her book. Tess realized she had been dismissed. They had only been back for a few weeks, but as far as she was concerned, Caroline hadn't been herself at all. Of course, they didn't know each other all that well. They had only been together for one term, and throughout that time, she had been involved with the best-looking boy from Harvard, living a whirlwind existence. Tess wondered if this more subdued Caroline was what she had been like before she had gotten involved with Carter, although Tess doubted it. It was a mystery, indeed.

Tess stood, glancing at the snow outside. She walked over to the window and unlocked it, pushing it open to get a breath of fresh air. An arctic breeze rushed in the room, and Caroline pulled her comforter over her quickly.

"Shut that window, will you?"

It was a demand, not a request. Tess inhaled the frosty air, watching her breath as she exhaled, and then closed it quickly. The room was decidedly colder, even though the window had been open for the briefest time.

"Sorry," she mumbled.

She took her sweater from the closet and threw it over her shoulders, turning to study her roommate, who didn't seem to notice anything she was doing.

"I'm going downstairs," she said. "Maybe you could come down later if you feel like it."

Caroline didn't answer, so Tess opened the door and stood for a second in the hall before tapping on Evie and Merritt's door.

"Enter, whoever you are," Evie called.

Tess went inside and shut the door behind her, leaning against it and crossing her arms. Evie was sorting through her wardrobe again, reorganizing everything, it seemed, by color. She smiled at Tess as she took a handful of clothes and began putting them back on hangers.

"What's the matter?" Merritt asked, raising a brow.

She was working on a drawing. From where Tess stood, it appeared to be a view of the ocean. Merritt had been drawing constantly since she had returned from Christmas break and had hung a number of her sketches on the bulletin board over her desk. One of them was a nearly perfect rendition of the Cambridge Bookshop, which Evie said she had drawn from memory.

"It's Caroline," Tess said, turning her attention back to the matter at hand.

Merritt stopped sketching and looked up. "Is she all right?"

"I don't think so," Tess replied, sitting on the edge of Merritt's bed. "She won't go down to eat, she won't get dressed. I don't know what's wrong with her."

"Carter Gray is what's wrong with her," Evie answered, giving them a look. She picked up her knitting basket and took out her current project, a crocheted pot holder fashioned with thick yellow yarn. She looped the long side of the yarn around her pinkie and twisted it around her index finger, working quickly and skillfully. "They shouldn't have broken up, as far as I'm concerned."

Tess nodded. "He's rich, he's gorgeous, and he likes her. I mean, what more could she possibly want? Doesn't that check all of her boxes?"

"Did you ever find out what they were fighting about?" Evie asked.

"No," Tess answered. "She hasn't confided in me."

She hadn't told them her suspicions about the night of the dance. It was possible she was wrong, and yet it was so mysterious. If Caroline had been as focused on her studies as much as she had focused on Carter Gray, Tess wouldn't have to worry about her so much.

"You know she left the dance with Ken the night of the Christmas dance," Tess said tentatively, looking from Merritt to Evie.

She let that information sink in for a second.

"But she wasn't home when we got here, remember?" Evie said, looking confused. "I wonder what—"

"Girls," Merritt interrupted. "We don't want to gossip about Caroline. There's a good explanation for what happened, I'm sure. If she wanted to tell us, she'd tell us."

Tess put her hands on her hips. "Yes, but what if what they're saying is true?"

"Are there rumors about Caroline?" asked Merritt. She stood, setting her pencil on the desk. "What are they saying, Tess?"

Tess looked to Evie for help, but Evie bent her head over her crocheting as though her life depended on it.

She cleared her throat. "They're saying just what you think they're saying."

Evie looked up again and for a moment, no one uttered a word. Merritt closed her sketchbook and gathered her pencils, dropping them into the cup. Then she slipped on her shoes and took down a sweater from her closet.

"Are you coming downstairs with me?" Tess asked. "I thought we could take a look at some of the activities that are going on."

"I'll go," Evie said. She stuffed her crocheting into a bag and hung it over the edge of her chair. "I can work on this anytime. Are you coming, Merritt?"

Merritt shook her head. "I have something else to do."

Tess knew better than to ask. She'd hoped they could sympathize about their situation—that Caroline had subjected them all, in some way, to scandal. Perhaps she should even be thrown out of Radcliffe. But Merritt stood unmoving, waiting for them to leave.

Tess shrugged and went downstairs with Evie, who paused halfway down and took hold of her arm.

"What exactly do you know?" Evie asked, glancing up the stairs in case Merritt was behind them.

"Not much," Tess replied in a low voice. "Ken left the party with Caroline. Then she never made it home. People are talking."

That was an exaggeration, but Tess didn't let it stop her. It was clearly a scandal, and Merritt suggesting otherwise just proved how little she knew.

"Oh my God," Evie gasped. "I don't know why I didn't realize this before. If this is true, it could sully all our reputations."

"'If'?" Tess repeated. "What other answer could there be?"

One of the third-floor girls was coming up the stairs, and they moved to make room for her to pass. They waited a minute to resume their conversation.

"She said she had a sprained ankle," Evie said doubtfully. "But how does that make sense with the rest of what we know? Did she fall on her way to the car and he had to take her to the hospital or something?"

"But wouldn't Mrs. Schwartz have known if that were the case?" Tess asked. "And if she had known about it, she would have told us. As far as I know, Caroline doesn't have any friends in Boston."

"Well, you can't be so sure about that," Evie replied, shaking her head. "She did mention that she and her mother went to Boston regularly on trips. Maybe they had friends who met them when they came into the city."

"Maybe," Tess admitted.

"I have to say, I'd feel much better if that were the case. If only we could know for sure." She looked at Tess. "Do you think we should just ask her?"

"Of course not," Tess snapped. "I don't want her to know I'm even thinking about it. Besides, isn't that exactly the sort of thing someone would lie about?"

"That's terrible," Evie answered. "I mean, do you really think she would do such a thing?"

"I don't know," Tess said. "But people do it every day."

They went downstairs, both lost in their own thoughts. In the dining room, they watched as some of the others worked on their aprons.

"Want to join us?" one of the girls asked. "There are lots of fabrics to choose from."

Tess shook her head. "No thanks. I'm just watching."

"I think I will," Evie replied, avoiding Tess's eye.

The small gesture irritated Tess, making her uncomfortable. She wondered if she had said too much, but surely she hadn't. Anyone would want to know if something untoward was going on. If only she could find out what had really happened.

She wandered into the salon and found a group of girls sitting around, discussing books. Ordinarily, it was a conversation she would have liked to join, but under the circumstances, it felt like she was being disloyal to her own book club, although it was possible their small group would shrink if what she believed about Caroline was true. On the other side of the room, one of the older girls waved her over.

"We need a fourth for bridge," she said. "Can you play?"

Tess nodded and took a seat at their table. Her grandmother had taught her years ago, and she rarely had the occasion to play. See, she told herself, there are other people to do things with.

You don't have to stick with one small group of girls.

It probably wasn't even advisable.

Nodding to herself, she lifted the cards that were dealt and sat back in her chair. Looking at the others, she tipped her cards back to shield them from view. You had to be careful in bridge, she thought. You never knew who was watching.

17

After Tess left the room, Caroline took the book she was pretending to read and threw it against the wall. It landed with a thud on the rug she'd brought from home. She forced herself to get out of bed and retrieve it, even though she didn't want to. It was undamaged apart from a few bent pages. Tossing it on her desk, she went and stood in front of the mirror in their room and examined her face, tracing the hollow of her cheek with her finger. She had lost weight—that was evident—but she was still somehow surprised that the face in the mirror looked much the same as it had for the last year. It was impossible, really, to be so unchanged on the outside when one was completely different on the inside.

She tried not to think about that night. Memories sprang to the surface several times a day, even several times an hour, but she pushed them back as well as she could, murmuring one of her mantras that had become second nature to her after all these weeks.

You survived that night, Caroline; you could have been killed.

That alone spurred her on. She might hate her life now, but she was still alive and there was still life to live. That had to count for something. In the meantime, she had to figure out how to get through the day.

However, it was difficult to carry on as usual. She was no longer the person she was before, an innocent college student with the whole world ahead of her. The thought of that night made her physically ill. Caroline closed her eyes, waiting for the feeling to pass. Sometimes she wondered if she would always feel this way. She wasn't sure how much more she could take.

A rap on the door interrupted her morbid thoughts.

"Who is it?" she asked.

"It's me," Merritt replied.

She didn't want to see anyone, although Merritt might be the exception. Caroline took a final glance at her unkempt appearance. She hadn't been out of her pajamas in days; her hair hadn't been washed; she hadn't eaten much at all. In fact, she refused to go down to the dining room during mealtimes, preferring to get up in the middle of the night and grab a hot roll or a sleeve of crackers or something else that wouldn't upset her stomach. She turned away from the mirror and sighed.

"Come in."

Merritt opened the door, looking her usual self: relaxed, in no rush, thinking everything through in a measured way. She was the opposite of Tess and Evie, when it came to that, both of whom were emotional and dramatic in one way or another. Evie chattered endlessly, and Tess's stony, judgmental silences were drama enough on their own. And for now, Caroline was sick to death of drama.

"I'm just checking on you," Merritt said, closing the door behind her. "Is it all right if I come in?"

"Yes, of course," Caroline answered. "How are you?"

It was her way, like her mother's, to preempt questions by asking some of her own. She had learned from the master how to cover up pain.

"I'm fine," Merritt replied. "I'm just worried about you."

"Why?" Caroline asked, turning away from her and pretending to look through the clothes in her closet. If she had her way, she would take a pair of shears to them all and cut them into tiny pieces, like confetti. "I've just been feeling a little lazy lately. It's not like we have any classes this week. Nobody needs to worry about me."

She regretted the sharpness of her tone. She might feel brittle, but it wasn't her place to take it out on Merritt.

"I know. It's just..."

"Just what?"

Merritt shrugged, trying to collect her thoughts. "You've gone quiet, as my mother used to say. I miss you at meals especially. You know if you aren't there, I'm stuck listening to Evie and Tess drone on and on about the most boring things."

Caroline didn't comment. Privately, however, she agreed, although she knew it was important to keep her college friendships as strong as possible. You never knew when you might need someone's goodwill. Not to mention, Tess was socially awkward enough without adding to her burden by making their relationship difficult, but Caroline was sick to death of all the questions.

"Listen," Merritt continued, folding her hands in her lap. "I think we might have a problem on that score."

"What sort of problem?" Caroline asked, turning to face her.

Even as she said the words, she knew. Her behavior wasn't going unnoticed. For a second, she toyed with the thought of going home for the rest of the year, but that wasn't really an option. A few weeks with her parents at the holidays had been difficult enough, though she was lucky that neither of them had looked at her too closely. In some ways, they didn't know her well enough to realize the change that had come over her. Still, her father's overbearing nature irked her even more than usual, and she had been desperate to leave. In January, she had chosen Radcliffe as the lesser of two evils.

"Tess says there is some sort of gossip about you."

Caroline went over and sat down at her desk. That wasn't what she had expected. "What sort of gossip?"

By the look on her face, Merritt clearly dreaded wading into the topic. "As far as I can tell, it's about the night of the Christmas dance."

"What about it?" Caroline demanded.

If it were anyone other than Merritt asking the question, she would have turned on her heel and left the room. As it was, she sighed again, resigned to the battery of questions.

"Where were you that night?" Merritt ventured. Then she shook her head. "It's presumptuous of me to ask, I know."

"Where was I that night?" Caroline asked in an arch voice. "I went to the dance and then I went home. What do you care?"

"You're forgetting what we learned in Psychology 101," Merritt said, sitting across from her on Tess's bed, drawing her legs up underneath her. "When someone is lying, they repeat what you just said to give themselves an extra five seconds to formulate a response. But I'm not giving you the third degree, Caroline. I'm just telling you that I care about you. I'm here for you if you want to talk and even if you don't."

"I know," Caroline said. She stared at her hands in her lap, wanting to close her eyes and wish her reality away. "I just can't talk about it, that's all. If you want to use psychological terms, I think I'm depressed."

"Why are you depressed?"

Caroline shrugged. "I can't really say."

"Have you ever been depressed before?" Merritt sat forward and studied her, truly interested in the answer.

Caroline shook her head.

"So something happened that has had a major effect on you," Merritt answered. "Would you feel more comfortable speaking to someone else? Maybe Mrs. Schwartz could talk to you about how you're feeling."

"God no," Caroline replied, distressed at the idea of sharing her grief with the breezy housemother, who hadn't appeared to have any depth when it came to human relations. "I don't want to discuss my feelings with Mrs. Schwartz."

"Then the campus infirmary might have someone you could talk to." Merritt frowned. "They're professionals. They're used to dealing with things like depression and anxiety. They mentioned it in orientation last fall. If you talked to someone, you wouldn't feel so alone."

"Absolutely not," Caroline said, shaking her head.

Merritt looked her in the eye. "They're talking about that night, Caroline. Tess said she wanted to know what happened after Ken took you home. They know you didn't come back here after the dance."

Caroline gasped. Tess was getting so close to the truth, it hurt. The last thing she needed was for her friends to spend every waking hour speculating about the worst night of her life. She simply couldn't stand it.

"Who is talking about it?" she choked out. "Just Tess? Or does everyone in the dorm have an opinion on the subject?"

"Tess is the only one I know for sure," Merritt admitted. "But she told me and Evie. I don't know if she would go so far as to share her suspicions with anyone else."

"I didn't like the way Ken spoke to me," Caroline said carefully. "And I got out of his car so quickly, I fell and twisted my ankle. When it happened, there was only one person I thought might be able to help."

"Alice Campbell," Merritt guessed.

"Yes," Caroline answered. "She let me spend the night at her apartment, and that is the honest truth."

She hadn't told Merritt everything, but neither did she want to lie.

Her friend sighed. "That's a relief. Why don't you tell Tess so she can let the whole thing drop?"

"Maybe I will," Caroline said.

"What can I do for you in the meantime?" Merritt asked. "Surely there's something I could do to make you feel better."

"Switch places with Tess and move in here with me," Caroline said. "She's such a busybody, I can't stand it. Let's let Evie take her on."

Merritt ran her hand over a pillow. "You're mismatched as roommates, that's for sure. But something tells me she wouldn't go."

"I know she wouldn't," Caroline admitted. "It's just that she's so...you know. Intense, for lack of a better word. You wouldn't badger me constantly, for one thing. You'd sit at your desk and draw all the time."

"Maybe if you talk to her, it will calm things down." Merritt picked at a piece of lint on the sleeve of her sweater. "But for now, I think you should take a shower and go downstairs. We'll get something to eat and play a game or something. If you act like nothing's wrong, people might forget about it."

It was the last thing Caroline wanted to do, but she knew Merritt was right. Things weren't going to improve by themselves. If she wanted to survive, she was going to have to act as though her life hadn't been completely shattered.

"All right," she conceded.

Merritt nodded, satisfied, and Caroline gathered her things so that she could shower. Perhaps she would feel better if she cleaned herself up. It was even possible that she could move past the horror of that night if she distracted herself temporarily and tried to pretend nothing had happened.

But by the end of the week, Caroline knew something was terribly wrong. The snow had stopped falling and was melting in the streets, which had been cleared by screeching city snowplows. Her fellow dorm mates were heading out into the bright February sunshine with a plethora of activities to do: sledding, going to the library, heading down to Harvard Square bundled in coats and galoshes—anything to relieve the boredom of being stuck inside for nearly a week. Caroline did her best to make appearances at meals and yet stay out of everyone's way. But by Friday, panic overtook her. Not only was she still feeling sick every day, but she hadn't had her period since December. When she had awoken that morning, her breasts were tender. Tears sprang to her eyes. She wanted to tell someone, but her suspicions were fodder for gossip throughout not only their dorm but the entire community.

What if I'm pregnant, she wondered. *Eighteen years old and pregnant by a man who attacked me?* It was hard to fathom, even though she had lived through it. Of course, she couldn't have a child that had been conceived in such a way, although there was no way to get rid of it. She had hoped that turning a blind eye to the situation would help her move past it. Now she realized nothing could change the terrible trajectory her life appeared to be on.

If only she were dead, she thought. Then she wouldn't have to face the consequences of that night or see the pity on her friends' faces when they realized her life was ruined. She couldn't breathe a word to anyone, of course. No one ever believed the girl in a circumstance like this. Everyone would say that she had been easy and now she was trying to ruin a man's college career as well as his life. Carter hadn't told her much about Ken, but judging by his clothes and mannerisms, he had been raised in a wealthy family like her own. If she were an ordinary girl, she could force him to marry her, knowing there would never be another option. No decent man would marry a girl who had gotten pregnant by someone else—no one. Caroline, however, was no ordinary girl. She knew her future prospects were likely to marry for convenience, but she would never marry someone who could behave brutally toward her or anyone else.

The other option was to force his family to help her and buy her silence. However, this posed different problems. If his family was wealthy, it was likely they had some connection to her parents' world. And she would do anything to keep this from her parents. Anything at all.

The following morning, she got dressed as if she were going to class, but when they left the dormitory, she turned and went to the library, hoping it would have the information she needed. The building, thankfully, was nearly empty. A few librarians were drinking coffee behind their desks and chatting about the previous weekend. Students wouldn't fill the rooms until after classes, and Caroline was relieved to have the place to herself.

She went to the card catalog, flipping through the carefully typed index cards until she found what she wanted and then wrote the call numbers on a piece of paper. Then she wandered the rooms until she found the biology section, taking a heavy book on female reproduction to an abandoned desk. It took several minutes, but she finally found what she was looking for. According to the book, her assumption was correct. She flipped pages until she discovered another piece of vital information: the average gestational period was two hundred and eighty days.

Caroline slammed the book shut and took out a piece of paper, counting the days from the Christmas dance, arriving at September 12. Even if she could hide the pregnancy until the end of May, when classes were out, she had nowhere to go for the last four months.

Numbly, she stood, leaving the book on the desk, and walked out of the building and back to her dorm. When she reached her room, she closed the door behind her and sat on her bed, trying to calm herself.

After a moment, she stood and then went over to Tess's desk, where a chocolate bar rested atop a magazine. She suddenly had the urge to eat it. Perhaps she needed to get some food inside her after all. She reached for the candy and nearly upset the pile of books and papers it rested on, putting out both hands to steady everything. As she straightened them on the desk, she noticed a photograph jammed between the books.

Taking the photo from the stack so it wouldn't get wrinkled, she froze when she recognized it as a picture of herself. It was a glossy print, taken a year ago in Capri when she and her mother had traveled to Italy. In it, she wore a white buttoned blouse with cap sleeves. She had undone the bottom two buttons and tied it around her midriff, showing a few inches of her tan above her pink A-line skirt. She'd been wearing her favorite sandals, white espadrilles that wrapped around her ankles and tied in a bow. She had a mesh market bag slung over her shoulder, and she was smiling at the camera. Behind her were the colorful houses that were perched on the hillside, looking out onto the Amalfi Coast. It had been a good day, she remembered. One of her favorite days with her mother. And now, the photo was lying on Tess's desk. Caroline hadn't brought it with her to Cambridge, of course. Her face went hot as she realized that Tess had removed it from the silver frame from the guest room and stolen the picture.

Caroline knew she was not a perfect person. She had many flaws, but snooping on others was not one of them. And she had never stolen anything, either, certainly not as personal as a photograph from someone else's home. Her cheeks flushed with anger. She was debating what to do when Tess suddenly opened the door.

Caroline spun around and held it out for her to see. "What are you doing with this?" she demanded.

Tess didn't answer. She stared at the photograph for a few seconds and then turned and fled the room.

18

"Is Caroline here?" Merritt asked as she tugged off her blue woolen coat at the Cambridge Bookshop.

It was a bitterly cold day—Alice's only complaint about living in New England. She was from Chicago, of course, so she was well acquainted with snow and brutal winds and the ravages of winter, but today, she couldn't quite shake the cold. A radiator hissed in the corner, but no matter how much she turned it up, she couldn't make the bookshop warm enough. Perhaps it was the building itself, with the drafts and frozen windows with condensation trapped between the panes, or even the view she had late at night looking down at the pool of light cast by the streetlamp onto the corner, where the piles of slush and snow sat.

Alice took Merritt's coat and hung it on a hook near the door. She turned back and looked at her, frowning.

"Isn't she with you?" she asked, studying Merritt's face. "Don't the four of you usually walk over here together?"

The dreaded feeling returned as quickly as it had left the last time she had seen Caroline. And who would she reach out to if something was wrong?

"I haven't seen her in a few hours," Merritt answered, reaching into her pocketbook and extracting a piece of paper that was folded in quarters. "She left this note."

Alice unfolded it and read: *Things to take care of. I'll see you later.* She puzzled over it for a moment and then handed it back to Merritt, who slid it into her bag.

Merritt rubbed her arms against the chill. "I'm not even sure what she meant."

"There's coffee," Alice said, walking over to the percolator and pouring her a cup.

Merritt took it gratefully, closing her hands around it for warmth. "Thank you, Miss Campbell."

"Is everything all right?" she asked in as light a tone as possible.

"Well, I'm not really sure," Merritt answered.

"Would you like to talk about it?" Alice asked.

Evie and Tess weren't there yet, either, and for some reason, Alice felt a sense of relief. She was glad to have some time alone with Merritt for a while. It might help her gain some insight into Caroline's mental state. The girl wasn't her responsibility, yet she couldn't help feeling concerned after what she had gone through.

Merritt hesitated and then nodded. "I'm worried about her, if you want to know the truth."

"Why is that?" Alice asked.

She sat down in the reading-group circle and gestured for Merritt to join her. The girl sat and leaned forward.

"I don't know exactly," she said. "Something has been bothering her, but she hasn't confided in me about anything specific. I mean, we're close, but I have the definite feeling she's holding something back."

Alice sighed. If Merritt didn't know what had happened, she couldn't be the one to tell her.

"How do you know something's troubling her?" she asked.

"During the first term, she was so happy and confident," Merritt answered. "There was nothing she couldn't do. She was fearless and fabulous, everything I wish I were."

"And now?" Alice prompted.

"Now she's completely different," Merritt said, shaking her head. "Something must have happened, maybe when she went home for Christmas. She hardly gets dressed. She never eats a thing. She's lost weight since we got back to school, I'm sure of it."

"You haven't tried to talk to her?"

"I haven't pried, but I've been trying to think of ways to help," Merritt said. "I try to get her to eat and do things, but I feel like I'm fighting a losing battle. You know, she did mention that she was feeling depressed."

Alice stood. "I think I need a drink. What about you?"

Merritt hesitated for a fraction of a second and then nodded. "Yes, please."

Alice poured them each a glass of wine and brought one to her. She settled into her chair again and frowned.

"What do you think we should do?"

Merritt took a sip of the wine. "I'm not sure, Miss Campbell. Sometimes I think I should be patient for a while longer. I keep hoping whatever cloud she's under will pass and things can get back to normal."

"And if they don't?"

"If they don't, I'll have to come up with another solution." Merritt paused. "By the way, she's not getting along with Tess particularly well either."

"I'm sure they'll be fine," Alice said with more confidence than she felt. "They're roommates, right? Sometimes there are conflicts between people when they live together, but they are both levelheaded girls. They should be able to work things out on their own."

"But what if they don't?" Merritt asked, learning forward. "That's what I'm worried about."

"You share a room with Evie, don't you?" Alice asked. "You two probably have similar situations from time to time."

Merritt sat back in her chair. "We've never had any major disagreements, though. I've been irritated with her sometimes, but I just get out of our room and do something else for a while until the feeling passes."

"They'll probably do the same thing," Alice replied. "I don't think Caroline is a confrontational sort of person."

However, she had her doubts about Tess. She'd hoped to be able to crack the girl's shell eventually and come to some sort of understanding, but Tess's guard appeared to be impenetrable.

Merritt nodded. "I wish I could believe that."

The door suddenly swung open, tinkling the bell attached to the top. Evie stepped inside and shut it behind her quickly, brushing the snow from her sleeves and removing her hat.

"Hello, Evie," Alice said with a brief glance at Merritt before she stood to take Evie's coat.

"Hi, Miss Campbell," the girl replied, shrugging it off her shoulders.

Alice hung it on the hook and turned to look at her. Evie's cheeks were red from the cold, and when she removed her knit gloves, Alice could see her hands were just as frozen as the rest of her.

"Would you like some coffee?" she asked. "It's fresh."

Evie nodded. "I usually don't like coffee very much, but a hot cup sounds nice right about now."

Alice poured her a cup and handed it to her. They went to sit down, but Evie paused when she caught sight of Merritt having a glass of wine.

"What are you doing?" she demanded in a tone that reminded Alice of her mother. "Not you too."

"I'm just having a sip," Merritt answered, shrugging. "It's taking off the chill."

"I expect behavior like that from Caroline," Evie said. "But certainly not from you."

Although she didn't give an obvious reaction, Alice could see that Merritt was upset by Evie's remark. She thought back to her own college days, wondering if the women then were as judgmental as some of the young women in this group. She didn't think they were. Alice remembered her college days as fun and stimulating. Everyone she went to school with felt incredibly fortunate to be able to follow their hearts and get a college education. In the not-too-distant past, most women didn't go to college. Women like Alice knew they were among the lucky ones. In some ways, she thought, the twenty years that passed since she had started college had caused the younger generation to take their opportunities for granted. In her opinion, it was a shame.

"You're not only breaking the law, you're failing to uphold the standards of a Radcliffe College student," Evie continued.

Merritt eyed her before setting down her glass. "You're sounding a lot like Tess tonight."

"Maybe Tess is right," Evie replied, holding her ground. "She believes in honoring traditional values, in case you haven't noticed."

"No one here is against traditional values," Alice said, sitting

down between them. "I hardly think Merritt deserves to be casti-
gated for having a sip of wine. But perhaps that's not really what
you're talking about. Could it be that you're concerned about book
club?"

Evie shrugged, glancing up at her and then down again. She
seemed almost to have forgotten Alice's presence in the room. "I
don't want her to get in trouble."

Alice nodded. "That's commendable, I'm sure. But do your personal values extend to others in your circle? Or are we, ultimately,
responsible for ourselves alone?"

"I think we are responsible for ourselves," Merritt said, pulling
her sweater closer around her.

"I'm not sure," Evie said.

"Well, put it like this," Alice said. "There's a hierarchy involved
in a situation like this. Merritt is responsible for herself, first and
foremost, and then in descending order, to her father, her family,
friends, and then society at large."

Evie looked from Merritt to Alice as if gauging their reaction.
"You forgot God."

"My point is," Alice continued, "even well-meaning friends
who love you shouldn't be judging you for your behavior. Especially
over things that aren't important."

"You think drinking alcohol under the legal age isn't important?"

"Do you honestly think I'd become a drunk?" Merritt asked,
shaking her head. "I don't know about your family, but in mine, my

father would occasionally pour me a small glass of wine on special occasions, if only for a sip. It was meant as a nice gesture. It didn't corrupt me or anything."

Evie shrugged and then stood. "I don't think we're going to discuss the book tonight, so I think I'll go. I have a sociology test tomorrow that I need to be studying for anyway."

"Evie..." Merritt began, but her friend ignored her.

She collected her coat and buttoned it quickly before turning around. "I'll see you back at the dorm."

Merritt nodded miserably and stood as well. She looked at Alice and sighed.

"I'm sorry there was a dustup tonight," Alice said.

"It's not your fault," Merritt answered. "But I think I should go. Maybe I can catch up with her."

"Of course."

Alice walked her to the door and watched as the girl gathered her things and left. When they had gone, she locked the door behind them and went over to her desk. She pulled the phone directory from the bottom drawer and opened it to the girls' dormitory building. Sliding on her spectacles, she peered at the number for a moment and then dialed it, waiting for it to ring through.

"Duncan Hall," came a young voice on the other end of the line.

"May I speak to Caroline Hanson?" Alice asked.

"Hold a moment, please," the girl replied.

Alice could hear the receiver being set down with a thud,

and then she could hear murmured voices in the background. She glanced at her watch. It was only twenty minutes after seven. Supper had been served and most of the girls were probably in their rooms studying. She waited a few minutes, wondering after a while if she had been forgotten, and then a breathless voice came back onto the telephone.

"I'm sorry," the girl said. "She doesn't seem to be here at the moment. May I take a message?"

"No, thank you," Alice replied. "I'll try again later."

She didn't want to raise suspicions by leaving her name, and neither did she want the other girls, Tess in particular, to know she was trying to reach Caroline.

Sighing, Alice set down the receiver and began to clear the glasses from the counter. Merritt hadn't deserved Evie's wrath. Her wine had hardly been touched. They were peculiar creatures, college girls. They could seem so grown-up at times and like adolescents at others, trapped between the constrictive rules of their childhoods and the freedom of being an adult.

On the surface, Evie appeared to be the most pliant of the girls, but she might have the worst temper. In Alice's opinion, it was because she feared change. She was the most likely to go back to her home after college, however long she stayed, and most likely to adhere to whatever guidelines and rules her parents had established during her growing-up years.

Caroline had a mind of her own and was enjoying independence at Radcliffe, at least until the night of her attack, but Alice was confident that she would eventually rebound from the hurt and pain and grasp life once again. Merritt seemed disconnected from her normal life, though unsure what to make of the year ahead of her and eager for a role model to help her make decisions. Tess, ever the mystery, would never go home in Alice's view. She eyed a future far beyond the perimeters of small-town Ohio.

Frustrated, Alice sat at her desk and pulled out a sheet of paper. It was newly arrived from the stationery shop two streets over, with the simple heading:

THE CAMBRIDGE BOOKSHOP
Simpson Street, Cambridge, Massachusetts

Then she took out a pen and began to write:

Dear Caroline,

You've been on my mind lately. I was sorry to miss you at book club this evening. I hope you know if you need anything, I am here.

With regards,
Alice Campbell

She read it to herself once or twice, dissatisfied. There was so much more she wanted to say, but should the letter fall into the wrong hands, it was important that it was brief and didn't allude to what had happened that night. She wanted to add that she hoped to hear from Caroline in response but decided that hope was implied. Caroline had been given a traditional upbringing that surely included the answering of private correspondence in a timely fashion. Alice would have to trust that Caroline would reply when she received the note.

Two days passed, then three. She had mailed the letter at the local post office, going directly to the desk instead of leaving it in the mailbox on the corner. By her calculations, it should have arrived two days ago, having only a short distance to travel to reach its intended recipient. However, by the fourth day, Alice could stand the waiting no longer. She walked over to the bookshelves and found the books that she had intended to give the girls a few days earlier. Of course, Merritt and Evie had left out of sorts, and Tess and Caroline hadn't attended book club that night. She pulled one from the shelf, *Bonjour Tristesse* by Françoise Sagan.

The book had pricked even her own more liberal conscience when she had read it a few months earlier. The author was an eighteen-year-old girl from France, and the novel had been quickly translated into English, catching the attention of American book-sellers. Alice sank into a chair and flipped through the chapters. It was a short book, only a hundred and fifty pages, but while its brevity would appeal to busy college girls, its promiscuity was certain to offend.

How set we are in our ways, Alice thought, *even when we try to open our minds.* She rose from the chair and placed the book back on the shelf, looking for a more palatable substitute. In the end, she pulled out another small book, *Gift from the Sea* by Anne Morrow Lindbergh. She had skimmed it herself, planning to read it later, but the newly published nonfiction title promised to elucidate readers on the benefits of solitude, simplicity, and the importance of a woman nurturing her own soul. It was written from the perspective of a mother having a holiday from life and its attendant responsibilities, which might be a little mature for her group of girls, but perhaps they would find some nuggets of wisdom inside. At any rate, it couldn't be construed in any way as inappropriate for an intelligent group of young women. *Bonjour Tristesse*, along with several other choices, like *Lolita*, *Lord of the Flies*, and *The Catcher in the Rye*, were best read by those who were ready to have their opinions challenged. The four young women in her book club may have begun that way a few months before but were all brittle and stressed at present.

Alice wrapped each of the four copies individually with paper and string and then tucked them inside her waterproof bag. She pulled on her coat before settling her hat on her head. Although she had never been to the Radcliffe campus before, she knew it wasn't far. If she couldn't find a taxi, she would walk.

The day was fair, if cold. She stopped after a minute to take her gloves from her pocketbook and put them on before locking the door behind her, trusting that within the hour, she would be able to assure herself of Caroline's state of mind and help in any way she possibly could. If everything went well, her young friend would be fine and they would be on track for book club the following month. If it didn't, Alice had no idea what to do next.

19

MARCH 1956

> "Woman must come of age by herself... She
> must find her true center alone."
> —ANNE MORROW LINDBERGH, *GIFT FROM THE SEA*

It was a Friday morning. Evie made her way downstairs and into
the dining room, where she poured a glass of orange juice and then
took her plate to the buffet table. She loaded it with scrambled
eggs, bacon, and toast, and at the last minute, spooned on some
oatmeal as well. She had a healthier appetite than her friends, but
having been raised on a farm, she knew a proper breakfast was the
key to a productive day.

She sat at their usual table, listening to the hum of quiet conversation around her, wondering if her roommate would appear. A
few minutes later, Merritt came in, wearing her camel wool coat

and a red stocking cap on her head. Her arms were loaded with books.

"Aren't you going to eat?" Evie asked disapprovingly.

Merritt shook her head, her blond hair swinging about her shoulders. "I'll get something later. I need to look up a few things in the library this morning before class."

"Are you sure?" Evie persisted, thinking the least she could do was keep her company. It wasn't right to change schedules and abandon your friends. "You don't want to get a headache from hunger, you know."

Merritt smiled. "Don't worry so much, Evie. I'm fine."

Evie watched as she headed out of the dining room and then glanced around the room. Every other table had two or three people sitting together, laughing and talking, getting ready for their day. She was getting tired of eating alone. After all, she'd eaten on her own yesterday as well. She wasn't quite certain what had happened, but there seemed to be some strain between Caroline and Tess that was contributing to the problem. As far as she knew, they hadn't argued or had a major disagreement. Nothing she could put her finger on, at least. Merritt claimed not to know anything, but everyone had noticed the two of them had started eating at different times. It irked Evie that they were ruining their cozy foursome with some petty disagreement, whatever it was.

She sighed, finishing her breakfast in silence, thinking that if this went on much longer, she would have to join another group of girls. College was hard enough without starting the day off having no one to talk to. Just as she stood to put her plate on the kitchen cart, Tess walked into the dining room. She barely nodded at Evie before getting a plate and turning to the buffet.

Evie shrugged it off, deciding to check her mail cubby in hopes that there was a letter from Matthew. He'd been too busy to write much lately. Her mood lifted when she saw there were a couple of letters inside as well as a flyer. She pulled them from their slot and looked at the return addresses eagerly. The first was a letter from her mother. Flipping the other around, her shoulders sagged when she saw that the second was merely a letter from a high school friend, Mary Gardner. She reached for the letter opener in a nearby pen cup and slit both the envelopes open. Then she went into the lounge and found a comfortable chair.

The flyer was an announcement of a fundraiser that evening at Joe's Burgers to raise money for the spring dance. No one she knew had mentioned it, but with the state of things among her friends, none of them would likely go. She drew her legs up under her skirt and pulled out her mother's letter, eager to read the news from home.

Her mother was a faithful correspondent, which was probably where Evie had gotten it herself, and her letter was her typical newsy dispatch. Her youngest brother, Bobby, had won the science fair at school this month with his innovative idea for a cow milker; her brother Frank, who was two years older than Bobby, had asked his girlfriend, Millie, to go steady and had taken her to get a milk-shake and fries the Saturday before; her father was his usual quiet self, although his lumbago was acting up. Aunt Florence was planning a visit in mid-June, so Evie would have the chance to see her, too, and hear about her life in the big city of Albany. The last winter storm had knocked down one of the trees on the far end of the property, and her father and brothers were waiting for the snow to melt so they could chop it up for firewood. Miss Melcher at church had fallen on the ice and was in bed with a sprained ankle (thank heaven it wasn't more serious). The Plucketts had put their house up for sale, deciding to move near their oldest daughter in Virginia, where they wouldn't have to deal with another harsh winter.

Evie smiled, savoring every word. Her mother had written a week earlier, and that letter had been similarly full of news, but at the moment, she was most interested in the Plucketts' house. It was three blocks from their church, an old Victorian, and one she had admired for years. She was almost sorry it had been put up for sale now, before she'd had time to get engaged, because she didn't want anyone else to snap it up. Hopefully, she thought, it would languish on the market for a year or two until she got her chance to marry someone and they could buy it for their future life together.

Her mother's letter put her to rights after her disappointing start to the day. Smiling to herself, she pulled out Mary Gardner's letter from its envelope and opened it to see what her old friend had to say. The last time she had spoken to her was over the Christmas holidays, and Mary had been wildly envious of her Radcliffe adventure. Evie hadn't always been the object of admiration and found it exciting.

However, one glance at the letter, and her heart dropped to her stomach.

Dear Evie,

I hope this letter finds you well. I have thought of you often since seeing you at Christmas. I haven't forgotten what you said about Radcliffe being a good place to meet Harvard boys and hope you have found someone you really, really like.

Matthew was here about a month ago to see his mother while she was in the hospital...

Evie stopped reading, seized by a feeling of panic. Matthew had mentioned in his last letter that his mother wasn't feeling well, but he hadn't said anything about going home. In fact... She frowned, trying to remember when she had last gotten a letter from him. Had it been two weeks? Three? She had put his lack of writing down to his difficult schedule, but now she wondered. Turning her attention back to the letter, she began to read.

While he was here, we went out for a soda. I knew you wouldn't mind, since you are busy with your fancy college life and all the dances and events you get to go to.

I always liked Matthew, but of course, I didn't want to tell him as long as you two were dating. But since you have gone separate ways, I thought I should let you know that the two of us had a few dates that week and have started writing each other. I know you'll be happy for me since you have a different life now, but I wanted to be honest with you and let you know. Have fun at college!

Sincerely,
Mary

The letter fell into Evie's lap and she closed her eyes, a dizzy feeling coming over her. She tried to remember what she had said to Mary that would have given her the impression that she wasn't interested in Matthew but couldn't imagine what it was. Perhaps, in some small way, she had made more of the college boys' interest in her than was true, in an effort to appear worldlier than she really was.

"Damn," she muttered under her breath.

"Is everything all right?" a girl asked behind her.

She turned to see one of the third-floor girls reaching for a book on the tallest bookshelf. Evie couldn't bring herself to reply, so she simply nodded. Gathering the letters, she stuffed them roughly back into their envelopes and headed upstairs to her room.

Something had to be done, she thought. She couldn't just take something like this lying down. She had never skipped a class before, but suddenly, she couldn't imagine sitting through lecture after lecture when her world was falling apart. Matthew was hers. Matthew was safe and good and a perfect fallback if no one better came along. They had dated for three years, and she'd be damned if Mary Gardner was going to get him.

Had she made him feel like her affections were lukewarm? She would never knowingly be unkind toward any man who was potential husband material, especially not Matthew. She genuinely liked and respected him, even if he was a little conventional and perhaps even stodgy at times. But he was concentrating on his future. Serious boys could be like that.

Glancing at the clock, she saw it was only eight thirty. Unlike Evie, he had chosen a traditional schedule with early classes so he could spend the afternoons studying in the library. She knew his schedule well from his letters. He would have eaten no later than seven, packed his books into his knapsack, and arrived in his class by seven twenty to talk with some of his classmates before the professor arrived. They would have compared notes and quizzed each other on test days and scheduled formal study sessions.

Evie sat on her bed, thinking. Of course, they would straighten everything out. Matthew was a solid, caring person. He wouldn't let some flirtatious girl from home interfere with his lessons and his life plan. There was plenty of time to talk to him.

Although, she reasoned, if it were true and he had been writing someone behind her back, he owed her an apology. Nothing had been said between them that would dim the feelings they had talked about over Christmas break.

Suddenly, the room she shared with Merritt seemed stiflingly small. She stood and slipped on her plaid car coat and took her handbag from the desk. Peering down the corridor, she made certain that Tess and Caroline's door was shut before she went downstairs. She wasn't in the mood for questions.

Without any thought to her destination, she found herself walking to University Square, where she went inside a coffee shop and ordered a hot chocolate. She took the steaming mug to a seat by the window, watching the gray and cloudy day outside. Although she was usually stoic about most things, this year Evie was tired of winter. She was ready for sweaters and bare legs with sandals. She wanted to go to dances and be kissed in the moonlight as she had at the first dance of the year. In fact, she could hardly think of anything else.

"Is this seat taken?" a voice asked near her ear.

Evie looked up to see a handsome face smiling down at her and shook her head. As he sat down across from her, she pulled her coat about her shoulders nervously.

"Aren't you a Radcliffe student?" he asked.

He was a few years older than she was and draped himself in his chair casually, with an arm on the brick windowsill, studying her face.

"Yes," she replied, looking him over. He was sophisticated, she could tell that at a glance. His hair was properly Brylcreemed, and under his expensive overcoat, she could see he was wearing a nice gray suit with a tie.

"I work in the science department," he continued. "I've seen you around campus."

"It's Friday," she replied, narrowing her eyes. "Shouldn't you be at work, then?"

"Shouldn't you be in class?" he countered. Then he smiled. "Actually, I was picking up something this morning and decided to grab a coffee, and here you are."

"My classes start later," she mumbled, not wanting to tell him the truth—that she was ditching classes for the day. Possibly forever, if she couldn't get her life straightened out.

"Ah, kismet," he replied. "A good plan, if I say so myself. Wish I had thought of it when I was going to college."

She glanced down at his hand. He wasn't wearing a ring. That shouldn't make any difference, of course. He was older and clearly more experienced. She couldn't help blushing just speaking to him. Of course he noticed her look and lifted his hand and grinned.

"Feel like taking a walk?" he asked.

Evie looked up at him, a rumble of anxiety piercing through her. Naturally she would want to take a walk with someone so attractive, and yet he was entirely too old for a college girl. Older men weren't manageable like college boys. Making a snap decision, she gave a curt smile and shook her head, standing.

"I have things to do today," she said.

She walked to the door, leaving her cup of hot chocolate sitting on the table. Walking back to the campus, she turned and headed for the redbrick building where Carter Gray lived with his friends in a roomy apartment. She had never been there, but Caroline had pointed it out to her once. She imagined the luxury of living in one's own apartment when most of the other students were saddled with housemothers and constant adult supervision. Many times she had wondered if Caroline had been inside and, if so, what had gone on in the privacy of those four walls.

"What are you up to, Carter Gray?" Evie murmured to herself as she approached. Maybe she should find out.

She found herself walking up the steps to the apartment building, letting herself in the front door. On the right, mailboxes were lined up in two rows. She went over and looked for Carter Gray's name. There it was, Apartment 207. Under his name was Ken Blackburn's.

Without thinking, she found herself ascending the staircase, admiring the crown moldings and details. It had once been a fashionable residence and, in fact, still would be if some of the gilt details weren't slightly tarnished. All the same, it was a place she could never have afforded to live. When she made it to the top of the stairs, she went over and knocked lightly on the door.

She had no explanation ready, not even for herself. Inside, she was a mass of contradictions, wanting a stable, serious life with a boy like Matthew, buying a house and filling it with lots of children. But there was something else as well, something she had felt the night of the dance. She was away from home for the first time and wanted some adventure before she settled down. The sort of adventure Caroline must have from time to time, even though Evie judged her for it. Perhaps if she had an adventure, her emotions would settle down and she could get back to business with school and her life. When the door opened, an unfamiliar face looked quizzically at her.

"Carter's not here," he said, assuming she had every right to be there. "He and Ken have gone to Boston for the day. They said I could use their apartment to study. It's even quieter than the library."

"Who are you?" she asked, walking inside. Evie drew off her gloves and set them on top of her handbag on the table, turning back to him with a smile.

"I'm Richard Solomon. And you are?"

"Interested in a drink," she said.

He looked at her and then shrugged. "I'm sure Carter keeps the bar stocked. I would expect nothing less."

Evie waited as he found two glasses and opened one of the bottles. She had no idea what it was, but it really didn't matter. A minute later, he brought her one and stood next to her as he downed his quickly. She took a tentative sip, never having tasted anything but a bit of brandy in her coffee last Christmas to toast the fact that she was about to become a college girl. What her family would think if they could see her now.

She tapped the edge of the glass with her finger and gave a lopsided smile.

"I don't think you really want that," he said, looking at her closely.

Evie let him take it from her and then waited as he leaned in to kiss her. He tasted of the liquor, but it wasn't objectionable at all.

Two hours later, she left the building, pulling her coat closer around her, a skip in her step. This was what gave Caroline her confidence, she thought: to know one was desired by men. It was a heady feeling. When she returned to her dorm, she took a long shower and then polished her fingernails, avoiding conversation with Merritt, who seemed distracted anyway. When she was done, she went back downstairs. She had one more thing to do that evening: call Matthew and deal with the situation.

"Matthew Turner, please," she said after she had dialed the number.

She sat in the window seat of the lounge, which at that moment was empty, hoping that no one suddenly walked in. This was a private conversation if ever there was one. It took several minutes for Matthew to be located and to come to the telephone. Muted sounds sifted through the receiver of a busy dormitory much like her own but with deeper voices calling out to one another. She felt an unexpected thrill just hearing it. When he finally came to the telephone, he was out of breath.

"Hello?" he said.

"Matthew, it's Evie." She had never called him at college before. In fact, he had only called her twice since she'd been at Radcliffe, and then it was a special occasion agreed upon in their letters, not a surprise.

"Evie!" he said, shock evident in his voice. "Is everything all right there?"

"Everything's fine," she answered, a little relieved that he sounded so concerned. "I missed you. I haven't heard from you in a while."

"It's really busy here," he said. She could hear the bewilderment in his voice. "I'm sure you have the same situation there: classes, exams, so much to think about."

"I was sitting down to write you a letter," she said. "And I just suddenly wanted to hear your voice instead. I hope you don't mind."

"'Mind'?" he echoed. "Of course I don't mind. Is everything all right?"

"Everything is fine," she lied. "But you sounded out of breath when you answered the phone. Are *you* all right?"

"I ran down two flights of stairs," he admitted.

"Were you expecting another call?" She couldn't help feeling her hackles rise.

"My mother—you know she's been sick. She's been doing radiation treatments. I guess I'm a little jumpy right now."

"You should have told me," she said, her voice softening. "I love your mother. I hope everything will be all right."

"The doctor says the treatments are going well," he replied. "But I feel guilty not being there when she needs me."

"You haven't seen her since Christmas, right?" she asked.

There was a pause on the line. "Well, I did go back last month for a short visit. I think I forgot to tell you."

"Oh, that's right," she said in her cheeriest voice. "Mary Gardner mentioned she saw you in her last letter."

"Mary Gardner," he repeated, obviously trying to assess how much she knew.

"Yes, Mary Gardner. She wrote to tell me that the two of you were an item now."

"Now, wait a minute," Matthew protested. "We are most definitely not an item. She didn't have any business saying that to you. I did see her one evening at the burger joint. You know how it is. Everyone goes there on a Saturday night."

"I think she said that just to make me feel bad," Evie replied. "She knows how I feel about you. Some girls will do anything to wreck someone else's relationship."

"I'm really sorry, Evie," he said. "She must have gotten the wrong idea. Everyone knows you're the only girl I've ever dated. I'm sorry, I should have said something to you. You didn't deserve to be treated like that."

Evie felt a moment of alarm. She didn't want to push him away. She had to think fast.

"I'm not angry, Matthew," she murmured. "It's just that I thought we had an understanding, you know? And when you love someone, you generally think they love you too."

Love had never been mentioned between them before, however much they had spoken in general terms about their future. Evie wasn't even certain it was true. But what was true was that she didn't want to lose him, no matter the cost.

"Oh, Evie," he breathed into the phone. "You know how much I care about you."

Relief coursed through her. "Of course, if you want someone else..."

"No," he answered firmly. "I could never want anyone else. Can you forgive me?"

Evie thought about everything that had happened that day and sighed, pretending to weigh the matter carefully, as if she wouldn't take him back with open arms. It just needed to come from him.

"I'll always forgive you, if you really want me," she said in a low voice. "You know how much you mean to me."

"Thank God," he said. "I wouldn't want to spoil what we have between us."

"When can I see you?" she asked.

"This weekend," he answered. "I'll skip Friday classes so that we can spend some time together."

When they hung up, Evie gave a huge sigh of relief. She was lucky she had gotten that letter before things had gone too far between them. If Matthew wasn't sure of her feelings before, he certainly was now. And as far as she was concerned, Mary Gardner could go hang herself.

20

The next afternoon, Caroline found herself once again in the library, the one place she was certain where no one would look for her. On the upper floor, which appeared to be deserted, she found a small room with glass doors. She tried the handle, which wasn't locked. Slipping inside, she took a deep breath before looking around. Leather armchairs sat in front of a fireplace that likely hadn't been lit in years. A worn kilim rug was thrown on the floor, and there were heavy standing lamps on each side of the room. She went over and switched on the one that was farthest from the door and then sank into one of the chairs to think.

Her life was a shambles in every way. And now she had the annoying problem of Tess and her incessant curiosity. After she had finally returned to the room, Caroline hadn't an ounce of energy with which to confront her. There was nothing she could do about it now anyway. While she hated having her privacy violated, it was her own fault. She was the one who had taken them all to Newport and introduced them to both her family and her extravagant lifestyle. She had never thought about how it might affect them. Perhaps she had provoked Tess's jealousy, however unintentionally.

Caroline was used to being the subject of envy, of course; the prettiest girl always was. No one ever realized how difficult it was to be the center of attention all the time. She longed for anonymity, for a release from the pressure of always having to be the most charming person in any room. It was exhausting. And no one really liked the pretty girl either. Not women, anyway. Men, however, liked one altogether too much, but never the way she hoped. It made it all too easy to be the breezy blond who wasn't expected to think.

She couldn't stumble without it being discussed by everyone in sight. She couldn't slip in and out of a room without drawing attention. She certainly couldn't eavesdrop on simple conversations and find a way to join in. It was true: most of the time, she relished the power that her looks gave her. She could command any room she was in, no matter who was in it, regardless of their age. But whenever she felt vulnerable, it was unsettling to deal with constant attention. It was like being trapped under a microscope every day of her life.

Caroline lifted her handbag and drew out the photograph, studying it once again. She was smiling into the camera, but was she really happy? For that matter, she thought, had she ever been happy? She couldn't really be sure. But what was happiness, when it came to that? Life, as she knew it, consisted of getting through a series of boring events and responsibilities, feeling aimless and disconnected from everyone around her. She wasn't built for happiness, she supposed. Women generally weren't.

She had been given grand experiences in life, and yet they were forgotten so quickly. Perhaps that was because that day in Italy had been an anomaly. Elizabeth Hanson wasn't close to anyone, especially not her child. Normally, it didn't trouble Caroline, but she thought of Merritt and the close bond she'd had with her mother. A rare feeling of envy stabbed her as she imagined having a mother to go to when things went wrong.

Caroline started in her chair as the door suddenly opened and a young woman near her own age peered inside.

"I thought I saw a light on in here," she said. "I'm sorry if I disturbed you."

The girl looked at her directly, as if wondering why anyone would be sitting in a distant, empty room with no books in her hands or a composition notebook full of notes to study. Caroline looked at her, unable to think of anything to say.

"We're closing in twenty minutes," the young woman said.

When she got no reply, she turned and closed the door.

Caroline sighed, tapping the photo in her hand. She thought of tearing it to bits just so that Tess couldn't steal it again, but instead, she got up and went to the fireplace, where a handful of dusty books rested on the mantel. She drew one down and opened it carefully, placing the photo inside. Then she closed it and went to stand by the window.

After turning the latch, she opened it, letting the cool March air fill the stuffy room. Outside, buds had begun to form on the branches of the trees, reminding them that in spite of the temperatures, spring was not far off. But by then, it would be too late. Everyone would know she was pregnant. What should she do in the meantime? Ask Mrs. Schwartz for a new roommate? Or pretend for a while longer that nothing was wrong, to buy herself time to think?

A wave of nausea came over her. Throughout her life, she had rarely been sick, so the last few weeks had been particularly difficult. She waited until the feeling passed and then stepped back from the window, assessing its size. If she pulled over a chair, she could climb onto the ledge and jump. Glancing down, she wondered how far one had to fall before it killed you. Because nothing, she thought, would be worse than jumping from a window and living through the experience.

Lingering for a moment, she made a decision. She would go to Boston. She left the room, forgetting to turn off the light, and flew down the stairs to the lobby floor. There, she went to the shelf of phone directories and flipped through the pages until she found what she wanted, copying the name and number onto a scrap of paper from her handbag: *Harris Forsythe, MD, Boston.* There were doctors closer to Radcliffe, but she wanted to get as far away from the college as possible.

Making her way to the square, she found a phone booth and shut the door firmly behind her before she dialed the number with a shaky hand.

"Dr. Forsythe's office," came a woman's voice on the other end of the line.

"I'd like to make an appointment," Caroline murmured.

"Name, please."

"Hillary Brown," she replied. "Mrs. Hillary Brown."

"Thank you, Mrs. Brown," the receptionist answered. "Can you tell me the reason for your visit?"

Caroline hesitated. "I think… I think I'm pregnant."

"Is this your first pregnancy?"

"Yes."

She took a deep breath, waiting for the next question, or perhaps for the truth to be guessed by a complete stranger. Instead, the woman answered with a businesslike tone.

"I have an opening on April tenth at one o'clock."

"Couldn't I get in any sooner?" Caroline asked, a feeling of panic coming over her. "I don't want to say anything to my husband until I know for certain."

"Let me check," came the reply. There was a brief pause. "Let's see. We have a cancelation for next week. Does Tuesday at nine o'clock work for you?"

"Tuesday at nine is fine," Caroline replied.

When she hung up, another wave of dizziness came over her.

After regaining her equilibrium, she left the telephone booth and headed back to the dormitory. Gulping in large breaths of air, she tried to fix a normal expression on her face. She couldn't let anyone see her distress, not even Merritt. There were days when she wanted to confide in her, knowing Merritt would never judge her, but even just saying the words out loud was impossible.

If only she could turn back the clock, she would have stayed home on the night of the dance. *How often we do things we have no desire to do, simply for appearance's sake,* she thought. That night, that single night, was ruining her life.

On the day of the appointment, Caroline borrowed a chunky knit sweater she had given to Tess, pulling it on over her clothes. The dress was snugger than when she had worn it last, and she eyed herself in the mirror, wondering if anyone would notice. Slipping a coat over her shoulders, she crept down the stairs, and when she was certain no one was about, she opened the door and went outside.

In Harvard Square, she hailed a taxi and settled back into the seat, lost in thought as they drove through the city. Unexpectedly, Ken's face kept coming into her mind. Men were animals, she thought. They had everything so easy. Ken had forced himself on her and then left her lying in the road in the middle of the night, beaten and bruised, without any repercussions whatsoever. He knew she couldn't say anything to anyone without having the situation turned back on herself. People always blamed the woman. She had seen it before, and she was well aware that her looks as well as her beautiful clothes would mark her as someone who was easy in the eyes of most people. For the first time, she wondered if Evie was right: perhaps there was safety in marriage. People could stop thinking of her as a woman on the make.

When the taxi stopped in front of the medical building, she drew a few bills from her pocketbook to pay the driver and opened the door. She found herself shaking. It was terrifying to face this alone. She suddenly wished she had asked Merritt to come with her. With an unsteady hand, she opened the door of the building and went inside.

Two other women, both noticeably pregnant, were sitting in the waiting room. The older one was knitting, and the other, much closer to her own age, was reading a book for expectant mothers. Caroline took a deep breath and went up to the receptionist. She slipped one hand inside her coat and held her stomach, which was suddenly starting to lurch. She wondered if she would be sick right there on the rug.

"I'm here for my appointment," she said, clutching her pocketbook to her chest. She wondered if the woman noticed her distress.

"Mrs. Brown?" the clerk inquired, looking up.

Caroline nodded, wondering if her lie had already been discovered.

"First name, please?"

"Hillary." It was her grandmother's name, and she was relieved that she had thought of it should it be asked of her.

"Take this clipboard and fill out the information," the woman said. "Give it to the nurse when she calls for you."

Caroline nodded and took the clipboard, choosing a seat away from the other women. Taking out a pen, she almost wrote her own name on the top line and remembered just in time to write her grandmother's instead. There wasn't much to fill out on the form, and she looked at the blank columns, wondering whether to check boxes or not. She decided to stick with the truth, at least as far as her health went. When she was finished, she placed it on the chair next to her, trying to keep from looking at the other women. The only sounds were the clicking of knitting needles and the ticking of the clock on the wall. It was enough to drive one mad.

At last, a nurse came up to her and smiled. "Mrs. Brown? We're ready for you now."

She was shown into a room, instinctively touching the collar of her dress in fear. Everything was nerve-racking: Answering questions from the nurse about her last period and her drinking habits. Putting on a white cotton gown with flimsy ties in the back. Worst of all, the doctor came in and explained the examination. She was so horrified, she could hardly take it in.

"Lie back, please," he said. "Put your feet in the stirrups."

Caroline didn't move. She wasn't certain she could. Damn Ken Blackburn. What a disaster he had made of her life.

"Nurse Reilly," the doctor said. "Perhaps you could hold Mrs. Brown's hand."

Caroline was humiliated, but she allowed the woman to take her hand and held it tightly as she suffered the indignity of the examination. She was numb by the time she was allowed to go into the changing room to put on her clothing, nearly as traumatized by the exam as she had been by the attack. If this was what mothers went through, she thought, she wasn't going to do it. She could be an old maid, as far as she was concerned. Afterward, she buttoned her dress with shaky fingers and slipped on the sweater, then sat in the small room, trying to pull herself together. She could hardly face going in to speak to the doctor, but the worst had already happened. It was time to find out if she was right. She stood, straightened her shoulders, and opened the door.

"Right this way, Mrs. Brown," the nurse said, showing her into the doctor's office.

It was a handsome room with a bookshelf behind the large mahogany desk. If she hadn't been so nervous, she would have tried to look through the titles, though they were certain to be tedious medical journals and textbooks.

Dr. Forsythe came in through a side door and sat down at his desk. "Well, I have some news for you," he said, settling back into his chair. "You're pregnant."

Caroline could almost feel the color draining from her face. "Are you sure?" she asked.

"Quite sure, Mrs. Brown," he replied.

When she didn't answer, he leaned back in his seat and tented his fingers, searching her face. "You're very young," he said. He lifted her file from his desk, looked at her date of birth, and closed it again. "Eighteen, I see. How long have you been married?"

Her cheeks grew warm. That was a question she hadn't been prepared for. "Not long."

"Young lady," he said gently. "I don't want to distress you, but you don't seem pleased with this development."

"It was…unexpected, I'm afraid."

He narrowed his eyes. "Does the father want to have a child at the present time? I can assure you that most men aren't eager for the first child, and yet they are completely captivated by it once it makes an appearance. You needn't worry on that account."

Caroline moved uncomfortably in her chair.

He leaned forward. "Does the father even know?"

She leapt to her feet and began walking toward the door.

As she did, Dr. Forsythe stood as well. "There are ways that I can help young women in a situation such as yours, if you want to discuss it," he said. "Please, come back and sit down for a moment."

"I can't," she murmured.

She wasn't entirely certain of his meaning. He might have been ready to suggest the name of a home for unwed mothers or even something more sinister, but she wasn't able to discuss it for another minute. She flung open the door and ran through the waiting room, certain of only one thing: she would never come back.

Caroline raced through the streets, barely aware of her surroundings. Several blocks from the doctor's office, she found a café and went inside, where she ordered a cup of coffee. As the cup was placed in front of her, she stared at the wall and thought. Something had to be done. Someone had to be told. Didn't they? Or should she just ignore things for as long as possible? Should she talk to Miss Campbell? Her mother was out of the question. Caroline didn't even want to think about what would happen if she told her mother the truth. She wasn't as afraid of her mother's reaction as much as her father's, because Elizabeth Hanson would tell him immediately, unable to deal with the situation herself. She could talk to Merritt, of course, but all that would do was bring stress and anxiety into her friend's life, and there was nothing she could do about it anyway. There was nothing any of them could do.

She sat there for two hours, the coffee long cold. Eventually, she stood and called for a cab and had him deposit her a block from the dorm.

"There you are," Evie said when she finally opened the door.

Caroline looked up in surprise. She hadn't expected any of them to be waiting for her, but Merritt and Tess were right behind Evie, concerned looks on their faces.

"I had a dentist's appointment," she murmured. "I had a toothache."

Lying got easier the more that one did it, she discovered. Looking up, she saw that Tess had raised an eyebrow, her eyes on the sweater that Caroline had given her in Newport. She probably wondered if Caroline was taking her things back since their relationship had taken a terrible turn.

"What are they going to do about it?" Tess asked.

"About what?"

"Your toothache."

"I'll schedule a filling soon," she answered, heading for the stairs. If she felt like skipping classes another day, at least that would be an alibi. And alibis were all she had at the moment.

21

The bookshop had been dusted and swept for book club, and Alice was more than ready to begin. Her trip to Duncan Hall at Radcliffe a few weeks earlier had been a disappointment. She had seen Tess and Evie, to whom she presented the wrapped copies of *Gift from the Sea*. Both of them had seemed to regard her as completely out of place in their dormitory environment. She had waved at Merritt, who breezed through with a friend and had seemed pleased to see her, but she hadn't gotten so much as a glimpse of Caroline. Her time at the University of Chicago didn't seem that long ago, and yet the twenty-year age difference between herself and the book club girls was glaring from their point of view.

Shrugging, she'd pressed two books into Evie's hands.

"Could you give one to Caroline for me?" she had asked.

"Sure," Evie had said, nodding. "I'll see her later today after classes."

"Thank you," Alice had replied. She clutched her bag to her chest. "I'll see you on the thirty-first."

Evie nodded and Alice had turned to leave, wondering at her own motives, if she should have let the book club wind down on its own due to lack of interest or if she was right to deliver the books to these young women, who obviously had very busy lives and far less interest in reading than she had. She hadn't imagined herself having much of an influence on them, but now, she realized her impact was probably even less than she had thought. These girls were strangers, really—people who weren't interested in investing emotion into books the way she was.

Caroline was the first to arrive a few minutes before seven, and she was on her own.

"Hello, Miss Campbell," she said when she opened the door.

"Caroline!" Alice greeted.

She pushed back her desk chair, where she had been working on an order, and watched as Caroline hung up her coat. March was supposed to come in like a lion and go out like a lamb, but so far, there had been no break in the weather. It was still cold and slushy from last week's snow.

"I wasn't sure I'd see you tonight," Alice admitted as Caroline stepped out of her rubber boots.

"Why not?" Caroline inquired.

The question left her tongue-tied. She stared at the young woman's face, which was paler than usual, but her beauty was unchanged.

"I didn't see you when I dropped off the books," Alice ventured. "I was a little worried about you."

She didn't mention the letter she'd sent, wondering suddenly if Caroline had blocked out the memory of what had happened the night of the December dance or if she was simply trying to. Inwardly, Alice chastised herself. It wasn't her business, and no matter how much she was concerned for Caroline, it certainly wasn't her place to dredge up anything painful at this point.

"You know how college is," Caroline replied, her face revealing nothing. "You're always so busy with classes."

"Of course," Alice said, nodding. "May I get you something to drink?"

"Do you have coffee?"

Alice smiled. "There's always coffee around here. I'll get you a cup."

The other girls breezed in a few minutes later, Evie and Merritt together and Tess shortly afterward. They settled in quickly, without much conversation between them.

"I liked the book," Merritt said, holding up her copy. "I even made notes in the margins."

"Anne Morrow Lindbergh is an interesting figure, isn't she?" Alice asked, settling into her chair. "If you weren't already aware, her husband is the well-known aviator Charles Lindbergh."

"The first man to fly solo across the Atlantic Ocean," Tess added.

Alice nodded. "That's right. And when I was about your age,

perhaps a little younger, he and his wife were prominently in the news when their young son was kidnapped."

"I've heard of that," Merritt said. "It was a famous case."

"Yes," Alice replied. "It dominated the news for years."

"What happened?" asked Evie.

Alice leaned forward. "Someone climbed a ladder to the upper floor of their home one evening and left a ransom note on the windowsill. The child's body was found a couple of weeks later. Perhaps it was because I was at an impressionable age at the time, but it was difficult for me to separate the young mother that Anne was, despondent over the loss of her child, with the mature woman who bares her soul on the nature of relationships in this book."

"May I read the first quote this time, Miss Campbell?" Evie asked. "There was a passage that really impressed me."

"Why yes, of course," Alice answered, delighted at her interest.

Evie turned the pages in her copy until she found the passage. "Here it is. 'It takes as much courage to have tried and failed as it does to have tried and succeeded.' I like that. I feel like it means our efforts aren't wasted."

"That's a lovely passage, and an excellent thought, Evie," Alice said. "If we aren't trying in our lives, we aren't learning and growing. In order to be a fulfilled woman in the world today, we'll have to attempt many things before we succeed. But the effort is always worth it."

"How do you think she was able to recover from such a tragedy?"

Merritt asked. "I can't imagine what she went through. I think if you lose a child, nothing could help you overcome the loss."

"Probably some women can't overcome it," Tess said matter-of-factly. "It probably depends on their temperament and life situation."

"I agree with you," Alice said. "Everyone handles problems in their own way. I remember a phrase I heard a long time ago, 'kicking against the goads.' Some of us fight the hard things that come into our lives to our detriment, while others are able to move on and heal and go on to help others."

Evie shrugged. "Anne has an independent nature from what I could see. Maybe she wasn't as bonded to her husband as she might have been. She talked of whether or not to let a marriage go."

"Seeing things clearly doesn't mean you don't care," Merritt argued. She looked at Alice. "She stayed married to her husband, didn't she?"

"Yes," Alice answered. "And I certainly think she was able to move on due to maturity and understanding and dealing with her grief rather than because she didn't care. It was an absolutely devastating event in her life. They even left the country for a few years to get out of the headlines and to try to put their lives back together again."

"But didn't they become involved in subversive politics?" Tess asked. "Weren't they friendly with the Nazis or something?"

"You do your homework, Tess," Alice said, nodding. "You're

right. During their stay in Europe after their son was killed, they lived for a while in England and later moved to an island off the French coast. For whatever reason, they began to advocate for isolationism. That didn't sit well with most Americans."

"What's isolationism?" Evie asked.

"It means they don't think America or any other country should be involved in the politics—or particularly, the wars—of other countries," Alice said. "And Americans knew that if they didn't get involved in the war, Hitler and the Nazis would continue their violent quest to take over the world." Alice looked around the group. "Charles also holds to a view called Nordicism, which maintains that the lighter-skinned Norwegians are superior to other races, even other Caucasian ethnicities. He's written papers on the subject. Anne's written a booklet that included a defense of Hitler. So combining those two stances, isolationism and Nordicism, was problematic and made them deeply unpopular for a while in the United States."

"So if they are Nazi sympathizers, why are we reading her book?" Evie asked.

"Well, for one thing, this book is not in the least political," Alice replied. "It's simply a look at a woman's experiences through the lens of marriage and motherhood, something most women experience in their lifetime. Perhaps the most important question is whether or not women have a right to a life and opinions of their own."

"She certainly has opinions," Tess said archly.

"Putting aside her political beliefs, what rights do women really have?" Alice asked. "What autonomy should they claim for their own lives?"

"I agree that women need time alone to think and to evaluate their lives," Caroline replied, finally weighing in on the conversation. "Anne set the example."

"She walked out on her family to do it," Tess said.

"Oh, you know they had maids to run everything," Evie remarked. She glanced at Caroline. "It must be nice to be rich."

Merritt sighed. "She was lucky to have a cottage at the beach, where she could go and do her in-depth contemplation."

"I don't think it matters so much where a woman goes to be alone and get her thoughts together," Alice ventured. "I just think it's important that they do."

None of them had a reply to her statement. Or if they did, none shared it.

"I have some news," Tess announced suddenly, looking around the group. "I found out today that I'm going to be the newest cub reporter for the *Radcliffe Promoter*. I've had a couple of articles published, but this is an actual position. My first column will be called 'Chaste, Hardworking Cliffies Get the Job Done.'"

Caroline made a derisive noise. Merritt simply stared at her. Tess shifted uncomfortably in her seat.

"That's great," Evie said, jumping in to smooth things over.

"Maybe you can work your way up to writing for the *Harvard Crimson.*"

Tess colored a little. "I know it's a smaller publication, but—"

"It's the front and back of a mimeographed sheet," Caroline inserted, unexpectedly critical. "They have paragraphs about how to groom yourself to look like a proper student and job listings for those about to drop out. Oh, and a few weeks ago, there was a quote about how to be a good secretary. I think it went like this: 'Dress like a woman, think like a man, and work like a dog.' Really, Tess, I wouldn't brag about it."

"I'm not bragging," she insisted.

"We all know how much Tess wants to be a writer," Alice said, once again feeling the need to intervene. "This is the first step along that path. Everyone has to start somewhere. It's really nice when you get to do something you really want to do."

"Thank you," Tess murmured.

"What about you, Merritt?" Alice asked. "Is anything new happening with you?"

The girl sighed and then drew an envelope from her pocketbook. She lifted it up for them to see. "I got a letter from my father."

No one spoke, waiting for her to continue.

"He married his girlfriend, Penelope, whom I hardly know." She stopped and looked at Alice. "And that's not all. He's signed onto a two-year research expedition to a country called the Central African Republic to study the centaurus beetle in its natural habitat. I have no idea what to make of all of this. It's just so…extreme. And there's a finality to it. I won't see him before he leaves, and he won't be back in the country for two years at least, maybe longer if the grant is extended."

"What about you?" Alice asked, her brow creasing. "Where are you supposed to go when you're not here in Cambridge?"

Merritt shrugged. "He suggested that I might want to stay with his sister in Nevada. She runs a bar in Reno. You might say that it's the one place I'd rather go to less than the Central African Republic."

"But at least it's family," protested Evie. "That must count for something."

"I think if you met her, you'd agree she's not what you consider family."

"You could just stay here," Caroline said firmly. "You could enroll in summer school. Then you could graduate early. Or maybe you could double major in something. What do you like besides art?"

Merritt shrugged. "Thank you for trying to help, but I just need time to think about things, that's all. I mean, this wasn't completely unexpected. Well, Africa was; I never thought he'd go back. But he and Penelope looked serious when I was home for Christmas. I'll just have to look at my options."

"Take your time and think it through," Alice cautioned. "Think about what you really want with your life."

"It must be nice to be older and have your life figured out already, Miss Campbell," Tess said.

Alice resisted the desire to react. "Does anyone really have their life figured out?" she countered. "You can make plans all you want and then find yourself facing unexpected circumstances in spite of everything."

Evie cocked her head and looked at them. "That's so true. Right now, when no one expects it, someone is going to die or let them down in a major way. Some wife is going to come home to lipstick on her husband's collar or find out that he embezzled money from the bank. Life is completely unpredictable."

"Perhaps that's true," Alice said. "But if you know what you want and go after it, some of the bad things that happen can be mere distractions."

"Maybe in your world," Tess said, a touch of bitterness in her voice.

"What shall we read for next month?" Alice asked, glancing at the others.

They looked at her blankly.

"I thought you chose the books!" Evie said.

"Well, I've had more than my fair share of turns," Alice answered. "This time, why don't you all have a look around and make a suggestion or two?"

They all murmured their assent and stood, walking over to various shelves. Alice wondered about their future. All four of them were probably only delaying the marriage process by a few months, a couple of years at most, and then, if they weren't careful, many avenues of thought would close to them. How likely would they be as young women to read books that challenged or interested them when there was a household to run and pregnancies to endure? They'd be reading Dr. Spock instead of Simone de Beauvoir or Margaret Sanger. They weren't in a position to consider whether or not birth control should be legal or even a viable choice when their entire futures were planned to provide a family and a home for the man who married them. They probably didn't even know how outraged they should be to find themselves in that position.

Hadn't Alice herself held traditional views before she met Jack? She had expected to have a partner in marriage, not another substitute for a parent, someone who felt he had to control her every move. She shuddered, refusing to let the past dominate her life. It was time to think about the future. And that future began this very minute, in a bookshop in Cambridge, Massachusetts.

"Here's one," Merritt said, walking over to her. "Let's read this."

It was a copy of *Emma* by Jane Austen. Alice nodded and smiled. However, if these girls thought that there was no controversy in a book simply because it was a hundred and forty years old, they were sadly mistaken.

22

APRIL 1956

**"You must be the best judge of your own
happiness."**

-JANE AUSTEN, *EMMA*

The days were blurring one into another. Caroline fretted, uncertain
of what to do. Some days she toyed with the idea of finding a place
to stay for her confinement and telling her parents she was going
to Europe with a friend for the summer, but even then, her mother
would expect her to come home and pack a suitable wardrobe for
an overseas trip. By May, however, she wouldn't be able to disguise
the pregnancy any longer. Her breasts were growing, and there was
already a firm roundness to her belly. Even the sweaters she had taken
to wearing wouldn't cover it up much longer. She thought of running
away, but she had no idea where to go. She certainly wouldn't go to

a home for unwed mothers and wait out the next few months with other unfortunate girls. That was as demeaning and humiliating an experience as she could imagine. She couldn't confide in anyone, least of all the nurse at the college infirmary, whom she had seen once and who had behaved like a hardened military officer. Her friends were too young to understand; her parents too unforgiving. Caroline realized for the first time in her life that there wasn't a single person she could count on in times of distress, and it was terrifying.

Sometimes, she was furious with Ken. Other days, she was furious with herself. She'd been too arrogant and self-assured, never for a moment believing something like this could possibly happen to her. But after a few months, fear took hold, edging out anger and replacing it with emotional paralysis.

Her grades were suffering as well. The dean had called her into his office the day before, gingerly asking questions about her happiness at Radcliffe, clearly aware of her parents and their position as donors.

"I'm fine," she'd lied. Of course, she couldn't possibly tell him what had happened. "Just a little run-down from having the flu recently."

"Oh, I see," he had answered, relieved that there wasn't a serious problem. Like everyone else, he probably believed she was marking time at Radcliffe for a year before getting married. "You can check with the infirmary if it doesn't clear up, but it sounds like you have things under control. Let me know if I can do anything."

Caroline had resisted the impulse to laugh. People were

ridiculously deferential to the wealthy. She'd seen it her entire life. Grown men sputtered in apology for minor infractions toward her father, which had the effect of assuring her of her own place in the social paradigm. The Hansons were accustomed to respect, if sometimes grudging, and it had shaped her entire world view.

"I will, thank you," she had replied, taking her leave.

Back at Duncan Hall, she took a book downstairs to the salon to avoid sitting in her room all evening with Tess. She couldn't concentrate on a single word, but she could hold it in front of her to ward off conversations. A few minutes later, Merritt came downstairs and walked over to join her.

"Oh, there you are!" she said. "Can I talk to you if you're not too busy?"

"Of course," Caroline answered.

Merritt was the only person who didn't irritate her these days. Besides, she thought, she could use the distraction.

Merritt went over to sit across from her on the yellow chintz settee. She had an unusually solemn look on her face and pushed her hair back behind her ears, something she only did when she was nervous.

"What is it?" Caroline asked, feeling a twinge of concern. "Are you all right?"

"I want your advice," Merritt replied.

Caroline placed the book on the table in front of her. "I'm not sure how valuable my advice is, but I'm happy to listen."

Merritt clasped her hands together. "I'm thinking of leaving Radcliffe."

"Leaving Radcliffe?" Caroline repeated, surprised. "Why would you do that? You're a wonderful student, and you're doing well in all of your classes. There's nothing wrong, is there?"

"Not really," Merritt said, shrugging. "It's just that sometimes I wonder if I should do something more practical than art. It's not going to be a way to make much of a living."

"Evie would say that's what husbands are for."

"I want to be able to take care of myself," Merritt insisted. "I was thinking I should get a job. My father even suggested secretarial school."

"I can't see you in a typing pool with a hundred other girls," Caroline said, frowning. "That's not who you are. That's not the girl who got into Radcliffe."

"At least a typing job would pay for half a tiny apartment in San Francisco."

"But what about your art?" Caroline protested. "Your drawings are beautiful. I'm a little jealous, you know. At least you're good at something."

"The truth is," Merritt said, lowering her voice, "I'm not like some of the others. I don't want to get married to the first person who asks me and let a husband humor me by allowing me to paint and draw for an hour every weekend in the garage. I'm not ready to turn my life over to a family and lose all hope of trying to make it. But on the other hand, I can't just paint and paint and never sell anything and waste my life wishing I could make it."

"Who says you couldn't make it?" Caroline asked. "You're really good at what you do. I can't imagine quitting if you think you'll regret it later. You know, you could find a job in the art world while you work at your craft. Something like teaching, or working in a museum or in a gallery. Have you thought about that?"

"That's possible, I suppose."

"You know what you want," Caroline replied. "And I think if you know what you want and don't go after it, you'll never forgive yourself. I wish I knew what I wanted. You're lucky that you do."

Merritt nodded. "My mother gave up painting to get married, and I always thought she was sorry she had. In some ways I feel guilty because she gave it up for me."

"Children are a huge responsibility," Caroline said, the import of her words striking her so suddenly, she drew in her breath.

"What is it?" Merritt asked, her eyes narrowing.

"Nothing," she answered, taking her book from the table. "I just realized how late it is. I have to get to work on a paper."

Merritt stood. "Thanks for talking with me. I'll think about what you said."

"I didn't mean you had to go," Caroline replied.

"That's all right, really. I have work to do too. Thanks for talking to me."

Caroline sighed as she watched Merritt leave. She almost

followed her. Perhaps she should confide in her and then Merritt would understand why she was so touchy. Instead, she walked to the window and looked out at the burgeoning blossoms on the trees. Nothing had stopped spring from arriving in full force, and nothing would stop this pregnancy either. As much as she wanted to tell Merritt what had happened, it wasn't fair to thrust a burden of this magnitude on someone who had their own problems. She held the book tightly, aware of just how much she needed someone to talk to. Miss Campbell came to mind. She'd trusted her once, and although she would rather not depend on anyone at the moment, it seemed she had no choice but to trust her once again. She slipped into the corridor and went to the telephone table, dialing the number of the bookshop.

"The Cambridge Bookshop," Alice answered.

"Miss Campbell, this is Caroline Hanson. I wondered if I could come by and talk to you."

"Of course," she replied. "How about this evening?"

Caroline hesitated. "Would tomorrow afternoon be all right?"

"That would be fine. I'll see you then."

It was raining the following day. Caroline was thankful for the chance to wear a raincoat. In fact, she wished it would rain every single day until she could leave the campus. She pulled it on and left the dorm. Two blocks away, she hailed a cab and leaned back

against the seat as it sloshed through the streets until it pulled to a stop at the curb outside the bookshop.

Caroline paid the driver and stepped through the door. Alice shut it behind her.

"I'm so glad you called," Alice said, turning the sign to read Closed. "You've been on my mind."

The bookshop—with its narrow, uneven shelves and the large desk—was a comforting sight. Caroline shook off her raincoat but made no effort to remove it. Miss Campbell gestured upstairs.

"Why don't we go up and have some tea?"

Caroline followed her up the stairs and quickly collapsed into an armchair tucked into the corner. For a few minutes, Miss Campbell busied herself with her task, cups and saucers clinking together rhythmically.

It was a pleasant sound, probably the first that hadn't jangled her nerves in weeks. Caroline closed her eyes, nearly lulled to sleep. She was tired. In fact, she had been tired since this whole nightmare began. She opened them again when she heard Miss Campbell put a teacup on a table next to her and watched as she sat down across from her on the chaise.

Caroline lifted the cup and looked at Alice, taking a deep breath. "I'm afraid I'm in trouble, Miss Campbell."

From the look on her face, it was clear that she had suspected as much already. In fact, Caroline wondered why no one else had guessed. She had all the symptoms.

"What are you going to do?" Alice asked gently.

"That's the problem," Caroline answered. "I have no idea."

"So, I suppose you would be about four months along," she said. "Have you seen a doctor yet?"

Caroline nodded. "A few weeks ago."

"What did he say?"

"I…I lied about my name, but he wasn't fooled," Caroline said. "He asked me if I wanted to talk about it, but I just couldn't. I was afraid he of what he was going to say."

"Did you think he would talk to you about an abortion?"

"Maybe."

Miss Campbell waited as Caroline took a sip of tea to calm her nerves. Alice lifted her own cup, giving her all the time she needed to compose herself, for which Caroline was grateful.

"Right now, I don't know which is worse: that or giving it up for adoption," Caroline continued. "This is all just too awful. I don't know what to do."

"You are hardly the first person to find yourself in this situation," Miss Campbell said. "Many innocent girls have suffered the same fate."

Caroline looked up. "If I was ever innocent, that's over now."

"You're too hard on yourself, you know," Miss Campbell said, setting her cup on the old trunk. "You've been taught that you need to be perfect all the time. The truth is, no one is perfect, and no one can please everyone around them. This is the time you have to think of yourself."

"What do you mean?"

"I mean you have to think hard about what you want right now."

"I want to not be pregnant," Caroline said. "And after this experience, I can't see myself ever wanting to be pregnant again."

"All right," Miss Campbell replied, settling back in her seat. "Let's talk about your options. First, you could go home and tell your parents you're pregnant and get their opinion. I assume you haven't told them yet."

"No, I haven't," Caroline answered, "and I don't intend to. I can't go home, Miss Campbell. My father would hit the roof, and my mother would take to her bed for the next six months. Honestly, neither of them would understand."

"All right, we can cross that off the list for now. The next option is that you can stay with a friend for your confinement or perhaps find a home for unwed mothers. Would you want to keep the baby? Have you thought that far ahead?"

Caroline shook her head miserably. "I've been shutting it out the best I could."

Miss Campbell smiled. "That tactic will only work for so long, I'm afraid."

"No," Caroline said, shaking her head suddenly. "The answer is no, I don't want to keep it. He raped me and then dumped me on the side of the road. I won't go to him and I won't go to my parents. But most of all, I won't keep this child."

Miss Campbell turned to look out the window.

"Let's look at this from a different perspective," she said. "If you weren't pregnant, what would you want your life to be like right now? Or even six months from now?"

"I wish I were like Merritt. She has her art." Caroline gripped the cup tightly in her hands. "But even she has problems. She knows she wants to pursue it, but she's afraid she'll make the wrong move."

"What would your advice be to her?"

"I've told her she should stick with it," Caroline said. "I don't think you could regret following your heart and doing something that you love. At least you'd know you'd tried. The problem for me is that I've never wanted anything like that before."

"Perhaps that's because you've been living with your parents' expectations rather than your own."

"All I had to do was be pretty, as if that would solve life's problems. Someone would marry me and I would have his children and then pass them off to a nanny to raise. I've been dreading it since I was fifteen. That's not the life I want, but I have no idea what I really want to do."

"I think you should spend some time figuring it out," Miss Campbell answered. "You know what you don't want, but it sounds as if you were resigned to doing it anyway."

Caroline raised a brow. "I never thought of it that way before."

"A couple of years ago, I was facing a dilemma of my own," Miss Campbell said. "The only way I could get through it was to imagine what I wanted my life to be and try to get there one step at a time."

"The bookshop?" Caroline asked. "Was this your dream?"

Miss Campbell smiled. "It was. I'd loved books all my life, but my parents expected me to settle down with someone who made a good living so that I would be one less mouth to feed. When you have that sort of pressure on you, I'm afraid you don't always make the best decisions."

"But you went to college!" Caroline exclaimed.

"Yes, I won a scholarship to the University of Chicago, which delayed the inevitable. I studied English literature, but the truth was, when I finished, I lacked confidence in myself. My parents were still pushing me to hurry up and marry, and it was the lesser of two evils. Going out into the world isn't always the easiest thing you can do. There's a lot of room for failure."

"How did you end up here?" Caroline asked.

"I married the first suitable man that came along and tucked my diploma in the back of a closet. To say we were mismatched would be a gross understatement. I had taken a job in a shop so that I could work with books, and he insisted that I quit and get pregnant. He felt shortchanged and put upon having a working wife. I eventually moved in with a friend to contemplate my options and had decided to look for a teaching job when I found out that my aunt, who had passed away earlier that year, had left me a small inheritance. It was enough to board a train and come to Boston and open this shop. I've never had security before, and I've never been happier. No matter how it turns out, I've charted my own course and I plan to see it through."

"That's inspiring," Caroline said. "It really is. All I've ever wanted was to escape from all of the ties that bind me."

"Perhaps if you did, you would discover what your passion really is."

"Thank you for talking to me."

"I'm not sure I helped," Miss Campbell said. "And we certainly haven't fixed your current situation."

"You did help," Caroline replied. "I'll go back to the doctor and tell him the truth. I'll see what options he thinks are available. But one thing is for certain: my life belongs to me. I need to start figuring out what to do with it."

They stood and Miss Campbell walked her downstairs.

Caroline turned toward her and tried to smile. "Thank you, Miss Campbell."

"Come back if you want to talk."

"I will."

Caroline tugged her raincoat closer around her as she walked back to the campus. Something was going to change—she knew it. She just wasn't certain yet what it was.

23

"I can't believe it's April already," Tess moaned over breakfast.

She buttered her toast and then picked up a spoon, pushing her oatmeal around the plate.

Evie settled her napkin on her lap and nodded. "The year's almost over," she said. "It won't be much longer, thank goodness. I've never been so tired in my whole life."

Tess glanced up and squinted at Evie through her lenses. "So what are you going to do after school is out? Have you decided?"

Evie smiled and dipped her fork into her eggs. "Everything is going fine with Matthew. We're going home at the end of the term to discuss our options. I'm pretty sure he's going to ask me to marry him."

"What happened when you went to Princeton?" Tess asked, as if she didn't know. There was only one thing Evie was interested in. It was practically the only thing she had talked about all year.

"We had a nice time together," Evie said vaguely. "You know, he showed me around the campus and the town. He introduced me to a few of his friends and took me to his favorite restaurants, things like that."

"Where did you stay?" Tess persisted. "I imagine hotels are expensive in New Jersey, just like they are here."

"A friend of his let me stay with his parents," Evie replied smoothly. "They live only a mile from the campus."

Tess noticed that Evie's eyes dropped down to her plate and she took a sudden interest in her scrambled eggs. One thing she knew for certain: Evie hadn't stayed with anyone's parents at Princeton. She had stayed with Matthew. She wondered why girls were so intent to ruin their lives by risking pregnancy when they could focus on their education. Or perhaps, she thought, that was the objective—to force an obligation to give one security in life. Plenty of young women had done it before. Something had changed in Evie over the last few weeks, something important. But no matter what it was, Tess wanted no part of it.

Merritt hadn't been herself lately, either, which was even more unusual. Sometimes Tess felt she was the only one who had come back from Christmas break unchanged in both attitude and ambition.

"I feel a bit lost, to be honest," Merritt had told her one evening when pressed on the subject. "About art, I mean."

"Maybe you should get a more practical major," Tess had

advised. She had always thought art to be a frivolous, unproductive pursuit, hardly worthy of a Radcliffe student. "You're right, Merritt; you do need to think about the future. Painting is a good hobby, but training for a practical job like a teacher or secretary is a way to ensure you'll always be able to be employed. You could major in business. Of course, you'd never get the sort of job a man would, but you would be a good asset in a business office."

Merritt had shrugged. "That's what my father says. Be practical."

"You should always listen to your father," Tess had answered, though she herself had no intention of doing any such thing. However, most young women needed guidance from a superior intellect, if one was available. She didn't, of course. She'd had to think for herself for most of her life.

But if Evie and Merritt had been acting suspiciously, Caroline was more so every single day. She'd come home from Christmas break withdrawn and depressed. She had none of her usual verve, and while Tess knew she was partly at fault for taking Caroline's photo from the Hansons' home, which had caused a strain between them, it didn't change how oddly Caroline was acting.

Privately, Tess tried to analyze her own motives for taking the picture but couldn't satisfactorily explain it. She wasn't a thief and she had never taken anything before, certainly not to keep. Perhaps the motive was a simple one, such as admiration for her friend or the desire to achieve some of the things her roommate had done, although everything had always been given to Caroline from the day she was born. Life was unfair sometimes, Tess often thought. People who didn't deserve things got them, and others who worked so hard rarely did.

Tess sat at her desk, thinking. Caroline's was next to hers, and she glanced over to see if the diary was on her friend's desk. She hadn't seen it recently and she had the sudden urge to read it. Something was going on, she was certain of it. Not only had Caroline stopped wearing her beautiful dresses, she hadn't even worn her pearls. In fact, Tess couldn't remember the last time she'd seen them, unless it was at the Christmas dance. Perhaps she'd left them in Newport, Tess thought, although that seemed unlikely. Caroline had worn them nearly every day for an entire semester, even to classes and on casual Friday-night outings to the cinema. From time to time, Tess had picked them up, stroking the luminescent strand with her fingers. It was irresistible. She had even thought of buying a fake pair to wear herself—on special occasions, of course—but when she had looked at them in shops, it hadn't been the same. Even though they were only five dollars, she wouldn't spend the money on something that anyone would know was a fake.

Tess stood and began digging through the books on Caroline's desk. Everything was in disarray, as it had been all year. She had always wondered how anyone could work in those conditions, having to search for every textbook and notebook each time she sat down to write a paper. Caroline even lost important essays and syllabi and study notes. Occasionally, Tess would weed through the mess and find them for her. Honestly, she thought, what would Caroline do without her? How was she going to cope in the real world?

The diary wasn't there. Glancing toward the door, she pulled out the drawers of Caroline's dresser, looking through the silky garments to see if she could find it. Then she remembered that Caroline had a box under her bed full of old notes and composition books. She pulled it out from under the bed and found the diary sitting on top.

She pulled it out, replaced the box, and slipped the pink leather book between two of her textbooks before grabbing her sweater. She would go to the library and find a private spot where she could read it, and then she would return it immediately.

It was a cool, sunny day. Tess was glad she had worn a sweater, and she stopped to tie a scarf over her ears. Then she proceeded to run up the library steps and went into one of the empty reading rooms. There was a well-worn sofa at one end of the room, and she sat, pulling the diary from between her pristine copies of *Blackstone's Humanities* and *Introduction to Psychology*. She opened it to find Caroline's familiar writing, flipping through the pages to the end. She frowned as she came to a spot where Ken's name had been written over and over, each one scratched out with thick black ink. The page before said only one thing: *Forsythe, Warren Street*.

She went over the last several pages, but nothing explained the cryptic entry. In fact, Caroline had hardly written in the diary at all since Christmas. There were a few notes about upcoming English tests and innocuous things, such as a complaint about the kitchen staff cooking a Sunday roast a little too long. The comments were so unlike Caroline's normal style that it was as if someone else had written them. Or perhaps she had jotted unimportant things to make it appear as if she were carrying on as normal. Clearly, she wasn't.

Across the hall were reference books, and Tess searched until she found the shelf of telephone directories. She found the one she was looking for. Turning the pages, she looked for the name Forsythe. Had another man come into the picture after Carter Gray and Ken Blackburn? But that didn't seem likely. Caroline hardly ever left their room anymore. It could be the Hansons' mysterious friend who lived in Boston, whom Caroline had visited once or twice. When Tess couldn't find anyone with the name Forsythe at that address, she turned and spied a telephone. Pulling a nickel from her coin purse, she inserted it in the slot and dialed 0.

"Operator," said a thick Boston accent. Although she had been in Cambridge for months, Tess still hadn't gotten used to it. "How may I help you?"

"Could you please get me the number for a Forsythe on Warren Street?"

"Just a moment, please."

Tess pushed up her glasses, glancing around the lobby. There were several people going about their business, none of whom were paying any attention to her. She didn't know why she felt so guilty. After all, if something was wrong with Caroline, she would merely try to help.

"Ma'am?" came the voice again. "I have the number for you."

"Go ahead."

She scribbled the number as it was read out, wondering who it belonged to. She hung up after she had the number and then steeled herself before dialing again. A woman answered after the first ring.

"Dr. Forsythe's office."

Tess froze. She had expected a suitor, not a doctor's office. She frowned, trying to think.

"This is a doctor's office?" she repeated.

"Yes, this is Dr. Forsythe's office," the woman answered. "Do you need to make an appointment?"

"What sort of doctor is he?" Tess ventured.

"Dr. Forsythe is an obstetrician."

Tess gasped. This explained everything: Caroline's reticence, her refusal to socialize, her sulking, keeping to herself instead of running them around constantly as she had during the first semester. She was pregnant. Tess could hardly breathe just thinking about it.

"Ma'am?" the woman inquired.

Tess hung up the receiver. She'd noticed that Caroline had taken to borrowing some of the sweaters she had given her in Newport, and Tess thought it was because Caroline no longer wanted Tess to have her things. Instead, she was hiding a pregnancy. And if she had gotten pregnant the night of the Christmas dance, she wouldn't be able to hide it much longer.

Tess gathered her things, stuffing the diary into her bag. She left the library quickly, ignoring the clerk who called out to her, asking if she needed to check out anything at the desk. She had suffered a shock, a shock nearly as great as if finding out she were pregnant herself. But questions began to gnaw at her. Why hadn't Caroline and Ken gotten engaged? Or was she already pregnant with Carter's child? This she doubted because Caroline's demeanor hadn't changed until she saw her again in January. No, Ken was the father, which made Tess wonder. Did he know about the baby? Or was Caroline hiding it from him, too, the way she was hiding it from her roommates?

Tess flew back to the dorm, running up the stairs to her room. She pulled out the key and hastily slid it into the lock. Thankfully, Caroline wasn't there. Retrieving the diary from between her books, Tess knelt and placed it under the bed where she had found it. Then she stood and went to the window, thinking. Had Caroline told her parents? If not, they were in for a mighty blow. People of their ilk didn't have daughters with unplanned pregnancies who were, what, four months pregnant and still not wed? That was unconscionable. They should have eloped as soon as they had learned about the baby. Instead, Caroline had refused, for whatever reason, to do the right thing. Someone would have to intervene.

What did they really know about Ken, anyway? Little apart from the fact that he had asked her to the Christmas dance and left her sitting there when he decided to rescue Caroline from Carter Gray's foul mood. Tess hadn't been interested in him at the time, resenting the way Caroline and Evie were always chasing men. She'd been pleased to be invited to the dance, it was true. It proved that she was worth asking just as much as the other girls. Ken was handsome too—tall and slender, with dark hair and perfect features. But something about him didn't feel right. He was too smooth, too self-assured, a lesser Carter in a designer suit. They were the sort of college men who would take a girl out for a while and then dump her when someone better came along. And to have been set aside for Caroline was even more demeaning. She always had to command every ounce of attention at any event.

Tess's curiosity got the better of her. She slid her key into her pocket and went downstairs, looking about for her friends, who were nowhere to be seen. Leaving the dorm, she walked in the direction of Ken's apartment building. She knew where he lived because Caroline had mentioned it once, months ago.

Tess sat on a bench a few yards away, watching the entrance of his building without being observed. After nearly three-quarters of an hour, Ken walked briskly through the door of the building, his textbooks under his arm. His stride was one of confidence. He turned and began to make his way toward the campus.

She rose, following him, although she tried to stay far enough back that if he suddenly turned in her direction, she would have time to react and avoid him. He didn't stop, however. Increasing her pace, she glanced at her watch. It was nearly ten o'clock. He had left his apartment at the last-possible minute before his class.

Her emotions roiling with each passing step, Tess vacillated between jealousy and anger. Jealousy that she had not kept the attention of a man who had asked her out to a dance, anger that he proved what she had long believed—that few if any men were worthy of the admiration they were given.

Even from behind, he was the picture of self-assurance. His stride, the way he flexed his neck muscles from time to time, the muscular arms that were evident under his letter sweater. He flicked his hair back with a hand, nodding from time to time at pretty girls that he passed, even whistling at one. Tess's ire was inflamed by the time they reached his building, and she stopped just short of following him inside.

He had done something terrible, stealing Caroline from Carter Gray and getting her pregnant. Tess wondered if he knew about the baby and had deserted her for that very reason. It wasn't fair, using women and ruining people's lives. Men were bullies and women had to sit back and take it. She knew it from her own experience. Well, she wouldn't have it. She would get to the bottom of what had happened if it was the last thing she did.

She followed him for the next three days, always at a different time of day. His behavior never altered. He was always confident, smiling and flirting with every girl that caught his eye. It wasn't lost on Tess that she had nearly come into contact with him twice and he hadn't even noticed her. It was almost as if she didn't exist at all.

Following him, however, lost its thrill after a few days. She wanted a confrontation. Of course, she couldn't go up and talk to him. He would no doubt laugh and then push past her, brushing off anything she had to say. She wanted him to be sorry, if she was honest. She wanted him to pay for what he had done. That evening, she decided she would place a call to his apartment and speak to him herself.

Tess went downstairs and dialed his number with a shaky hand, glancing about the room to make certain no one had followed her. She felt a moment of thrill as she waited for someone to pick up the line.

Carter happened to be the one to answer the phone. "Hello?"

"Ken Blackburn, please," she said.

She waited to be questioned or asked her name, but Carter didn't even acknowledge her on the telephone. That's how little she meant in the scheme of things. Instead, he called for Ken to come to the phone.

Tess shivered, anticipating Ken's voice on the line. What was she doing? She could hang up now, but her curiosity was too strong.

"Who is it?" she could hear Ken ask Carter. "I was in the shower."

"Some girl on the phone," Carter answered. "Sounded like a nobody."

Her nostrils flared at the very word.

"Yeah?" Ken said into the receiver.

For a moment, she didn't say anything, willing herself to stop. But she couldn't. After a few seconds, she spoke quickly into the phone.

"I know what you did that night."

There was a long pause at the end of the line.

"Who is this?" he growled at last.

"It doesn't matter, does it?" she asked in a breathless voice. "You're going to pay for what you've done."

She took a deep breath and then hung up the line. When she looked up, Caroline was standing in the doorway. Tess's heart raced as she wondered if her roommate had heard what she said, but before she could utter a single coherent remark, Caroline turned and walked away.

The secrets were thick in this place, Tess thought. Trysts and lovers' quarrels and pregnancies. People like the Hansons and the Blackburns of the world did as they pleased, and all because they had money. It wasn't fair.

She started to go into the salon and then went back to the telephone, waiting for a minute as some of the third-floor girls wandered through and stood near the doorway, trying to decide if they needed a coat before they went out. Eventually, they chose sweaters and left the dormitory. Tess fished in her pocket and took out a slip of paper, studying it carefully. She tapped it against her finger as she tried to decide what to do. Eventually, she dialed the number she had written earlier and waited for someone to answer.

"Hanson residence," said a crisp, efficient voice.

Tess recognized it as that of Pearl, the Hansons' maid.

"Mrs. Hanson, please," she replied.

"May I ask who is calling?"

She paused for a split second. "This is Evie Miller. I visited the house last fall with Caroline, just before Thanksgiving."

"Oh, yes, Miss Miller, I remember," Pearl answered. "I hope everything is all right with Miss Caroline."

"She's fine," Tess lied. "I just wanted to speak to her mother about a surprise."

It was certainly a surprise, she thought.

"Just a moment, please."

Tess waited, twisting the telephone cord around her finger. If Mrs. Schwartz were in the room, she would have scolded her. One wasn't to damage the property belonging to the dormitory, the other girls, or, God forbid, Radcliffe itself. Still, she couldn't help it. Her nerves were tied in knots.

"Evie?" said Mrs. Hanson a moment later. "How nice to hear from you. Pearl says you would like to discuss a surprise for Caroline."

Tess cleared her throat. "I'm afraid the surprise is really for you."

"I'm sorry, I don't quite understand."

"Caroline is pregnant, Mrs. Hanson," she said, plunging in headfirst. "She's been afraid to tell you."

"Why, I..." Elizabeth Hanson began in a strangled voice. "That's impossible. It can't be true."

"Oh, it's true all right," Tess continued. "She got pregnant on the night of the Christmas dance and is already four months along. She's getting away with it, Mrs. Hanson. Something needs to be done."

"Dear God," Caroline's mother replied. "Is she there? Put her on the line and let me speak to her at once."

"She's refusing to talk to you," Tess answered. She couldn't still her ragged breathing. "I wasn't sure what to do about it, and then I decided that you needed to know. I hope I did the right thing."

Elizabeth Hanson was at a complete loss for words.

Tess felt a chill running up her spine.

"We'll be there in the morning," came the reply, followed by a loud click on the line.

After hanging up the receiver, Tess went into the kitchen, unable to face Caroline. She was going to have to wait until she was certain her roommate was asleep before she ventured up the stairs.

24

It had been a quiet week in the bookshop, so quiet and uneventful that Alice might not have opened the doors at all. The days were blustery and wet, but while she never minded being confined to the shop on rainy days, it kept everyone else at bay. The foot traffic through the area was never heavy during good weather and almost nonexistent during a storm, which left plenty of time for reflection and thought. On the morning of book club, after three solid days of rain, she put on her raincoat and her stoutest boots and ventured outdoors.

Three blocks away was La Fleuriste, a French-style flower shop that specialized in tiny bouquets. She sloshed her way through the streets and bought three posies of pink roses tucked into small zinc cups. It was an extravagance, and though she rarely indulged in luxuries, once in a while a woman has to have flowers, even if she buys them for herself.

"I'll put these in a box for you," the owner said, taking one from under the counter. "Then we'll wrap them in plastic so they don't get ruined. I didn't think we'd see anyone out and about on a day like today."

"I have a bookshop on Simpson," she replied, smiling. "And I haven't seen a soul in nearly forty-eight hours. I needed flowers and to talk to another human being."

"You're only the second person I've talked to today, myself," he answered. "You should have seen the first, some poor schmuck who forgot his wife's birthday."

Alice laughed as she paid the florist and clutched the plastic bag to her chest as she left the shop. She was glad she had gotten out and that she had decided to start living. One of the best things she had done in recent weeks was to accept Eleanor's invitation to dinner. It had been an unexpected pleasure to have the opportunity to talk books with someone of her own age and temperament. Their first evening, spent over a plate of spaghetti Bolognese and a bottle of pinot noir at Giuseppe's, had become a weekly ritual. The intellectual stimulation of novels and poetry, the change of scenery, and not least the opportunity to meet a like-minded friend had changed her life, making her wonder why she hadn't sought a connection like this before.

She made her way back to the shop, where she took extra care to arrange the delicate blooms around the room. Her mood flagged a little at the thought of that evening, wondering if the girls would trouble to come if the storm didn't abate and knowing that what she was truly interested in was Caroline's welfare when she wouldn't have the privacy to inquire after her health.

She was looking forward to discussing *Emma*. Although it was a comedy, there were useful lessons to draw from the story. In particular, Alice reminded herself that meddling in the affairs of others—as the title character, Emma, was wont to do—often led to failure. Her book club girls were so young and desperate to see how life would turn out, just as she had been at their age. The four of them stood at the precipice of life, where they were about to find out if their reality would match their dreams or if they were to be crossed in love and life. Was love easy for anyone if it was a tangle for Emma Woodhouse, who had it all? But then, Caroline Hanson had it all, only to lose everything in the blink of an eye. Alice had the vantage point of experience to guide her, but all the same, any advice she could give them would likely fall on deaf ears.

Restless, she put out a tray of shortbread and turned on the electric kettle for tea, sorting cups and saucers and teaspoons. It would be uncivilized to discuss an elegant novel like *Emma* without tea. Jane Austen had recorded the importance of the ceremonies her characters undertook, the backdrop to momentous occasions and secrets whispered between friends. Alice resolved in the future to observe the little graces in life as often as possible.

Jane Austen was one of Alice's favorite authors. There were some, Mark Twain among them, who belittled her work as romantic nonsense, books about nothing of importance. But in truth, Miss Austen dissected human nature with a sharp eye and a wit that was unsurpassed. Of course, the subject of the books were often love and romance. But in 1814, when *Emma* was written, women were dependent upon the capricious nature of men. They were beholden to husbands and fathers to provide food, shelter, and clothing. Without them, women could hardly survive. In many ways, Alice decided, the female characters in Austen's books learned to navigate the system and turn situations to their advantage, a skill that many women still practiced when they lived within the confines of a male-dominated system.

Students at Radcliffe College might feel they were long past such antiquated habits. Although they were being given the opportunity to pursue an education, there was little doubt that they would adhere almost as strictly to societal norms as their mothers had. Alice was an exception, she knew. As Virginia Woolf had so aptly said, if one has a little money and a room of one's own, therein lies freedom. But even in the modern era of 1956, nearly a hundred and fifty years after *Emma* had been written, it was still difficult for a woman to obtain money and have a life determined by herself. Alice looked forward to discussing it with the girls, anticipating a lively conversation.

Tess was the first to arrive. She held the door open as she shook out her umbrella before propping it inside the door. After taking off her slicker, she hung it on the hook.

"Hello, Tess," Alice said, stealing a look behind her to see if any of the others were with her.

"Good evening, Miss Campbell," Tess answered.

"How have you been since I last saw you?"

"Fine," she answered.

Alice thought her response a little abrupt. She had not been alone with Tess since the first day the girl had arrived in the shop and taken one of her flyers. Her observation at the time was that the girl was not a kindred spirit, although when Tess had asked about the book club, Alice wondered if she had been wrong about her. But after all these months, she realized that her first impression had been correct.

"I've made tea," she said. "Lapsang Souchong. It seems fitting when we're reading Jane Austen, doesn't it?"

"That's nice," Tess replied. "I suppose this is our last book club night."

"I'm afraid it is," Alice agreed. "I'm sure everyone is going home for summer vacation."

"That is, if they come back at all," Tess remarked.

Alice was nonplussed. "Is someone not coming back?"

Tess shrugged. "I expect so. Of course, I intend to be here. I've got my eye on bigger things than husbands, no matter how important Jane Austen seems to think they are."

"Are the other girls coming tonight?" Alice asked, unable to control her curiosity a moment longer.

Tess shrugged. "Everyone except Caroline, I presume."

"What do you mean?" Alice asked, trying not to betray her emotions.

"Her parents came to see her this morning," Tess answered.

Alice brought a hand to her throat. "That's unusual, isn't it?"

Tess looked uncomfortable. "Something is going on. I think she's probably leaving early."

"'Leaving'?" Alice echoed. "Did Caroline pack her things?"

"No, nothing like that," Tess answered. "I assumed they went out for coffee, but they've been gone all day."

Alice stepped back from Tess, wanting a little time to think.

"I've left something upstairs," she said, stalling for time. She didn't want to begin the conversation about the book before everyone else arrived, and certainly not with Tess, who was the most contentious if she didn't like a novel. Sighing, she turned to Tess and forced a smile. "Please help yourself to refreshments, if you like. I made shortbread cookies especially for tonight."

She went up the stairs slowly and shut the door behind her, glancing out the window to see if anyone else was coming. The rain had slowed slightly and the street was empty. Alice perched on the edge of the chair, wondering what to do. Caroline must have told her parents about her pregnancy, even though she'd vowed not to do it. Alice could only hope they had taken the news well. Perhaps it meant that Caroline had come to some sort of decision. After a few minutes, she began to hope that Evie and Merritt would arrive soon. If Tess were the only one present, it would make for an awkward evening.

She heard the bell ring as the door opened downstairs, but did not immediately move. Tess could greet whichever of the girls had arrived, and she would go down in a minute. The sound of voices below told her only one person had arrived, and as it was not likely to be Caroline, she picked up the book on her bedside table. She and Eleanor were reading Patricia Highsmith's new title, *The Talented Mr. Ripley*. It was thrilling in a way few books were. Highsmith, she concluded, was a master of suspense, and Alice was thankful that she had someone with whom to discuss this highly interesting book. She almost picked up the phone to call Eleanor now—for a dose of encouragement, perhaps—and then decided not to. Sighing, she put down the book and stood just as she heard voices rising from below.

Alice swung open her door and realized that Tess was having an argument with a young man. She paused on the stairs, trying to decide whether or not to intervene. Tess, she knew, could hold her own in most situations. Alice couldn't tell what the disagreement was about and decided not to interfere unless it was called for.

"You're not the only one who can follow someone," he suddenly snapped, grabbing her by the arm.

Alice gripped the rail, shocked. Perhaps he was a threat after all. He hadn't noticed her yet, and she hoped she could use the element of surprise to stop him from doing whatever it was he intended to do.

"You've got the wrong person," Tess insisted, although the color had risen in her cheeks. It was clear from where Alice stood that Tess was lying.

"Oh yeah?" he argued. "Carter followed you the last two

days when I told him some pathetic girl wouldn't leave me alone. Everyone's laughing about it."

Alice gasped. They were standing near her desk, and she eyed the door, wondering if help could be found if she were able to make it outside. Perhaps not. Not only was it a quiet street, but also he would have enough time to react if he wanted to stop her. She decided to go back upstairs and call the police.

"We know what you did," Tess replied. "Everyone does."

"You're just jealous," the man continued. "Pathetic and jealous and stupid. I can't believe I even bothered asking you to the dance. It was really only to get closer to Caroline."

He reached out and shoved her. Alice darted down the steps, but she was too late. Tess grabbed the knife that Alice kept on her desk for opening letters—a knife Alice admired for its pretty, carved handle, which felt so nice in the hand—and stabbed the boy in the shoulder.

He staggered backward, stunned, and then fell onto the floor, moaning.

"Dear God," Alice cried as she fell to the ground beside him.

Just then the door burst open, and Evie and Merritt came inside. Alice looked up at them and pointed at the telephone.

"Call the police," she ordered, but no one moved. Everyone seemed riveted to the spot. "I said call the police!"

Evie was the first to recover from the shock, and she ran to the telephone and started to dial. Alice bent over the boy and looked up at Tess.

"Get me something to stop the bleeding," she said.

She wouldn't pull out the knife, which was lodged just below his shoulder. If she did, it was possible she could do more damage than had already been done.

"There's nothing here," Tess said weakly.

"There's a towel in the powder room," Alice ordered. "Bring it to me."

When Tess didn't move, Merritt ran to get the towel and brought it to Alice.

"What happened?" Alice demanded, looking up at Tess as she pressed the towel as close to the wound as she could without dislodging the knife. "Who is he?"

"His name is Ken Blackburn. He and Caroline are having an affair," Tess sputtered. "And she's pregnant."

"She can't be," Merritt protested, shocked. "She would have told me."

"Are you sure?" Evie asked, looking at Tess.

"Yes," Tess answered. "And she's been carrying on with him. It's disgusting."

"You don't know what you're talking about," Alice replied in a cold tone.

Tess nodded, her face pale. "Yes, I do. She's been going to an obstetrician on Warren Street. She's definitely pregnant. Haven't you noticed how different she looks lately?"

No one said a word. Ken tried to sit up, clutching his shoulder.

Two police cars had arrived outside the shop, and the wail of an ambulance could be heard in the background. Alice felt like she was in a fog. She answered questions, although later she would remember none of them. Ken was taken away on a stretcher, after which Tess had broken down during questioning and had been handcuffed by the police officers. Alice followed, watching as an officer took her out to the squad car, holding her head as she was helped inside.

Alice stood in the rain, rubbing her arms against the cold night air, until the police cars were out of sight. As she went back inside the shop, a chill came over her.

"Is Caroline really pregnant?" Evie asked Merritt, searching her face for the answer. "I didn't see her today, did you?"

"No," Merritt answered, although Alice had no idea which question she was referring to.

"There's blood on the floor," she said, in no mood for gossip. "I'll fetch a mop."

"I'm sorry, Miss Campbell," Merritt said. "Would you like some help?"

"No, that's all right," Alice answered, flustered. "It will only take a few minutes. You girls should go back home."

After they had gone, Alice locked the door and went upstairs. She didn't even clear away the tea. Pulling a blanket over her, she sank onto the chaise. So that, she thought, was the man responsible for attacking Caroline. He was tall and muscular and aggressive.

None of them would have been a match for a man that size. She realized she had been holding her breath and exhaled, trying to calm down. It seemed that Tess had figured out part of the story and jumped to the wrong conclusion, and now her life, as she had hoped to live it, was in jeopardy too.

The final book club had ended with tragedy, one that could have been prevented if only common sense had prevailed. For a moment, Alice thought about closing the shop permanently to prevent anything else from happening under her watch. But of course she wouldn't. One couldn't prevent all pain and suffering; it happens in spite of the best of intentions. Nevertheless, life goes on. It proceeds in spite of the breaking of human hearts.

25

MAY 1956

"It isn't what we say or think that defines us,
but what we do."

—JANE AUSTEN, *SENSE AND SENSIBILITY*

In the end, everything was decided for her. Throughout April, Caroline had taken to getting up an hour past normal, if only as a way of avoiding Tess, so it wasn't unusual that she awoke on the last Thursday of the month at eight thirty, after everyone else had gone downstairs. Throwing back the covers, she decided to take a long, hot shower. Afterward, she took her time with her makeup and hair, mustering her courage to see Dr. Forsythe that morning.

She went downstairs and walked into the dining room just as the last two people were leaving. Breakfast was still sitting on the sideboard, and she poured herself a cup of coffee before taking two pieces of toast from the rack and buttering them. It was a momentous day. She had finally made a decision. There were telephone calls to be faced, arrangements to be made. Caroline wondered why it had taken her so long to determine what to do and decided it was because none of the alternatives were acceptable. Suicide had been an option, but the truth was she wanted desperately to live. The other choices were equally terrifying. Some might have suggested an abortion, but there were serious risks involved, both health and legal, along with psychological trauma. She could have the child and give it up for adoption, but that idea, too, was fraught with problems and required a secrecy that would gnaw at her forever, always wondering what had become of the life she had created. The most impossible option, in her view, was to have the child and try to raise it on her own. She couldn't imagine being less equipped to take on the task, without a husband or support of any kind. Her parents would blame her for destroying their lives, of that she was certain. But even worse, she couldn't give a child a stable, decent life.

Caroline scraped butter across the cold toast and sipped her coffee, feeling she had come to the only conclusion that she could stand. She relished the peace and quiet of the empty dormitory, for there would be little of it to be had once she set everything in motion. Pouring a second cup of coffee and stirring in a teaspoon of sugar, an indulgence of which her mother would doubtless disapprove, she drank it in silence and then cleared away the dishes, smoothing the tablecloth before she went upstairs.

Reapplying her lipstick, a fortification designed to steel her against the difficulties ahead, she took her pocketbook and went downstairs to call a taxi to take her to the doctor's office. She had just lifted the receiver when she heard a commotion at the front door. Her mouth flew open in surprise when she realized her parents had just walked into the dorm.

"Where are you going, young lady?" her father demanded, eyeing the pocketbook in her hand and the sweater draped over her arm.

Every muscle in her body tensed at the sight of them. Caroline could have told him that she was going to class, but she could not tell such a pointless lie. She had planned to explain everything in a letter. If her father became as angry as she expected him to be, she would have been shielded from the worst of it. But now, there was no escape from Richard Hanson's flaming temper. It was clear from not only his tone but the veins bulging on his neck that he had already worked himself up into a rage. They couldn't know, she thought desperately; there wasn't any way they could have found out the secret she held inside.

"Father," Caroline said, stalling. She clutched her pocketbook, trying to calm her nerves as she worked out what to say. "What brings you here today?"

"What brings us here?" he repeated, looking at her mother, eyes wide open. "Elizabeth, can you believe this? Caroline wants to know what brings us here."

"Why don't we sit down?" Caroline asked, turning toward the salon. She hoped Mrs. Schwartz was watching television in her private rooms and not aware of the commotion that her father was making.

"I don't want to sit down!" her father snapped.

Caroline frowned, glancing at her mother, who didn't attempt to intervene.

"What is the matter?" Caroline asked, looking from her father to her mother. "Why are you here?"

"I received a telephone call from your friend Evie yesterday evening," Elizabeth answered coldly. "We were hoping you could explain yourself."

"Evie?" she repeated, bewildered. "Why on earth would Evie call you?"

"To notify us that our own daughter was pregnant." Elizabeth's color rose. "Obviously, you didn't have the courage to tell us yourself."

Caroline sank onto the sofa, stunned. How had Evie known? Tess, of course, was a snoop but not Evie. She had kept everything to herself until she had finally confided in Miss Campbell, who would never breathe a word to a soul. Caroline struggled to sort it out. Tess must have realized she was pregnant and told Evie; that was the only thing that made sense. And probably not only Evie; she had probably told everyone she knew. Caroline should have made her decision earlier, but her mother was right. She hadn't had the courage.

Looking at Elizabeth, she searched for a hint of compassion in her face, finding none. Whatever her father thought would be echoed by her mother, she knew without asking.

"This is inexcusable, Caroline," her father said, raising his voice. "Say something. Have the guts to break your mother's heart to her face."

Caroline stood and took a deep breath. "It's true, Father. I'm pregnant. I've let you both down."

"How could you, Caroline?" her mother said shrilly. "Of all the horrific things to do to your father and me. It's inexcusable."

"Lower your voice, please, Mother," she replied, worried that someone would hear.

"Don't tell your mother what to do," her father growled. "You, of all people, should have known better. We gave you everything you ever wanted, and then you pay us back by running around like a slut. Now look what you've done. Do you realize what this means for your mother and me?"

Caroline had known her father had a cruel streak, but his language came as a shock. If she hadn't suddenly felt dizzy, she would have walked out the door. She struggled not to hyperventilate, putting a hand on her chest.

"Yes," she answered.

When she refused to elaborate, he slapped his hand on a table.

"It could ruin us," he said. "What a mess. What a goddamned mess."

She would never tell them what happened, she realized at that moment. Knowing she was a victim wouldn't make a difference when they were intent on punishing her for something that wasn't her fault. She'd shown poor judgment, of course. She should have never gotten into a car with someone she hardly knew. But she didn't deserve what had happened. Her parents stared at her defiantly, waiting for her to speak, but she held her ground.

"Wait until our friends find out," Elizabeth sputtered. "We'll be the laughingstock of Newport. We'll lose our standing in the community."

"Say something," her father ordered, taking a step toward her. "Who's the father of this bastard, or do you even know?"

Every word was a slap in the face. She wanted to tell them the truth and receive the comfort any daughter needed at a moment like this, but they were too furious to listen. Someone had to pay for their humiliation.

"Stop," she said, gasping for breath. "Please, stop."

She had seen her father vent his anger many times, although it had seldom been directed at her. Business associates, neighbors, slow taxi drivers—sometimes it seemed everyone had been a target of his wrath. She'd always known that one day, she would overstep the bounds and it could all fall directly onto her. Today was that day.

"You're the one who should have stopped," he snapped. "You could have prevented all manner of injury to your mother and me."

"Do we know the boy?" asked her mother.

Caroline looked up at her. For once, Elizabeth's makeup wasn't entirely perfect. They had been up before dawn, driving all the way from Newport to have this showdown. She gave Caroline a pleading look, hoping there was some way to salvage the situation.

"Is it Carter Gray?" Elizabeth continued. "Because one thing I know, the Grays would make him marry you. We could find him a job overseas for a few years, and you could come back when the scandal has died down. It wouldn't mitigate all of the damage but at least over time, some people might forget what you've done."

"What I've done?" Caroline said, her voice rising. "How could you possibly know what I've done? You've never cared about anything but yourselves. You've never spared a moment to think of my feelings, especially at a time like this."

"Don't you speak to your mother in that tone of voice, young lady," Richard snapped. "All we've ever done is think of you. And look how that's turned out."

Caroline started to make her way toward the door, but her father followed her, taking hold of her arm. He spun her around to face him.

"We expected so much more from you," he said, his fingers biting into her arm. "You're a Hanson. There are standards to abide by, both for your mother's sake and mine. We've done everything for you, and now you've repaid us like this."

"I have done nothing to you," she answered. "Nothing at all."

His nostrils flared. "Have the decency to answer your mother's question."

Caroline looked at Elizabeth. "No, Mother, it wasn't Carter. He's a stupid drunk, if you want to know the truth. I would never sleep with someone like that."

Richard slapped her across the face. "Don't speak to your mother like that."

"Really?" she said, turning back to face him. "If you cared about using language in front of her, you wouldn't have called me a slut."

He took a step toward her, hand raised. Caroline could hear her mother make a weak protest in the background. Even Elizabeth knew her husband had gone too far. Caroline turned on her heel to leave, but suddenly, a strong pain gripped her across her abdomen and she doubled over, gasping.

"You can try to get sympathy all you want," her father said. "But it won't work with me."

She didn't answer. The wave of dizziness that had threatened before came back with a vengeance. Her mother cried out as Caroline fell, her handbag tumbling to the floor.

She awoke disoriented as ambulance medics were strapping her onto a gurney. They wheeled her outside to a waiting ambulance. Her parents hovered just behind them, so she shut her eyes tightly, gritting her teeth as the gurney was lifted into the waiting vehicle.

One of the medics put his hand on her arm as the other slid the door closed.

"Try to relax," he said. "We'll get you to the hospital in a few minutes."

Caroline turned away, crying out as a sudden contraction wracked her body. She clutched her belly, moaning. She had rarely touched it over the last few months, preferring to ignore the changes that were taking place inside her. Certainly, she had felt the baby move, although she couldn't remember the last time. Had it been today? This week? In the fog of pain, she wasn't certain.

One of the medics inserted an IV into her arm. She tried to protest, but he held her arm in place. In a minute, he had injected something into it that made her drowsy. The rocking of the ambulance as it raced down the street combined with the numbing sensation of the medication took its toll, and blissfully, she drifted to sleep.

Sometime later, Caroline woke in a darkened hospital room. She struggled to sit up but couldn't quite manage it. As she was trying to decide what to do, a young nurse came into the room.

"How are you feeling?" she asked. "I'm Jeanie, your nurse on call this evening. Are you in any pain?"

Caroline shook her head, still groggy. "I don't feel much of anything."

"That's normal after a procedure, miss."

"What procedure?" Caroline asked, trying to focus on the nurse. "What happened to the baby?"

"We don't have to talk about this now," the girl answered.

She was young, not much older than Caroline herself, but she had a comforting manner. Caroline put her hand across her stomach and frowned. "No, tell me, please."

"I'm afraid you lost the baby," the nurse said quietly. "But for now, we need you to get some rest. Do you need anything?"

"Was it a boy or a girl?" Caroline asked.

"Sometimes people don't want to know," the young woman answered. "It might make your suffering easier if you don't."

"I want to know."

The nurse came over and stood next to her. "It was a girl, Miss Hanson. A perfect little girl."

Caroline nodded, trying to swallow.

"There's a button here on the side of your bed if you decide you need some water or extra blankets or anything. Please press it if you need me. I'll check on you in a little while."

Caroline waited as she closed the door, clutching the rails of the hospital bed. It was over. The child she had carried in her own body, whom she had resented and wished away and regretted, was now dead. Her problem was over now, but she felt no relief, merely guilt over the way she had denied the child's existence for months, thinking only of herself.

She would never tell Ken. He didn't deserve to know. But still, she wondered if he had any concept of the suffering he had inflicted on her. Would he have been sorry if he knew? She doubted it. He didn't seem capable of remorse. As she rolled onto her side, thinking, she heard the door open. Caroline tried to sit up as her parents walked into the room. Her father turned on the light.

"I can't talk right now," she said, turning away from the light.

"Well, this is a horrible state of affairs," her father pronounced. "It's unfortunate, but it's done. We'll take you home in the morning."

The last thing she wanted was to be driven home like a child and consigned to her room until she was twenty-five. In fact, she never wanted to speak to them again.

"Do you want to pack your things, or shall I go to the dormitory and do it for you?" her mother asked.

"Don't pack for me," Caroline managed to say.

She looked for the button the nurse had shown her to press if she needed more pain medication. She pressed it and then sat back, ignoring her parents as they tried to engage her in conversation. A minute later, the nurse came into the room. She walked up to Caroline and took her pulse.

"Did you need more pain medication, Miss Hanson?"

Caroline shook her head. "I'm not feeling well. I'm not up to company right now."

Jeanie's brow went up, and she turned around to face the Hansons. "I'm afraid you'll have to leave," she said. "Our patient needs to get some rest."

"We're her parents," insisted her father.

"I'm sorry, sir, you'll have to go to the waiting room," the woman replied. "She's not up to talking right now, as you can see."

With a few muttered complaints, they turned to go and the nurse shut the door behind them. "Shall I turn off this light again?" she asked, her hand hovering at the light switch.

"Yes, please," Caroline replied.

"You know, first pregnancies sometimes end in miscarriages," she said in a quiet voice. "It doesn't mean you won't be able to have a child later."

When Caroline didn't answer, the woman walked to the door.

"I'll check on you in a while," Jeanie answered. "I'm on duty all night."

Caroline nodded and turned toward the window, where she could see the moon between the parted curtains. The nurse understood, she was certain of that. She wondered how long her parents would wait before they gave up. But that, she decided, was not her concern. Let them believe what they wanted. Let them hate her if they chose to do so. She knew well the Hanson stubbornness, of course. She had it herself.

They would never have a change of heart.

26

Caroline slept for a long while, dozing at times, startling awake at others. Each time she opened her eyes, she remembered what had happened all over again. That poor little life, she thought. Not even wanted by her own mother. She would have cried if she'd had the strength. Instead, she lay completely still, staring at the ceiling. Her life, as she knew it, was over. Nothing would ever be the same again.

Sometime later, Jeanie cracked open her door. "There's someone here to see you if you feel up to it."

Caroline shook her head. "I don't want to see my parents again."

"It's a friend," the nurse replied. "She said her name is Merritt Weber."

"All right," Caroline replied after a pause. "I'll see her."

A minute later, Merritt came in the room. Caroline watched as she pulled a chair up to the bed and sat down.

"I hate you seeing me like this," Caroline finally said, pulling the bedsheet nearly to her chin. She had hardly budged from the bed after waking from the procedure. "It's the worst day of my life."

"You don't have to talk, Caroline," Merritt assured her. "I just came to sit with you so you didn't have to be alone."

Tears stung the corner of her eyes. Alone. She had never felt more alone in her life. Not even that dark day in December, when she was brutalized by Ken Blackburn and thrown onto the street in the middle of the night, having to struggle for miles in the freezing cold back to Cambridge. Nor, indeed, the day she stood at the window of the library, wondering if she should jump and end it all. Or even the night after she first found out she was pregnant, listening to Tess's breathing in the bed across the room and being afraid the truth would be exposed. No one could possibly understand what she had gone through.

She nodded, turning away from Merritt. She couldn't discuss it now. She couldn't discuss anything at all. Closing her eyes, she let exhaustion overtake her.

Sometime later, she awoke in the darkened room. She looked at the clock and saw it was half past one. Turning, she realized Merritt was still there, fast asleep in the chair by the bed. It was strangely comforting to know that Merritt hadn't left her side.

A few minutes later, Merritt stirred, stretching.

"You're awake!" she said, sitting up. "Can I get you anything?"

Caroline nodded. "Some water would be nice. I was about to ring the nurse."

Merritt stood. "I'll get it," she said.

She returned shortly with a plastic pitcher in hand. Caroline watched as Merritt poured water into a cup, and she took it gratefully.

"How are you feeling?" Merritt asked. "Do you need any pain medication? Another blanket? The nurse has heated ones I can bring you."

"No, thank you," she answered, sitting up on the pillows. "I'm all right."

"I saw your parents around midnight when I went to find a vending machine."

"Are they still here?" Caroline tensed at the thought.

Merritt shook her head. "No, they were about to leave. I gather they were giving the hospital staff a difficult time. Your mother did take me aside and say that they expected you to pack and go back to Newport at once."

"Well, I'm not going," Caroline answered.

Merritt's eyes widened. "What do you mean?"

"We have a couple of weeks left here, and I don't intend to leave until Radcliffe makes me."

"What about classes?"

Caroline shrugged. "What about them? All we really have left are finals. If I don't take them, the whole semester won't count."

Merritt nodded. "I've been thinking about that too. I guess I supposed that you wouldn't bother. I mean..."

"You mean, how could I possibly face anyone after what's happened?"

"We don't have to talk about it," Merritt replied. "It's too soon."

"I need to talk about it," Caroline said. "I was raped, Merritt. I got pregnant and I was afraid to tell anyone. I lost the baby. End of story."

"Except I'm afraid that's not the end of the story," Merritt said, pulling on her cardigan. "You don't know what happened at book club last night."

"What do you mean?" Caroline asked, frowning. "What could have possibly have happened at book club that has anything to do with me? Was Evie telling everyone I'm pregnant?"

"Evie?" Merritt frowned. "What makes you think Evie knew you were pregnant?"

"She called my parents," Caroline stated. "That's why they drove up here and confronted me. She told them I was having an affair and hiding a pregnancy from them."

"Did you tell your mother and father the truth about what really happened?" Merritt asked.

"No," Caroline replied, pulling back the blankets. "They were too angry to listen. And my father said unforgivable things, Merritt. Things that I will never forget."

"What about your mother? Wasn't she understanding?"

"She took his side, as she always does," Caroline replied. "I don't want to see them for as long as I can help it."

Merritt stood and walked to the window, looking out at the moonlight-drenched park below. "It wasn't Evie who called your parents, Caroline. It was Tess. She probably told them she was Evie so she could avoid responsibility for it."

"What happened at book club, then?" Caroline asked, confused.

Merritt turned around and crossed her arms. "Tess was stalking Ken Blackburn. She connected him to you and had been following him around Cambridge for days."

Caroline was shocked. "How did she know?"

"I'm not sure," Merritt admitted. "All I know is that he found out who was following him, so he showed up at the bookshop last night and confronted her."

"Did they have an argument in front of everyone?" Caroline was horrified just imagining it.

"Oh, they had an argument, all right. Raised voices and strong language. Evie and I had just arrived, and Miss Campbell was coming down the stairs when it happened. But you haven't heard the worst part. Tess found a knife on Miss Campbell's desk and stabbed Ken in the shoulder."

"Oh my God!" Caroline exclaimed, genuinely shocked. "Is he dead?"

"No," Merritt answered. "He was taken to the hospital last night in an ambulance. I haven't heard anything else."

Caroline shivered. "What about Tess?"

"She was arrested."

Caroline was shocked. She'd never imagined Tess capable of anything like this. And to think, her parents thought she was the scandal.

"I shouldn't have told you," Merritt said at last. "I should have kept it to myself instead of burdening you at a time like this."

"I can't believe it," Caroline murmured. "I want to know what happened to both of them. Will you find out for me?"

"You've been through enough."

"I have to know."

Merritt sat down next to Caroline. "I'm so sorry everything turned out like this. I had no idea you were pregnant. I mean, I knew you were unhappy, but I thought it had something to do with Carter. You know, if you had wanted to talk to me, I would have been there for you."

"I know," she answered. "You and Miss Campbell have been the only two people I could trust. It's just that I didn't want to burden you. You've been reeling since your father announced he was going away, and I didn't want to add to your problems."

"What are you going to do now?"

Caroline shrugged. "I have no idea, but I know it doesn't involve dealing with my parents anytime soon."

"You should get some sleep," Merritt said, taking Caroline's cup of water to set on a nearby table. "Everything can be sorted out later."

Caroline nodded, rolling over on her side. She had never been so tired. After a few minutes, she sat up on one elbow. Merritt was still awake, though lying back in the chair next to her.

"You know, the awful thing is," Caroline murmured, "I had come to a decision about the pregnancy."

"What were you going to do?" Merritt asked. Then she shook her head, sighing. "No, don't tell me, Caroline. It's none of my business. And it doesn't matter anyway. Nothing could change how I feel about you."

"I need to tell someone," Caroline insisted. "I need someone to know that I was planning to go to a home for unwed mothers so that I could give my baby a chance for a better life."

Suddenly, the tears came, tears she had held back for months. Merritt held her as she wept—for herself, for the child, and for just how devastatingly unfair life could be.

27

The next morning, Caroline was woken by the door opening. Merritt came in, carrying a newspaper under her arm.

"Sorry," she said. "I was trying to be quiet."

"It's fine," Caroline replied, looking out the window. The sun was already shining. She must have been in a deep sleep after being up in the middle of the night. "What time is it?"

"Just after nine." Merritt smiled. "The nurse said she'll bring your breakfast in a few minutes."

"The same nurse as last night?" Caroline asked.

"No, Nurse Wallace went off duty at seven o'clock. She checked on you before she left. By the way, she told me she left strict instructions with the nurse coming in on the new shift not to allow any visitors without your approval."

"Good," Caroline answered. "What about you? Have you had breakfast yet?"

"I stopped for a doughnut and coffee in the hospital cafeteria." She pulled the newspaper from under her arm and held it up. "I'm not sure if you want to see this, but Tess is in the paper."

Caroline shook her head when Merritt held it out. "Just give me the details, please."

"Ken's going to be all right," Merritt said, sitting back in the chair. "Tess stabbed him in the shoulder, narrowly missing an artery. He lost a lot of blood and there may be nerve damage, but he'll survive. He'll probably be charged with assault."

"What about her?" Caroline asked.

"The district attorney is considering charges." Merritt paused. "Although I'm sure she'll argue it was in self-defense."

The nurse came in with a tray and set it on the wheeled table, positioning it in front of Caroline. She lifted the lid from the plate.

"Good morning," she said, smiling. "We have scrambled eggs, toast, and bacon this morning, along with some black coffee. Although I might be able to bring you a packet of sugar if you want."

"This is fine, thank you."

"I also brought some pain medication, in case you need it."

"I think I do," Caroline replied. "Yesterday's medication has worn off."

Caroline took the pill and then waited until the nurse left the room. She lifted the cup of coffee and took a sip, then placed it back on the tray.

"I wish I understood what happened with Tess," she said. "What got into her, anyway?"

"I spoke to Miss Campbell last night," Merritt said. "She thinks perhaps Tess was jealous of the fact that you got the attention instead of her when Ken left her at the dance to take you home."

"If only I hadn't gotten in that car," Caroline said. "Then none of this would ever have happened."

"Don't blame yourself," Merritt said firmly. "You had every right to accept a ride home, especially when your own date was drunk out of his skull. Carter might have hurt you himself."

"I don't know…"

"Look, Caroline. Imagine if it had been me. Do you think I would have deserved the terrible experience you went through?"

"Of course not," Caroline said.

Merritt nodded. "The only fault here is Ken's. I think you need to talk to the police so they can get the whole story."

"But it's so awful," Caroline answered. "You can't imagine what it's like telling someone. I can't even tell you everything that happened."

"The trouble is, if you don't, he could do it again."

Caroline sighed. "My parents are furious already. This will only make it worse."

"After the way they behaved, you don't owe them an explanation," Merritt said. "I think the most important thing is to make

sure he never gets the chance to do something like this to someone else."

Caroline was in the hospital for three days. She had refused to see
her parents, and they had gone back to Newport without a word.
Merritt visited every morning and was there when she was ready to
check out so she could take her home.

"I called for a taxi," Merritt said as they gathered her things.

"I'm a little afraid to go back," Caroline admitted. "Although I'd
rather go back to Duncan Hall than go home."

"Evie's the only one besides me who knows what happened,
and she hasn't told anyone," Merritt said. "And Mrs. Schwartz told
me that your parents called to say you had burst an appendix."

"Of course they did," Caroline replied, shaking her head. "They
came up with a cover story all the way from Newport just to save face."

"I only told you so that you won't be blindsided if someone
mentions it."

"I'm glad you did. I suppose the fewer people who know about
this, the better."

At the dorm, they went inside, Merritt carrying the sack of
Caroline's belongings. Several of the girls were downstairs, and a
few came up to ask how she was doing.

"I'm fine, thank you," Caroline answered, knowing that not
a single one of them would have spoken to her if they'd known

she'd just lost a child conceived out of wedlock. However, she didn't need to waste her time worrying about it. "I'm tired, so I'm going upstairs."

Merritt followed her up to the second floor, where Caroline opened the door. Everything was as she'd left it three days earlier, apart from the fact that her pocketbook had been placed on the desk next to her bed.

"Do you want me to stay in here with you?" Merritt asked.

Caroline opened the window and shook her head. "I'm fine, really. I just want to be alone for a little while."

Merritt slipped out and Caroline crossed to Tess's side of the room and opened her window as well to allow a breeze. The space felt empty. She looked at the matching rose duvets, the twin desks, the two closets—one jammed full of frilly, beautiful clothes and the other as neat as a pin, with far fewer garments and two pair of shoes lined up carefully next to a small box.

Caroline had never felt even the most remote curiosity about Tess. One look at her all those months ago had told her everything she needed to know. Tess didn't have money or social status, two problems Caroline had tried to alleviate by giving her clothing and inviting her to every function she attended. Tess didn't want to talk about her past, although who could blame her for trying to focus on building a future at Radcliffe and beyond into the one she had dreamed of in New York? Caroline had money, but she wasn't a snob. She'd admired Tess's ambitious nature and her strong drive to succeed, even while not approving of some of her other harsher stances. She supposed most people had some good qualities and some bad. It was certainly true of herself. She'd tried to do what she could for Tess, but she had never engendered anything more than jealousy.

Caroline went over to her desk, where she pulled out one of her textbooks and sat down on the bed. If she was going to take her finals, she would have to get busy. She had gotten permission from the dean to make them up and spent the afternoon going through notes and reading chapters. For some reason, it was suddenly important to her to do well on them.

At five thirty, Merritt knocked on the door and brought in a tray.

"Mrs. Schwartz said you might want to eat in your room for a couple of days," she said, placing the tray on the desk.

"That's nice, thank you," Caroline answered. Although she hadn't had much of an appetite for the last few days, she knew she needed to eat something. She looked at Merritt. "When did you take your finals?"

"Three yesterday and one the day before. I'm glad they're letting you take yours now. Do you have your schedule yet?"

"I have two tomorrow and two next Monday."

"I'll let you study."

Merritt let herself out of the room, and Caroline looked at the tray of food. She picked up a hot roll and carried it back to her bed, where she opened her sociology book and started making notes. She was fortunate. She usually remembered something when she heard it the first time, so studying was rarely arduous, even though it was sometimes boring. Now she tried to concentrate on identifying and comparing key sociological concepts such as social class, inequality, and mobility, instead of her own life. Halfway through, she realized the parallels between her and Tess. She'd been given social status, upper-class wealth, and certainly mobility compared to Tess's life with a lower-class background, modest financial means, and no mobility at all. At least, not until Tess had made it into Radcliffe before throwing it all away on jealousy and a fool like Ken Blackburn.

She worked for another couple of hours and had just put her books away when she was interrupted by a tap at the door. Evie stuck her head in.

"Your mother is on the phone," she said.

"All right," Caroline answered.

She pushed her books aside and went into the hall, ignoring Evie's curious gaze. She sat in the chair next to the phone and took a deep breath before answering.

"Hello, Mother," she said.

"How are you feeling?" Elizabeth asked.

"Fine," Caroline replied. It wasn't entirely true, but she was in no mood to confide in her mother about anything.

"I'm glad to hear it," her mother answered. "I was calling to find out when you are coming home."

"People are still taking finals," Caroline said. "The dorm is open until mid-May."

"You aren't seriously going to stay after what's happened, are you?" her mother asked. "I can't imagine facing such a humiliation. Of course, I told them you'd been ill. We wanted to avoid as much embarrassment as possible."

"Thank you for that," Caroline said dryly.

"What is the last day of finals?" her mother pressed, ignoring her daughter's tone.

"The tenth," Caroline replied with a heavy feeling in the pit of her stomach. She was in no mood to pack her things and go to Newport, where there was nothing to do but relive the worst day of her life over and over.

"Then I'll send Baxter on the eleventh." Elizabeth paused. "Your birthday is on the twentieth. Of course, it goes without saying that we won't be having a party this year. We'll manage with a small dinner at home."

Caroline sighed. "Mother, I honestly don't care."

It was inconceivable that her mother could talk about something as unimportant as a birthday after everything that had occurred between them. She didn't blame her parents for the miscarriage, but neither could she pretend it had never happened.

"I think you should have a quiet summer," Elizabeth continued, which Caroline correctly interpreted as *no social life*, though she had no interest in any such thing. "Then in the fall, we'll get serious about social opportunities and make arrangements."

"Arrangements for me to meet someone suitable and get

married as soon as possible?" Caroline asked. "Is that what you're saying?"

"It would be the best thing for all of us if you are settled down and married," her mother agreed. "Even you can see you need the sort of stability in your life only a man can provide."

"Mother," she began, but Elizabeth cut her off.

"Be ready on the eleventh."

Caroline heard her mother hang up the telephone and stared at the receiver. She set it carefully on the hook and then stood slowly. This was her own fault. Although she had done well at boarding school and even at Radcliffe, she'd never had anything spark her interest. She was biding her time, waiting for the inevitable, instead of making something happen. But what did she even want, apart from not being rushed into a marriage with a perfect stranger, who could very likely be as controlling as her father? She'd use a martini glass as a shield from life, the same as her mother always had. It was too awful to contemplate. But too much had happened in the last few days. She couldn't even think about making a decision now.

"When are you leaving?" Caroline asked Merritt at breakfast the next day.

She had been getting up at her usual time and was beginning to feel normal again. The breakfast room was empty, and many of the girls had already packed and started for home.

"Saturday," Merritt answered.

Caroline met her gaze. "You are coming back to Radcliffe, are you?"

She tried to imagine Merritt here at Duncan Hall in September. Perhaps they could have lunch once in a while, depending on where Caroline ended up, although her parents would likely fix her up with someone outside of their circle, to further bury their shame and resentment over what had happened. Her friends from Radcliffe would be shunned.

Merritt nodded. "You know, I think I've had enough. I'm going home, and I have an idea."

"What sort of idea?"

"I think you should come with me."

"Come with you?" Caroline repeated. She placed her fork on her plate and frowned. "I couldn't possibly."

"Why not?" Merritt replied. "We both need a fresh start, don't we?"

"But I have no idea what I'm going to do," Caroline insisted. "I'm not a fit companion right now. I've never held a job or done anything sensible in my entire life."

"Of course you have," Merritt argued. "You've just finished a year at Radcliffe. Besides, we could manage. It might even be fun."

Caroline shook her head. "I can't, really. It wouldn't be right."

Merritt shrugged. "Well, I won't press you about it. But I think it's a great idea."

Caroline took her finals and then spent the next three days

packing her trunks and cases. Her dresses, in particular, were arranged with care to protect the silks and tulle from becoming wrinkled. Pulling the box of textbooks and papers out from under her bed, she began to sort them. All the papers went into the trash, the books were boxed up, and the grades had even been posted. She had done better than she had expected, given her lack of enthusiasm over the past few months.

She was closing the last case when there was a knock at the door. Caroline opened it and found Mrs. Schwartz there with a woman she had never seen before.

"This is Mrs. Collins," the housemother said. "She's here to collect Tess's things."

Tess's mother—an older version of Tess, if perhaps more beaten down—looked at her curiously. She knew, Caroline thought. Of course she did. She would have spoken to the police and gotten every detail of that awful night, and here, in living color, was the girl she would blame for her daughter's reckless behavior.

"Come in," Caroline said, grabbing her handbag. "I'm all finished, so I'll let you pack in peace."

She walked to Harvard Square and found a café, ordering a cup of coffee, thinking about Tess. She couldn't help but compare their mothers, both of whom were trying to control the damage after being shamed and ruined. Tess's mother looked broken; Caroline's would survive. Caroline wanted to tell Mrs. Collins that she was sorry, although she wasn't quite certain what she was sorry for.

Everything, perhaps. Maybe even coming to Radcliffe in the first place.

Caroline put a few coins on the table and went outside to take a final walk through Cambridge. Radcliffe and Harvard were even prettier in spring than they had been in fall. She suddenly appreciated the walk between Duncan Hall and the Harvard buildings, the sight of students hurrying past, loaded down with books and knapsacks. Her fellow Cliffies and the Harvard men were having picnics on the grounds in Harvard Yard, enjoying the last remaining days of their academic year. Finals were finished, grades unalterably entered into their permanent records, notices were posted on every bulletin board of the dates that buildings and dormitories were closing. She felt an unexpected tug of sadness to let go of her college experience, wishing she could do it over and be the student she knew she could have been.

As she walked, she realized that she was making her way to the library. She went up the steps and pulled the door open, feeling a moment of relief that it hadn't already closed. She went to the elevator and took it to the third floor and then found the small room where she had been so miserable and alone just weeks earlier. As before, the room was empty. In fact, the entire floor seemed abandoned. She hesitated before pulling one of the books off the mantel. Opening the front cover, she pulled out the photo Tess had taken from her parents' house.

The girl in the photo stared back at her as she ran her finger along the edge. She'd been seventeen, a mere year younger than she was now, though she felt so much older. Tess had only seen a young woman of privilege, who had never wanted for anything, to whom everything had come easily. By virtue of her family's wealth, she realized that nothing she had done had ever shifted Tess's opinion. And now what was to become of her?

Caroline wondered about her own future as well. She thought about what Miss Campbell had said. What did she want her life to be like a year from now? Would she be married to a dull junior business executive her parents had chosen? And if not, what job would await her? What sort of future did anyone have if all she had been groomed for was to be a wife and mother who volunteered for the Ladies' Auxiliary Club and planned extravagant dinner parties where half the men were drunk and most of the women too? She wondered if there was any occupation that could be satisfying or meaningful. What, in fact, did she really want to do? At the moment, nothing came to mind. All she wanted was to escape the misery of the last few months and bury her head in a book. That was the one good thing that had come out of the last year: she had discovered reading.

She slid the photo into her pocketbook and put the book back onto the shelf, where it would remain undisturbed for the foreseeable future. Then she waited, unhappily, for Saturday to come.

The day, it turned out, was sunny and fine. Her parents' driver arrived at the stroke of nine, just as she'd expected, and she was ready, with all her cases on the pavement of the portico, waiting.

"Good morning, Miss Caroline," Baxter said with a slight bow.

If he knew anything was wrong, he didn't let it show. Caroline took off her sunglasses and smiled.

"Hello, Baxter," she said. "I have everything ready. It was good of you to come all this way."

"Not at all, miss," he said, returning her smile. "It's always my pleasure."

She watched as he went to the myriad suitcases and boxes and lifted them two at a time, carefully settling them in the trunk and the back seat of the car. When he was finished, he turned to her and smiled.

"If that's everything, then we're ready to go," he pronounced.

Caroline walked with him to the car, but as he went to open the door, she touched him on the arm.

"I'm not going with you," she said. "I'm just sending my things back to the house."

"But, Miss Caroline!" he stammered. "What do you mean, you're not going?"

"Just what I said, Baxter," she answered. "Thank you very much for coming all this way and taking care of everything for me."

"Will there be a message for your parents?" he asked.

"No," she replied. "No message."

After a moment, he nodded. "Do you need a lift somewhere, miss?"

"I have that taken care of, Baxter," she said. "Thank you for everything."

He hesitated for a minute and then tipped his hat before getting into the car. After rolling down the window, he waved as he pulled away. Caroline watched him, raising her hand in return. Then she turned and went inside to tell Merritt she had changed her mind. First, she would go to the police station and file a report against Ken Blackburn, and then she would leave Radcliffe College and begin the rest of her life.

28

————

Tess was led by one of the guards out of her cell and down a seemingly endless corridor. Her shoulders slumped as she followed him through the dim hall to the visitors' room, wondering who had come to see her. It was probably her attorney, who had been provided free of charge by the state of Massachusetts and whom she had already met on one occasion. He had decided to pursue a plea of self-defense for her case. It was true—she had never planned to harm anyone, certainly not to stab another human being. However, a single shove from Ken Blackburn had pushed her over the edge.

It was too familiar, being bullied. She had grown up with it all her life. Older brothers, an authoritarian father, even a boy in high school who had once slapped her. She'd long given up on the opposite sex. They were dangerous, in her opinion, and she'd never had any experiences that had convinced her otherwise.

The guard brought her to the door of the visitors' room and she walked in, if only to stand inside the less oppressive, lighter room, with windows that looked out onto the bluest sky. Two steps inside and she changed her mind as soon as she saw who was waiting to speak to her. She turned to go back into the dark hallway when she heard Caroline call out.

"Tess!"

Fear, anxiety, and shame overwhelmed her. She had been wrong to obsess over her roommate, no matter how terrible her own life had been. Her cheeks flamed as she paused, trying to decide what to do. It would be painful to hear Caroline gloat or ridicule her while she was in this helpless position, but every second out of the cell was precious. She steeled herself and walked up to the table where Caroline sat, afraid to sit yet curious to hear what she was going to say. Whatever it was, she deserved it.

"Please," Caroline insisted. "Just sit down for a minute."

Tess wrapped her arms around her waist, conscious of the prison clothes she was wearing. This moment would be forever burned on her brain. Caroline, however, looked none too well herself.

"Why are you here?" she asked, not caring how harsh she sounded. The events of the last few days had been traumatizing, and she wasn't in the mood to be polite.

"How are you holding up?" Caroline asked. "Are you eating?"

Tess was surprised. "You didn't come down here to ask if I was eating."

"No, I didn't," Caroline said. "I'm not really sure why I'm here at all."

"I'm leaving," Tess said. She took one last look out of the window, wishing she were walking free. *How we take our freedom for granted*, she thought. One day you can walk into a bookstore, and the next you're in handcuffs. Another example of how unfair life could be.

"Please stay," Caroline said. "We have things to talk about."

"Like what?" Tess replied. "Like how I deserved what I got? Thanks for telling me. Now you can go."

Caroline sighed, putting her hands on the table. "Don't you want to know what happened, Tess?"

"What do you mean, what happened?" she asked.

"Sit down so I can tell you."

Reluctantly, Tess slid back into her chair, staring at her room-mate, whose face was paler than usual and her cheeks had a hollow look. Surely Caroline hadn't been upset on her account. That was impossible to believe.

"I've been trying to work out what you were thinking," Caroline said, clasping her hands together. "You obviously found my diary and saw that I had crossed out Ken's name. I looked through it again and discovered I had written Dr. Forsythe's name in there too."

"I had no business looking at your personal things," Tess said quietly.

"I think it must have been misleading," Caroline replied,

ignoring her remark. "I think it gave you the impression that I'd had an affair with Ken."

Tess's head jerked up in surprise. "What do you mean? Were you carrying Carter's baby?"

She'd blurted out the words before she could stop herself. If Caroline hadn't slept with Ken, then she had gotten everything wrong. She had stabbed someone who was innocent. She shook her head in disbelief.

"You're going to be the second person I have told this story to," Caroline continued.

"Who was the first?"

"A police sergeant in Cambridge about an hour ago."

"I don't understand," Tess replied.

"Let me start at the beginning," Caroline said. "The night of the dance, Carter was being a jerk. He got drunk. He was being rough with me. He was tired of me saying no to him all the time, and he'd decided that he was going to get me in bed that night, one way or another."

"But I thought…" Tess began. Then she stopped herself, looking down at the table.

"I couldn't stand being mauled by him one more second, and I wanted to leave. When I stepped outside, Ken followed me and he offered to take me home. I told him he couldn't just leave you, but he said he'd told you that he was just going to drive me back to the dorm. Honestly, I was so grateful at that point not to be humiliated in public any longer that I got into that car. And, Tess, it was the biggest mistake I ever made, getting into that car."

"You expect me to believe that you weren't having an affair with Carter, after the way you were carrying on? I don't believe it."

"I don't know what you mean by 'carrying on,' but no, I wasn't."

"You're no innocent, Caroline," Tess said.

"No, I'm not," Caroline agreed. "I've made some questionable choices, it's true. But I didn't deserve what happened to me that night. I didn't encourage Ken, if that's what you were thinking."

Tess tried to take it all in. If what Caroline was saying was true, she had seriously misjudged her.

"He raped me," Caroline continued. "He ripped my pearl necklace off my throat. I have a scar on the back of my neck where the clasp caught. He punched me so hard, it broke a rib. And when he was done, he pushed me out of his car onto the road in the middle of nowhere. It was late, it was freezing cold. I sprained my ankle in the fall, but I had to walk back to Cambridge anyway. I was too ashamed and upset to go back to the dorm, so I went to the bookshop, where Miss Campbell looked after me for a few days."

Tess gasped. "Is that true?"

Caroline nodded. "You can ask Miss Campbell, if you like. She took care of me."

"I don't know what to say," she finally choked out.

"You don't have to say anything," Caroline replied. "I should have gone to the police, but I was too ashamed to do it. Women always get blamed for things that aren't their fault. And I knew my parents would be furious."

Tess knew she had been in the wrong, but she hadn't realized how far off her calculations were. By jumping to conclusions, she had not only hurt Caroline but had destroyed her own future as well.

"I didn't know what to do when I realized I was pregnant," Caroline continued. "So I didn't do anything. I couldn't tell my parents. I couldn't tell anyone at all."

"Oh my God, your parents," Tess exclaimed, lowering her eyes. She had never felt so awful in her life.

"They were furious, all right," Caroline said. "I haven't even told them what happened. They assumed I was sleeping around and got myself in trouble. My father, in particular, was brutal about the whole thing. We were arguing in the dorm when I began to miscarry the baby."

"You mean…" Tess said, eyes widening.

"Yes. I lost the baby," Caroline said in a low voice. "Just that morning I had finally decided what I had to do, and then my parents rushed in, accusing me of the worst."

"What a terrible thing to go through," Tess said, starting to feel numb. "And all of this happened because of me."

"Actually, all of this happened because of Ken," Caroline corrected. "But I've finally done something about it."

"What do you mean?" Tess asked.

"I told the police what happened to me. He's going to be charged with rape." Caroline eyed her for a few moments. "I think that will have bearing on you as well."

"What do you mean?"

"Your case for self-defense will be helped by my statement that Ken was violent and predatory toward me too."

Tess put her face in her hands. After a second, she looked up. "Why are you here? Why would you help me after what I've done to you?"

"You're not a bad person, Tess," Caroline said. "Too judgmental, maybe, but you don't deserve to go to prison for it. It's going to be hard at first, but we both have to go forward and try to start a new life."

"What are you going to do?" Tess asked.

"I'm leaving Radcliffe," Caroline said. "I took my finals and sent my things back home. The rest remains to be seen."

"I'm sorry for everything, Caroline. I really am."

Caroline stood. "I hope you're out of here soon and that things work out for you. Remember one thing: this can only destroy us if we let it."

Tess couldn't answer. She watched as her roommate extended forgiveness to her, asking nothing in return. Tess had done everything she could to ruin Caroline's life and didn't deserve her mercy, but she'd been given it anyway. She watched until her friend was gone and then felt a nudge on her arm.

The guard cocked his head in the direction of the cells. "Time's up."

Tess stood to go.

The next morning, she was given her own clothing and released from jail. Her mother was at the police station to pick her up.

"The charges were dropped," her mother said, sighing in relief. "Your father wanted to come, but I insisted I could do it myself. I've never driven this far before, but I made it."

"Thank you," Tess said, overcome by emotion.

"I've packed your things. I hope you don't mind."

Tess looked at her mother, feeling grateful. "No, I don't mind."

"Let's go somewhere to talk, if that's all right."

"Of course," Tess answered, surprised.

They got into her parents' old gray Studebaker, and her mother drove them a few blocks to a small restaurant. Tess was exhausted. It was terrifying to be in jail, even for a few days. It was an experience she would never forget. She hadn't slept more than a few hours and was still reeling from the humiliation of discovering that her impulsive, hateful actions had been based on false assumptions. She had thought she was smarter than that, but obviously she had some growing up to do.

Inside the café, they ordered coffee, sitting in silence as they stirred sugar and milk into their cups. Tess wished desperately that her mother was here for any other reason than to see her in this situation. There was no telling what she must think of her now. Tess had let her down. She'd let everyone down. And there was no way to make up for a mistake as enormous as this.

"I have something to tell you," her mother finally said after taking a sip of her coffee.

Tess tensed, wondering what her mother was going to say.

"I don't think you should come home," Harriet Collins said at last. "Your father would never let it go."

"But—"Tess began, and then she stopped herself.

The last thing she wanted to do was go home and bear the brunt of her father's anger and her brothers' incessant taunting. It would be better to be dead than to go back home. But something in her wanted to keep living, and she had nowhere else to go.

"I've talked to your aunt Dorothy in Cleveland," her mother said, a serious look on her face. "She's agreed that you can come and stay with her. I'll drop you off on my way home."

"Aunt Dorothy!" Tess repeated. Dorothy was possibly the only relation whom she liked. "Does she know what happened?"

"Not everything," her mother replied. "I just told her that things had become a little much here and that you needed a place to go while you sort yourself out. She's happy to have you. She even suggested that you apply to go to college there in the fall. I think that's a sensible idea. That way, you won't have to stop working for the future you're hoping for."

"But, Mother, I've let you all down. I can't even tell you how sorry I am."

"We all make mistakes, Tess," her mother said. "If you're lucky, you won't have to live with them forever."

Tess couldn't help but wonder what she meant but was afraid to ask.

"Thank you," she finally said. "I don't deserve your help."

"I hope I can see you sometimes," her mother answered. "Maybe I could come to Cleveland after you're settled."

"Yes, please," Tess replied. She stood and went over to hug her mother. "I hope you come soon."

"Let's have another cup of coffee," her mother said, putting her hand on Tess's arm. "We have a very long drive ahead of us."

EPILOGUE

———

The taxi pulled in front of a house that was nothing like anything Caroline had seen before. She might have called it Victorian, and she supposed it was, with its decorative trim—which needed to be painted—and its asymmetrical shape and three tall stories. It was perched so precariously on the street that she wondered if it would slide off come a heavy day of rain, although she knew better. Merritt had told her the house had been built in 1887 and had survived the earthquake of 1906, so it was sturdier than it looked. She glanced up at her friend, wondering what she thought of the house where she grew up, but Merritt seemed not to notice anything particularly unusual about it. Of course she wouldn't, Caroline thought, reproving herself for the thought. It was her home.

They pulled their luggage from the trunk and set everything

out on the pavement. Caroline took her wallet from her handbag and drew out a ten-dollar bill.

"I've got it," Merritt said.

"We have to share expenses," Caroline said.

"My father left money for me to get back home and to run the household," she told her once the cab had driven away. She reached down and picked up her cases. "You aren't a boarder, you know, Caroline. He was relieved that I had a friend coming to stay. He said I won't get lonely that way."

They hefted their things into the house as Merritt opened the door. "You should have let me carry that," she scolded, turning around. "You aren't supposed to be lifting anything for a while."

"I'm fine," Caroline replied. "You don't have to worry about me."

She pulled her two cases into the foyer of the large, drafty house and set them down, looking around. The inside was as neglected as the outside, giving the grand scale a humble appearance. But there was something appealing about it just the same.

"I know it's not much," Merritt said. "But there's all this space. And we can paint it and organize it any way we like. We could paint zebra stripes on the wall and I'm not sure my father would notice."

"It's perfect," Caroline answered, and it was. "It's on the other side of the world."

Merritt smiled. "Maybe not the world."

"Close enough."

Merritt showed her to her room, which was across the hall from her own, and Caroline sat down on the edge of the bed, testing the springs, finding it satisfactory. Then she stood and unpacked the few things she had brought with her. There were no crinolines or tea dresses, nothing fancy at all. Her beautiful things were back in Rhode Island, leaving Caroline to wonder what would happen to them. In the end, she supposed it didn't matter. Her life would be different now. From the little she had seen of it, California had little of the stuffiness and primness of the East Coast. It could be a little freeing.

"What should we do?" Caroline asked when she'd hung up her few dresses and tucked everything else into drawers.

Merritt smiled. "We'd better make a list of supplies."

When they were done, they walked to the nearest market, stocking up on staples for the kitchen: milk, eggs, bread, cheese, and peanut butter. Caroline knew without asking that there would be a lot of peanut butter, but she wasn't worried. They were embarking on an adventure, she knew—an adventure that would determine what they would do about the rest of their lives.

Within a couple of days, they had developed a routine. Breakfast at eight, which they took turns cooking. Then they tackled various jobs to organize the house. Merritt decided to organize the front sitting room while Caroline began in the kitchen. She had worked in the kitchen in Newport with Pearl on many occasions, although never to clean it. She had always been assigned tasks like cutting out cookies or stirring batter. Here, she put on an old shirt belonging to Merritt's father and emptied every cabinet and shelf, scrubbing everything thoroughly before putting back only the necessities.

"I'm throwing out the flour," she told Merritt, walking into the study as she rolled up her sleeves.

"It's old, I'm sure," Merritt answered, looking up. She'd tied a scarf around her hair to keep it back from her face. "In fact, throw out everything we won't use. It won't be any good when my father and Penelope come home in two or three years anyway."

Caroline scrubbed and cleaned and tossed. It was cleansing. She had never thought she could have enjoyed something like this, but there was something about taking possession of a place and making it habitable that was most satisfying.

In the afternoons, they explored the neighborhood. They also made a trip to several of the colleges and picked up applications, which they filled out together after scrambling eggs for dinner.

"I think I want to go to Berkeley," Merritt said one evening as they worked across from each other at the kitchen table.

Rain pattered against the window, which was cracked open, allowing fresh air inside. Caroline sighed, as content as she had ever been.

"Me too," she answered. "I thought the campus had a really nice feel."

"Will you have to apply for a scholarship?" Merritt asked. "If you do, you may have to apply for the winter semester. It might be too late for fall."

"You mean because my parents have cut me off," Caroline answered.

"I'm sorry. It was rude of me to ask."

Caroline shook her head. "I have a trust fund from my grandmother, which I can't touch until I'm twenty-five unless I plan to use it for college."

"That's great news," Merritt said. "I hope we'll both get admitted to the same place."

"Well, we got high marks this year, so that might tip the scales in our favor. Not everyone gets into Radcliffe."

"It was lovely," Merritt said. "Although I know I'll miss it."

Caroline arched a brow. "We got an education there, anyway."

"Have you decided what your major will be?"

"I'm thinking about English literature," Caroline answered. "I'd like to learn more about Virginia Woolf and some of the other authors we read over the past year. I think I've become a more disciplined reader than I was in the beginning."

Merritt put her hands on her hips. "Won't Miss Campbell be proud!"

Caroline smiled. She had been changed by the events of the last year, though she wanted to focus on the positive things that had occurred. She tried not to think about the trauma of the last few months, although it was impossible to avoid it entirely. Nights were especially hard. At times, she placed her hand across her stomach, wondering what would have happened if she hadn't lost the baby.

She hadn't been ready to be a mother, but neither had she wanted to lose her in such a terrible way. Her life was changed because of a tragic mistake, one she would never make again.

After a couple of weeks, the house looked far less neglected than when they had first found it.

"Do you miss home?" Merritt asked her one morning as they were folding towels at the kitchen table.

"I've hardly even thought of it," Caroline admitted. "I usually spent my summers traveling or staying with friends."

It was true. She'd avoided being home as much as possible for the last few years. It wouldn't do to think about that too much now either.

"I thought I should start looking for a job," Merritt remarked. "That's what I usually do in the summer."

"What sort of job?" Caroline asked.

Merritt shrugged. "I've done all sorts of things. You know, walked dogs, sold hamburgers, handed out flyers. Last summer, I worked as a lifeguard at a local pool."

Caroline shook her head, trying to imagine it. "I've never done anything like that before."

"Let's check the paper," Merritt suggested. "We'll see if we can find anything you might like."

By the end of the week, they were both employed. Merritt resumed her job at the local pool, and Caroline was hired part-time to shelve books at the library. For the rest of June and July, they worked, explored the city on the weekends, and waited for a response to their college applications. In the end, they were both admitted to Berkeley. The day the letters arrived, they celebrated by ordering sandwiches from a nearby deli. They sat on the floor of the living room, the box perched on the coffee table as they ate.

"Look at this," Caroline said, holding out an envelope embossed with Evie's name. "We forgot to look at the rest of the mail today. It looks like an invitation."

"Let me see," Merritt said, taking the letter. She ripped it open and sighed as she held it out for Caroline's inspection.

Mr. and Mrs. John B. Miller
announce the marriage
of their daughter
Genevieve Marie
to
Mr. Matthew Gordon Turner
on
Friday, August Sixteenth
Nineteen Hundred and Fifty-Six
All Souls Cathedral

"I'd say I'm surprised, but I'm not," Caroline said. "All she ever wanted was to get married."

"It's awfully fast," Merritt said. "You don't suppose…"

Caroline shrugged. "Either that or they're just getting married before the fall semester. He'll surely go back to Princeton, and it looks like he's taking a wife back with him."

"Will she ever go back to school?" Merritt asked.

"I doubt it," Caroline answered. "I feel terrible for her, giving up Radcliffe to chain herself to a man and a kitchen sink."

Merritt put down her sandwich and dusted her hands. She looked at Caroline seriously.

"We're not man-haters, are we, Caroline?"

Caroline stopped and looked at her. "Of course not. We'll both meet the right person and fall in love one of these days. We're just not ready yet. Who is at eighteen? But when the time is right, the perfect man will be waiting for us."

"Name one perfect man," Merritt insisted. "Just one."

"Oh, that's easy," Caroline said. "Rossano Brazzi."

Merritt laughed and Caroline couldn't help joining in. She laughed until tears sprang into her eyes.

"What shall we do about this invitation?" Caroline asked at last, wagging it in the air.

"We'll buy her a loud tablecloth and send a card with our best wishes," Merritt answered. "That should be the last we hear of her."

"By the way, there's a letter here from Miss Campbell too," Caroline said, holding it out. "It's for both of us."

She sat in one of the battered leather chairs and then opened it carefully and began to read.

Dear Caroline and Merritt,

Thank you for sending me your address. I am so happy to hear you're settling in there in San Francisco. The weather sounds perfect and I almost envy you. In fact, I would if I weren't so happy to be here in my alcove above the bookshop. I'm busy ordering titles and looking forward to fall, when I plan to host another book club.

I have a word of advice for the two of you, if you would like to hear it. Find a bookshop near you. Find several, in fact, and a good library as well. Spend a little time every week discovering new books. Read them; discuss them; let them inform you about life; let them seep into your spirit. Women from the past and even the present have so much to teach us about life and living and about what it means to be a woman.

Let me hear from you now and then! I shall think of you sunning yourselves in California with a good book in hand. Stay well, my dear friends.

Affectionately,
Alice

Caroline folded the letter and placed it back into the envelope. "She's wonderful. I'm going to miss her."

"I hope we're as wise as she is when we're her age," Merritt answered.

"Remember what we learned in Psychology?" Caroline asked. "'The only true wisdom is knowing you know nothing.'"

"Socrates."

"If that's the case, it makes us very wise indeed."

"Come on," said Merritt, standing. "Let's clean this up later. We need to get out of here for a while. The sun's out and we should take advantage of it."

"Where do you want to go?"

"Let's get ice cream on the beach."

They went upstairs and changed. Caroline put on a sundress she had purchased with her first check from the library—a white dress with thin shoulder straps and a faint pattern of lilacs. She went downstairs and waited for Merritt, who appeared a minute later in a knit striped boater shirt with white shorts. They walked for a few blocks, stopping when a cherry-red Porsche Carrera Speedster pulled up alongside them. A young man about their age gave a long, low whistle. He was tan and blond, with startlingly good looks, and he grinned at them in appreciation.

"Anyone need a lift?" he asked.

"No," they answered in unison, smiling at each other.

"We already have a ride," Merritt answered.

Shrugging, he pulled away from the curb. "Your loss, ladies."

"What ride?" Caroline asked when he had gone.

READING GROUP GUIDE

1. Alice reflects that many times our most profound reading experiences come from books we wouldn't have expected. What book has had the most surprising effect on you?

2. How would you characterize Caroline? What effect does her wealth have on her relationships with the other women?

3. How does Alice select titles for discussion in the book club? Do you think her selections live up to her expectations?

4. Tess never expected to make friends in college. Why is she more comfortable on the sidelines? Does the newness of her relationships change the way she acts?

5. What are each book club member's expectations for marriage? How do their observations of their parents contribute to those assumptions? Whose views are changed the most by the readings in the book club?

6. How is reputation dangerous even when it doesn't contain

truth? What effect does reputation have on the events around the Christmas dance?

7. How does Tess handle her discovery about Caroline's secret? Why does she react this way? What would you have done in her position?

8. Caroline forgives Tess and even contributes somewhat to her criminal defense. Did Tess deserve forgiveness? What do you think is next for her?

9. By the end of the book, the principal characters have for the most part gone their separate ways. Do you think their friendships would have been more durable in other circumstances? What might have driven them apart if not the events of the Christmas dance? What do Merritt and Caroline do differently that allows them to stay close?

A CONVERSATION
WITH THE AUTHOR

How did you first begin writing *The Radcliffe Ladies' Reading Club*? What was your inspiration?

Several things led me to write this book. First, I love thinking back to the days of being a brand-new college freshman. It's such a time of discovering yourself: finding out which things you hang on to from the past and which thoughts and habits you adopt in a new environment. But this book actually begins with Alice and the Cambridge Bookshop. She's a dream mentor, someone who encourages and inspires these young women and helps them consider new ideas at a critical stage in their lives. Of course, I love bookstores, and it was exciting to create the one I'd own myself if I had the chance.

Alice is surprised that the girls' college experiences seem to be so different from her own. How did you research the attitudes of the first generations of female college students?

I interviewed several women a generation older than myself and found that they have as many varied experiences as we did when we went to college. That allowed me the freedom to write Alice's experiences as I wanted to imagine them. Talking with older graduates gave me an appreciation for those who were the first person in their families to go to college. It was inspiring to see how they courageously changed the trajectories of their lives.

One of the things I discovered while writing the book is that so many men did not want Radcliffe to be built at all. They thought it was dangerous to allow women to be educated because it would threaten their control. Even today, it's important to understand how vital education is and what an impact it can have in a woman's life.

Which member of the book club do you most identify with? Were any of the perspectives especially challenging to write?

What an interesting question! As is typical with my books, I see elements of myself in more than one character. I was the earnest student like Tess, the quiet observer like Merritt, and today I imagine myself more as Alice Campbell, someone who loves books and sharing them with others.

It was most challenging to write Tess, because I felt sympathetic toward her, but I could also see her impulses getting the better of her. And without having a firm anchor, someone she trusted whom she could go to for advice, she allowed her imagination to run wild with no one to rein her in.

What is the most challenging part of writing historical fiction?

I love writing historical fiction. I am a natural student, so I enjoy studying the time periods of my books, everything from pol-

older? Or do we rigidly hold on to beliefs we haven't examined in years because it is expected of us? I discovered this book after writing *The Radcliffe Ladies' Reading Club*, but it would have been a fine inspiration had I found it earlier.

itics to fashion. However, I never thought I would write historical fiction because I was afraid I wasn't an expert in a particular area. Then one day I realized my favorite books were all historical fiction, and I took a critical look at what I liked most about those novels. In the end, I decided I would be an expert on my characters and that studying the time period of each story was a wonderful perk of writing books set in a different era.

Alice's reading selections are intended to challenge the girls' assumptions. What book have you read recently that challenged you the most?

Good books really do change, challenge, and inspire you. A recent example of this for me was the book *The Prime of Miss Jean Brodie* by Muriel Spark, written in 1961. I expected a tame and possibly lackluster book about a teacher and her pupils in 1930s Edinburgh, but I found myself shocked at times and pulled into the story, fascinated by the complex behaviors and motivations of the main character. Certain quotes from the book resonated with me, such as: "Outwardly, she differed from the rest of the teaching staff in that she was still in a state of fluctuating development, whereas they had only too understandably not trusted themselves to change their minds, particularly on ethical questions, after the age of twenty."

That brought up a number of questions for me. Do we allow ourselves to really think? To change our points of view as we grow

split second to take Catherine with her and walk the other way. That split-second decision lingers long after the war ends, impacting the rest of their lives.

Perfect for readers of *The Guernsey Literary and Potato Peel Society*, *For Those Who Are Lost* is at once heartbreaking, thought-provoking, and uplifting.

"A compelling story of love, courage, and forgiveness. Highly recommended."

—**Historical Novel Society**

"A sure bet for readers of personal war stories and those who want to know, 'What about the women and children?'"

—***Booklist***

FOR THOSE WHO ARE LOST

On the eve of the Nazi invasion of the island of Guernsey, terrified parents have a choice to make: send their children alone to England or keep the family together and risk whatever may come to their villages.

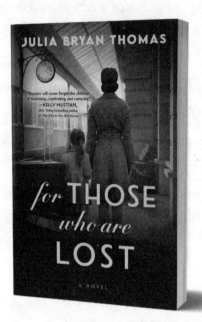

Ava and Joseph Simon reluctantly put their nine-year-old son, Henry, and four-year-old daughter, Catherine, in the care of their son's teacher, Helen, who will escort them on a boat to mainland England—or so they think. Just as the ferry is about to leave, the teacher's sister, Lily, appears. The two trade places: Helen doesn't want to leave Guernsey, and Lily is desperate for a fresh start.

So Lily is the one who accompanies the children to England, and Lily is the one who lets Henry get on a train by himself, deciding in a

ACKNOWLEDGMENTS

This novel was such a pleasure to write, and I owe a debt of gratitude to the amazing team of people who helped make it happen. First, I would like to thank my agent, Victoria Skurnick, whose encouragement and support have been invaluable. Much appreciation to my editor, Shana Drehs, who makes the editing process a true pleasure. I'd also like to thank my publicist, Anna Venckus, as well as the talented team at Sourcebooks, who do such a beautiful job from the unedited manuscript to the finished product.

A special nod to Kevin Thurwanger of the Harvard Radcliffe Institute, who kindly answered my questions about Radcliffe, which added to the realism in the story.

In addition, I appreciate all the family and friends who encouraged me along the way: Sherry Sides, Becca Scott, Christina Khaladkar, Joyce Deason, Lori Naufel, Leslie Purcell, and Connie Miller. Also, a special shout-out to my friends from Andersen who cheer me on. I am thankful for each and every one of you!

Finally, I'd like to express my appreciation to my daughters, Caitlin and Heather, and son-in-law, David, whose encouragement means so much. And as always, great thanks to my husband, Will Thomas. It's so much fun being partners on this writing journey together.

ABOUT THE AUTHOR

Julia Bryan Thomas is a graduate of Northeastern State University and the Yale Writers' Workshop. She is married to mystery novelist Will Thomas.

© Justin Greiman

"You'll see," Merritt answered.

They walked a couple of blocks, and then Merritt led her to a sign on a corner.

"This is a trolley stop," Caroline said, raising a brow. "Isn't this a little bit too touristy for us?"

Merritt grinned. "So be a tourist. You only live once!"

The green-and-white cable car rang a bell as it approached a few minutes later, and Caroline smiled. It was her first California summer and a chance for a whole new life. They climbed aboard and stood on the step, holding firmly to the poles. Caroline shifted her weight as the car began to move, the wind blowing her hair into her face. She laughed and pushed it back, watching as the famous hills of San Francisco dipped and bowed beneath them, ushering them into a brand-new world.

She closed her eyes and lifted her face to the sunshine. It was all right to begin again, she thought. In fact, it was better than all right. It was perfect.